Club Nero Series - The Reunion

Dale v Mcfarlane

Published by Dale v Mcfarlane, 2024.

CLUB NERO SERIES - THE REUNION

First edition. June 30, 2024.

Copyright © 2024 Dale v Mcfarlane.

ISBN: 979-8224469727

Written by Dale v Mcfarlane.

Table of Contents

Chapter 1
Prologue

I taly - 1987

DARIAN ROLLED ROUND feeling the bed no one there he opened his eyes Zeke not there Darian sat up the morning light shining into the window he stretched then leaning over to the side picking up his boxers putting them on and got up where is he Darian thought . The smell of paint hitting the bedroom Darian smiled he had had inspiration again Darian thought that's good .

The door to Zeke's study was slightly ajar Darian could see Zeke staring at one of the paintings arms folded Darian went into the room and stopped; he couldn't believe what he saw . Zeke looked round he was cross Darian saw when he came closer " Babe it was to be a surprise " . It certainly was a surprise Darian thought the painting of him lying in bed asleep naked covered half of him .So this is the secret painting he has been doing and not letting him see it .

" You hate it " Darian looks at Zeke he goes over to him laying his arm round Zeke shoulder " I don't hate it just surprised " Zeke smiled good he thought they both looked at the painting " it's for your birthday " " Really " Zeke looked round smiling at Darian " Yes really " .Darian smiles they bump heads and look round at the the painting again .

" it's a beautiful birthday present love " Darian wrapped his arms round Zeke's shoulders they kissed Darian tasted smoke from Zeke ahh he thought he had had a sneaky cigarette Darian thought . " Caught me " Zeke sniggered, cocking his head, smirking , Darian shook his head and sniffed the air Zeke chewed his lip. Shit he's goons smell something else to feel worried .

" SO WHERE WOULD YOU want to hang your painting? Zeke asked, changing the subject Darian touched his arm. Zeke looked round at Darian " Babe it was just a couple puffs it makes me think" " Mmm" Darian goes over to the painting inspecting it Zeke watching him .I really do hope he likes it enough that we can hang it somewhere for only us to see .

" I was thinking we could hang it in the bedroom. " Zeke smiled, going over to Darian, laying his arm around his shoulder. " You mean that " Darian nods, looks at Zeke, nods again and looks back at the painting it's growing on me Darian thought and since Zeke made it for him he will treasure it .

" Only for our eyes love " Darian kisses Zeke again, his arms around his waist " off course ".

DARIAN AND ZEKE STAND in the bedroom looking at the wall above the bedroom Zeke looks round at Darian I think it's the right place to put the painting " It's perfect " Darian said Zeke nodded he thought so to " I so love you right now " Zeke said kissing Darians cheek Darian sniggered looks at Zeke . " I certainly hope so " . Darian looks up at the wall at his painting Zeke whispers to Darian "You're so hot right now " Chews his lip he is so right about that Zeke thought .

Darian looks round at Zeke chewing his lip again and starting to unbutton his shirt " We have time right "while he strips Darian watching him " We do " Darian going nearer to Zeke and pinning him against the wall " They won't mind us being a little late right " Zeke asked Darian smiled who cares he thought his family was used to it by now it is his birthday anyway .

And they were a little late for Darians birthday lunch at his cousin's restaurant with some of the family. Their excuse was they lost track of the time, who are they kidding? His niece Cara thought of tucking into their meal and presents were given to her uncle .

" Lost track of time then " Cara snorted chatting to Darian he sat down his glass of wine looks at Cara and at Zeke who is chatting to Caras husband Carlo " You know how it is Cara " Cara nods looking over at Carlo her husband with Zeke he is so handsome that husband of mine and he can tell her uncle Darian is very much in love with Zeke . It has been at least seven years now with them on and off but there is something between them that is special, she thought .

Present Day

" PHILIP MACKENZIE FRASER Longstrome came back here " Cameron stopped writing and looked round he shook his head and sniggered into himself. It was Philip's first day at school; he couldn't believe how the first 5 years had passed so quickly their baby boy was going to school. He kinda felt sad but happy and it will be good for him. Cameron thought of meeting new people since he had a couple friends from nursery school . The study door burst open Philip ran inside followed by Lydia their nanny puffing away Philip hugged Cameron Lydia holding his school cap pouting shaking her head that boy will be the death of me she thought .But he and her had a good relationship which was good except for not wanting to wear his uniform for school which she had to practically bribe into it this morning .

" Daddy please don't make me wear it. "Philip stood in front of Cameron looking very cross. Cameron sniggered, looked up at Lydia and back at Philip who was wearing the school colours of burgundy and black he did look handsome, he thought . " Philip we talked about this didn't we " Philip pouted and looked up at his dad Cameron ruffled his brown locks Philip giggled Malcolm came into the study looked at Philip and smiled he looked so cute in his School uniform. He was a handsome boy and everyone had said he looked like the three of them .Maybe more Darians chin Malcolm thought he certainly got Darians temper that's for sure .

" Daddy " Philip ran to him Malcolm bent down to him as they embraced " No wany wear my hat " " Philip not wanting to wear your hat " Cameron scolded him he pouted again then Darian appeared god his son he thought he wasn't ready for this day he thought to he was so used to having him around .Bossing everyone around Darian leaned onto the door frame grinning at his handsome boy not looking happy .

" Aren't you handsome? " Philip smiled. Darian bent down to hug Darian. "What is all this noise about then? " Darian asked, pinching Philip's nose. He grumbled a bit leaning into Darian . It is a big thing starting a new school. He was excited about it which he kept going on about for two days .

" Do i have to wear it " Well son i'm afraid so you don't want to get into trouble your first day right " Philip nodded he took the hat from Lydia and put it on then Bill appeared to take them to the school ." Ok then " Philip grumbled again Malcolm shakes his head at what a boy he thought he would just have to learn to compromise on things and not get his own way all the time .

" Will get you at the club Bill the three of us are driving him today " Darian announced pinched Philips cheek " Ok " Bill leaves and goes out to the Merc driving off to the club for opening for the cleaners to get in first before this afternoon's opening .I don't want to miss my boys first day at School Darian thought .

After Philip was safely into his car seat they decided to take Cameron's car . Malcolm thought it would be ridiculous to take Philip in the fancy one since Bill was away in it to the club they didn't want to rock up to school on the first day showing off their fancy car .Mind you most parents are maybe like that to Malcolm thought but who cares which car you drive it's not a competition who has the best .

Malcolm sat in the back with Philip after Cameron would drop him and Darian at work "Daddy " " What buddy " Malcolm asking Philip he looked up at his dad " Ice cream later " .Philip smiled while Malcolm gave him his phone to look at some music videos .Philip watching the silly dance moves that he likes and imitates sometimes .

" Maybe getting daddy from work later remember " Philip huffed Malcolm lay his arm round Philip ruffing his hair Philip squealed Darian looks round at them giggling don't get him too excited for school Darian thought .Malcolm kissed Philips head Malcolm looks at Darian and still couldn't believe how incredibly lucky they were to have Philip .

ALL 4 OF THEM STOOD at the school gates while the mothers fathers took their kids into school the teachers stood outside to greet them Philip recognised Mrs story one his teachers who he liked he had said she had a kind face to his dads .They thought that funny " Ahh, Mr Mackenzie Mr Longstrom , Mr Fraser and Philip " Philip looked up at his dads and then looked over at the other children lined up to go inside . Mrs. Story knelt down in front of Philip. " Philip, why don't you go and line up with the others? "Mrs Story looked up at Cameron , Malcolm and Darian who looked worried about Philip starting his first day .

Philip nodded, looked up at his dads . Cameron knelt down and gave him a pound, Philip smiled " Thanks Dad " Then he went off to the other children wow Darian thought that was easy he thought looking at Cameron and Malcolm who were teary eyed he felt a bit emotional to they were used to having Philip around most the day he hoped he would like school . " Emotional day for everyone " Mrs Story explained she is definitely right there Malcolm thought it's going to be weird at first . While they watched the kids get all lined up to go into school proud moment Cameron thought he was going to send a picture of Philip in his uniform to his dad later .

All the kids went inside Cameron lay his arm round Malcolm while Darian still watched on until the kids disappeared into the building " Wow I can't believe he just went in without a fuss " Darian said Cameron and Malcolm thought the same .

SAM AND GERAINT WERE getting ready to go to work with Daisy Mae, their daughter who is now three and to drop her off at Nursery on the way. Two years ago they moved into their new house which was three doors down from Malcolm's home; they had more space now that they didn't have before . " Baby have you got your bag " Sam asked Daisy Mae while washing the dishes `` Yes Daddy " "Ready " Geraint asked Sam looked round at him and smiled Geraint looked at him " What " He asked Sam shook his head couldn't they have stayed in Spain longer thought there little girl was growing up to fast he thought just like Philip who was starting School today .

Geraint went over to him and squeezed Sam's bottom, hitting him off Daisy Mae giggled at the show of affection they both looked round at her then Geraint went to tickle Maisie " Daddy stop " Sam laughed as Geraint picked her up and swung her around he was so good with her Sam thought . Who would have thought years ago he would be married to the most amazing man and a child who they both adore .

SAM'S PHONE RANG OFF sitting on the counter it was his AuntbMae something must be up for her to call him this early in the morning " Aunt Mae what's up " " " Oh Sam I'm sorry to call you this early it's your dad " Sam looks at Geraint Sam opens the back door to go outside to talk " Sam he's had a stroke " "What when " That's not good Sam thought he did hope his dad would be ok. They hadn't spoken for a long while since Sam decided to move out .

" His neighbour was worried about him and went to check he's in intensive care son "

Oh god Sam thought it must be bad he looked round at Geraint watching him at the window " Aunt t Mae i gotta call work i'll call you back " Damn Sam thought many a time he had thought about going to visit his dad with Geraint and Daisy Mae .Make it up to him.if they could he wanted to before when Daisy Mae was born

.But decided against it Geraint didn't push him about it whatever Sam decided he would support him .

" Sam it's up to you whether you want to go to the hospital they did ask about next of kin "

Sam went back inside and told Geraint what happened with his dad " Ready " Daisy Mae announced they both looked over at her Sam wiped his nose and went over to her and bent down to see what was wrong with her dad Daisy Mae thought he looked Sad . " Daddy what's wrong " .cuddling into her dad .

" Allergies baby "He looked up at Geraint and smiled " Right missy lets go " Geraint announced " Daddy is not going to work " .Daisy Mae held onto Geraint both him and Sam looking at each other .

" Not yet honey got a couple things to do first " Sam kissed Daisy Mae's head and stood up Geraint touched Sam's face and gave him.a kiss on the cheek . " Love you " Geraint said first " Love you to i'll call you later " Sam nods and pinches Daisy Maes cheeks then kisses her cheek .

Geraint leaves with Daisy Mae leaving Sam with his thoughts about his dad. Am I ready to see my dad? He thought he picked up his phone to call his Aunt Mae. Well, I guess I had better go see him. Sam thought if he didn't he would regret it .

Mae stood outside the hospital waiting for Sam to arrive. He sounded tense on the phone the second time he called back and had reservations whether to come to the hospital to see his dad, which Mae understood just then she saw him walking across the forecourt to her . " Aunt Mae " Mae went to him and they embraced. She looked at him and he looked as if he had been crying " Are you ok " ." Yea just shocked me " That's understandable Mae thought

Mae lay her arm round Sam's shoulder reassuring him " Lets go talk to the nurse ok " .

Sam nodded he faltered she looked round at him" Aunt Mae is he really bad " Mae sighed no sugar coating it she thought and took his arm as they walked along " Your dad has his ways Sam you know that I told him to quite his drinking a long time ago or he will lose everything " ." I know I wished that " Sam exclaims he definitely wished things were different with his dad . Mae laid her arm round Sam's shoulder and nodded " c'mon then " .

THE NURSE TOOK SAM'S details and he did explain the situation with him and his dad which she understood "How bad is he " the nurse sighed many times she had witnessed patients neglecting themselves with drunks and other kinds of patients coming and going . "Your dad is very lucky the neighbours checked on him and it looked like he had been on a bender too " . Again Sam thought he should have taken more care of himself but his dad had his ways .

Sam looked round at his Aunt Mae and she took his hand he nodded " He has given my staff a hard time but we are used to dealing with difficult patients' ' Sam rolled his eyes his dad could be hard headed at times he thought that's just his nature . "Mr Mcvie it's up to you whether you want to see your father or you would rather your aunt dealing with him " Sam looked at his aunt Mae " it's ok I'd like to see him " .

Sam and Mae stood outside the ward he was willing himself to go inside Mae took his arm he looked round at her and nodded " Well I better get this over with "They went inside his dad was over at the far side Sam got a shock at how thin he was he didn't look happy Sam thought as he stood for a moment letting it sink in he was here well it's better now than later Sam thought staring at his dad .Sam took a deep breath try not stress to much he thought don't let him get to you Sam thought Mae took Sam's hand and squeezed it Sam looked round at his Aunt she nodded giving him a reassuring smile they both look over at Tom .

" About time " Tom said when Mae got to him she shook her head looked over at Sam " These damn nurses " " Tom enough " Mae scolded him and sat down drinks and food for him Tom looked up at a young man coming over to him his eyesight wasn't as good as it was Mae looked over at Sam and back at Tom .

"Oh it's you " Tom tutted Mae shook her head and looked round at Sam while he came over to the bed he was all wired up with a drip in " Come to claim your inheritance then " " Tom " . Mae scolded him. He huffed Sam, looked down at his feet and folded his arms. He looked up at his dad. Tom looked over at Sam and noticed a ring on his wedding finger. He remembered that Mae had told him about Sam getting Married to a man .How long ago was that Tom thought Tom looks over at Sam again Mae looks between them .

" How are you feeling dad? " Sam asked, sitting on the other side of the bed. Tom huffed, went to move and winced, holding his hand. The nurse did mention a slight paralysis on his left side . " What do you care about? " Sam took a deep breath. Mae nodded for him to reply " I do care, that's why I'm here " . Don't get angry Sam thought just keep calm he's I'll Sam thought and that's just the way he is .And he is bound to be feeling frustrated with the stroke .

" Still married then " Sam got his phone out and scrolled to find a picture of Daisy Mae . " This is your granddaughter. Her name is Daisy Mae " Sam held the phone up to his dad. He looked at the phone off a little girl in pigtail brown hair with Sam and the other guy . "Mmm" .

" it's her birthday soon she will be turning 4"

Tom looked round at Sam he did look good he thought by what Name was telling him before " I'm a grandad then " Tom looks over at Sam Sam nods "Hmm " the nurse comes over to Tom with his meds and to take his blood pressure " These lot don't give you peace " the nurse finishes his blood pressure them leaves . " Dad is just making sure you're ok " . Tom huffs again Sam's phone pings of a text he checks who it's from which was from Malcolm asking how his dad is he quickly texts him back he will update later .Tom noticing Sam texting whoever it was back .

" That boy you know " Tom asks Sam looks up at his dad " Malcolm yes he's Married now they have a son " " Everyone having babies " Tom huffs " They you say " Tom asks Sam looks at his aunt Mae she nods " Malcolm is in a throuple relationship " Mae explains " Jeez " . Sam looks at the time he should get to the centre soon " Am I keeping you " Tom asks huffing " I got to go to work at the drop in centre dad " .

" Drop in centre " Tom asks looking at Mae and back at Sam " Yes I'm a counsellor now " Tom nodded good for him he thought getting himself clean a husband and a daughter I've missed out on things Tom thought he was pleased about that Sam getting his life back by the sounds off it good for him he thought.

*That's good * Tom says nodding he coughed racking that doesn't sound good Sam thought looking at his Aunt the nurses did say he may have a chest infection from smoking wouldn't help either Sam thought while they chatted away .

" Hello " Malcolm looked round at Sam standing at the office door he looked tired Malcolm thought Sam came over to him and sat on the other chair and sighed " i'm not gonna ask i can tell " Malcolm said Sam nodded he sat forward and looked up at Malcolm. " He is looking terrible. Mal " Sam sat back in his chair. Malcolm thought, looking at Sam .Doesn't sound good Malcolm thought he hoped that Tom would make a recovery for Sam's sake .

" WHAT ELSE HAVE THE hospital said " " He had been lucky slight paralysis on the left side Aunt Mae said he had not been eating proper " Izzy Malcolms work mate came in to check stuff she could tell Sam was upset about something she left them to talk " Hospital is going to give him physio and medication " .

" That's good right? " Sam nodded. Malcolm got up and bent down in front of Sam. He patted his arm. Sam smiled and nodded. " Look at Geraint, we thought he wouldn't make it but he did your dad's will to Sam." Sam nodded he hoped so and yes Geraint was lucky to get into his remission thankfully .It did take a while with his set back and having his second dose of Chemo .

SAM HOPED SO MANY TIMES he had thought about going to see him with Geraint; he even discussed it with his Aunt Mae after Daisy Mae was born. Maybe they could have sounded interested when he had mentioned about being a grandad . " Have you time for a coffee? "" I am going into work said to take the week off when I called them " Malcolm's phone rang he checked who it was it was Darian calling him maybe for an update on Sam .

" Hey babe " " Sam any update " Darian asked sitting in his office going over the books for the membership's Malcolm looked over at Sam at the coffee machine " Hospital said Toms very lucky there gonna give him physio and medication he's been neglecting himself Darian " Darian hummed poor Sam he thought having to deal with his dad in a bad condition he also hoped that his dad would get better .Must have been a shock for Sam to see him like that .

" Dont sound good is he ok " " He looks drained Darian " . Malcolm explained looking round at Sam making his drink he felt sad for him but he has their support if he needs it like they always do .

AFTER THE CALL AND Sam having his coffee he left to go into work to organise time off to spend time with his dad and see what he can do with the flat and try sort it out whenever he comes home with his Aunts and Geraint's help hopefully it wouldn't take too long .He could deal with his grumpiness and maybe with taking Daisy Mae to visit her grampa might make his dad more happier he hoped .Sam wanted his dad to get to know his granddaughter if it didn't work out then so be it she had Geraint's parents who were great with her she loved going to see her grandparents they spoiled her rotten .

Malcolm stood outside the school waiting for the kids to come out. A few of the mothers and fathers had hung around chatting. He had noticed "Saw you this morning. " Malcolm looked round at the person who spoke. He kinda remembered her from the morning.but this time with full make up on hair done it looks like she just came from work " It can be nerve racking right, I'm Alicia " " Malcolm " .

They shook hands Alicia seemed a nice person he thought her phone pinged of a text she checked it and shook her head and a little giggle she looked up at Malcolm " Boy or girl " " Boy Philip " " Boy to Jacob we missed him today " Malcolm sniggered and so did he but at least they got things done without any interruptions instead of Philip wanting attention every five minutes .

" I bet his mum was relieved to get things done " " Dads ' Alicia looked at Malcolm surprised at what he said and she smiled " I am in a throuple relationship the three of us donated to our surrogate " . Oh wow Alicia thought that's pretty amazing to hear three dads .

" WOW, REALLY AMAZING! " Just then the kids came out. Malcolm looked at Philip. He was walking and talking with another boy. Great Malcolm thought he'd made a friend. " That's my Jacob. " Alicia announced the boy with Philip. Philip shouted and waved as they came closer to them, Philip hugging Malcolm .Malcolm thought Philip looked happy for his first day at School; he even made a couple pictures giving it to Malcolm . He inspected the picture, some scribbles he made and one off Philip with Frank cute he thought .

" MUM JACOB SHOUTED then rushed to her Alicia bent down to hug her son Jacob looked round at Philip " See you tomorrow Philip" " Bye Jacob " Wow Malcolm thought he would never have thought that he would have taken to being at school so quickly . And made friends which was also fantastic to which Malcolm was Pleased about Jacob's mum seemed nice which was great too .

Malcolm Buckles in Philip in his car seat then gets in himself " Daddy " "Yes buddy " Malcolm looks round at Philip " I think I'm going to like school I also made another friend too " " That's great Philip you can tell papa and Daddy C all about it to " .

" Jacobs is really nice, he has two mommies like I have three daddy's " "He does' ' wow Malcolm thought maybe Alicia didn't want to advertise it around the other mothers and fathers understandable though but it shouldn't be a problem unless other people do and for Jacob let Philip know on there first day she seemed Nice Malcolm thought .kids adapt to anything these days Malcolm thought starting the car up he looks in the mirror the little fella is tired it definitely won't take him long to fall asleep tonight hopefully .Driving off home Malcolm puts on the radio turning it down low kings of Leon comes on sex on fire Malcolm smiles he has always liked that song reminding him of Darian sex on fire .

DARIAN WAS IN THE OFFICE still checking on members payments which had been paid or still to be paid a chap at the door a little person appeared Darian looked up as Philip came inside running over to his dad and sitting on his knee followed by Malcolm holding a costa coffee for him just what he needs he thought the books are a nightmare to go over and a welcome distraction was needed .By his little man looks like he brought his drawings home with him to .

" Daddy did you miss me " " Of course I missed you " Malcolm sat downDarians Coffee and sat on the other side of the table sipping his coffee " How was school "" Great I made two friends Jacob and Molly and Jacob has two mommies too " . Malcolm sniggers Darian looks up at Malcolm shaking his head "That's great Philip "

.Interesting Darian thought and was good to hear he had made new friends as another bonus .

" I THINK I'M GOING to like school " " I'm pleased to know that " the door chaps again Cameron comes into the office Philips face beams he gets up and goes over to him Cameron picks him up " Well how was school " "Awesome " Wow Cameron thought for a first day he got on ok which was good he thought he let Philip down and he went over to Malcolm and sat on his knee .

 " How did your meeting go "Darian asked Cameron he had a meeting with his publisher his new book would be coming out soon highland fling 3 and was working on another " Good should be ready to launch in a couple months all the editing is done now in his hands " Darian was pleased to hear that and there was another possible movie off highland fling 3 that Cameron was in talks with Samantha about .And they should definitely do another movie project together Darian thought Cameron and Samantha worked great together .Cameron thought the same she had listened to what Cameron wanted when they both did the directing with Samantha's help and the movie was a success.

" CAN WE GET PIZZA? " Philip asked Darian, shaking his head. That boy thought " Course buddy, we can get pizza on the way home. " " Yeah. " Philip punched the air, hugging Darian at the table while he drew another picture sitting on Darians knee. It looked like a house with a dog. Hopefully Philip will be artistic when he gets older, Darian thought .

PHILIP RAN AROUND THE dance floor chasing the colours of the dance floor while Darian chatted with Claudia before he went home. Where does that boy get his energy from? She thought Darian looked round at him and shook his head . " Philip, get your jacket, we will be going soon. " Philip pouted and got off the dance floor over to Cameron who had been watching him dancing around the dance floor isn't he tired yet, Cameron thought .Exhausted watching him Cameron thought helping with his jacket on .

Cameron pinches Philips cheek he laughs Cameron also does a pouty face Philips tired he thought he will definitely sleep well tonight ." Are you tired? " Cameron asked Philip. He shook his head. They snuggled into his dad. Yep he is tired but did not want to admit it .It's been a long day for him Cameron thought about starting a new school .

LATER THAT NIGHT IT was Malcolm's turn to put Philip to bed which they all took turns each night and to read him a bedtime story before he went to sleep it was the story off the gruffalo turn tonight they both read each part like they normally did at bedtime read . Malcolm kissed Philip's head and went out of his light beside his bed "Daddy " " Yes buddy " . Malcolm leaned against the door, hands in his pockets, he went over to Philip lifting up his cover more .

Philip pointed to the door and the light for the landing. Philip didn't like it too dark and had always wanted his door and landing left on and open " I know I'll keep the light on love you loads " " Love you to daddy " . Malcolm kissed Philip's head lifting up His cover, Philip lifting up his snuggie while he settled in bed . Malcolm looks at him one more time leaving the bedroom door half open for Philip .

DARIAN WAS ON THE COMPUTER Cameron reading when Malcolm came into the room he shook his head and smiled at the sight of them he wouldn't wish it any different their nighty routine even though they sometimes had to schedule alone time sometimes . Malcolm got into bed Darian moved over Malcolm knew he was pissed off at. Couple members regarding their payments and had to schedule a meeting for one regarding their attitudes .He shouldn't stress about it too much Malcolm thought even though he and Cameron check the books with him it still plays on Darians mind .

"YOUR GONNA HAVE A WORD with the guy " " Will do " Darian sighed he sat down his laptop took off his glasses and rubbed the bridge off his nose "You shouldn't let it stress you love " Cameron said looking at him he looked round at Cameron as Malcolm checked his phone for any updates from Sam nothing yet hopefully let him know in the morning .

" I know I should " Darian said yawning and stretched he looked over at Malcolm on his phone texting Sam " How is he " Malcolm looked up at Darian "No update yet ":Cameron looked round at the monitor of Philips room he was sleeping now cuddled into his favourite teddy Cameron smiled . He got up, went over to the door and shut it and locked it. Philip knew to knock before entering. Cameron got back into bed and kissed each other before settling down for the night Darian had a hard on. He grunted snuggling into Malcolm kissing his ear Malcolm moving closer to Darian .Malcolm smirked he is always horny he thought sniggering into himself .

" Darian Longstrom " Malcolm looked round at him they kissed again " I can't help it " Cameron sat up leaned over Darian " I can't help it either " Cameron also had a hard on the three off them giggled snuggled into each other " raincheck " Malcolm said he just wasn't in the mood tonight Darian kissed him looked at Cameron he nodded "Defo " .Malcolm looked between Cameron and Darian they all sniggered and had a brief make out session. Then fell asleep holding each other quickies were good to Malcolm thought which can be good too.

GERAINT CAME INTO THE bedroom after reading Daisy Mae her night time story Sam was on the bed he had texted Malcolm an update about his dad he looked up at Geraint coming over to him and sat on the bed lifting up his arm Sam moved over to him . " Stressful day " Sam announced looking up at Geraint he smiled down at Sam and kissed his head "Try and not stress yourself babe " .

Geraint kissed Sam's cheek. He didn't want him to be stressed about his dad and how he is if he wants to take Daisy Mae to see Tom. That's ok by him just as long she doesn't get too upset .

Sam sat up and sighed , he thought he wanted to know his dad and for his dad to get to know Geraint and Daisy Mae to which they would have to talk to her about it. Hopefully she will understand what is going on .

" He seemed to be interested in Daisy Mae " " He did " That wasn't too bad Geraint thought hopefully he would accept the three of them since he didn't accept Sam's sexuality at the beginning when Sam told him about his dad and what he was like back then .

Sam scrubbed his face and yawned he felt exhausted by the days events they both lay down and turned to each other " I thought maybe we could tell her about him soon " "Up to you no rush " Geraint touched Sam's face he would do anything for his husband and if he wants to take Daisy Mae to the hospital he will support him on that .

" You're amazing, " Sam said to Geraint he smiled reaching up to kiss Sam's nose " And you have been amazing dealing with your dad try not stress about it Babe " .

He will try not to Sam thought laying on his back arms around his head

Chapter 2

P hilip ran into the school gates up to his friend Jacob Malcolm smiled Philip waved at his dad as he and Jacob went into the building " Jacob talked non stop about Philip on the way home yesterday " Malcolm looked round at Alice she looked at him " He did " They both looked over the kids had disappeared into the building Malcolm was about to go back to the car when Alicia stopped him .

" I'd like to apologise for yesterday " Malcolm looked at Alicia. What's she apologising for he thought she didn't say anything wrong "What t for " " I didn't react well to what you said about Philip having three dads when I'm in a partnership to " .

Malcolm huffed and shook his head he shook his head " Philip mentioned it and it's totally fine " " He did that's our Jacob oh Jacob asked if Philip would like to come over to ours on a play date sometime " " sure that be great " Malcolm thought that was a nice thing for Philip to do even though he still had a couple friends from nursery and Alicia seemed nice he thought. But it's good that he was making new friends from school and that was great too .

" Jesus look at this place " Sam was shocked at the state off his dads flat rubbish and cans vodka bottles message bags everywhere even though his aunt Mae did try to keep on top off it when she could " Where do we start " Geraint asked picking up some cans and putting them in the rubbish bag " Just work out way through " .

" What's that smell " Bert held his nose when he entered the kitchen sniffing the sink and going around checking " Smells like feet " Geraint announced lucky his aunt brought gloves Sam shook his head and they carried on adding rubbish into the bags as they went along finding clothes socks the washing machine was full to luckily they had stopped off at the supermarket for essentials .

" WHAT DID THE HOSPITAL say this morning? " Sam asked. " A comfortable night," The nurse said. " His Aunt explained while sifting through rubbish that Geraint thought it sounded like he was improving a bit hopefully .

" Well i guess i better start with the kitchen " Aunt Mae announced going to help Bert Sam and Geraint went upstairs to do some cleaning and wash down some things . Hopefully the place will look better soon for his dad when he comes out of the hospital. They will have to chat to his dad about getting a better place. Maybe the flat wouldn't be a good idea to use depending on his rehabilitation.

Malcolm chapped the office door, peeked his head in, Darian looked up from his Computer. He looked serious. Malcolm thought he cocked his head and smiled. " What's up? " Darian shut the computer when Malcolm came over " Nothing to worry about, just checking the books ". Darian sighed, sitting back in his chair when Malcolm came over to him .He had to stop worrying about the damn books Malcolm thought were getting annoying now.

Malcolm leaned against the table beside Darian he leaned down and they kissed " Darian we don't keep secrets you know besides its our Club to " Darian looked up at Malcolm he knew that he thought but didn't want him and Cameron to worry to not that he was worried about his club it was running well thanks to his staff for tha

" i know it's fine " Malcolm looked at the laptop Darian had an old picture of from the old days he looked at Darian and sniggered and remembered it would be his birthday soon he would be 80 . Darian glared and huffed "Ahh now I know what's up it's your big birthday soon " I will be 50 " Malcolm sniggered again only close friends and family know he would be 80 others pretend 50th " Honestly Darian age is just a number right " " I suppose " .Darian rolled his eyes swearing in Italian Malcolm huffed shaking his head he and Cameron were learning some Italian . And knew some phrases he and Cameron wanted to know more in Italian .

Malcolm stood up and said he would have to get to work soon Darian took his hand and smiled " What " " Stay a little longer " Malcolm bent down he kissed Darian " I can't meeting " Darian pouted Malcolm shook his head "Call in sick " Darian touched Malcolm's knee they looked at each other then Malcolms phone rang damn he thought not now . He checked the caller id it was work " Sorry " Malcolm stood up and connected the call from his work colleague Ryan " Ryan what's up " " where are you ".

Malcolm looked round at Darian and smiled " At the club doing some inventory that Darian wanted I'm leaving now " " We have a new review to discuss when you come in " which Malcolm was aware of previously and hopefully they can fix the problem.

" SORRY " MALCOLM KISSES Darian then leaves just as Bill was coming into the office Darian got up and went over to the drinks cabinet and poured himself a whiskey . " Boss " Darian looked round at Bill. He had a worried look on his face with Darian taking an early morning drink . " Don't worry all ok Bill " That's a weird thing to say Bil thought . Is everything ok? he thought .

" Can I have Saturday off ? " Darian smiled as he leaned against the table folding his arms. " Course you can have another date. " Bill cleared his throat, looked down and back up," he nodded . " Double dating with philip and Chloe " Darian had a feeling Bill liked the guy it would be their 4th date which was good he thought .

" You like him then " Bill looked round at Darian he blushed Darian smiled " I do " then Bill left Bill hadn't dated much Darian had thought not because he didn't want just the right person hadn't come along he did like much maybe the odd one night stand with men and women he was playing the field and why not Darian thought . And this new person that Bill was seeing seemed to be the one Darian thought that would be good for Bill .

Cameron went into the shower and soaped himself and let the water flow over him the shower door opened Darian came inside he wrapping his arms round Cameron he smiled and turned his head " You are supposed to be at work " " I'm playing hooky besides Claudia is there if she needs me " Cameron giggled Darian kissed his neck Cameron leaned into him . " I can make my own rules you know " Cameron huffed he certainly can, it's their business after all .Darian moved closer to Cameron feeling his hardness against him.Cameron leaned against Darian he wrapped his arms round Cameron kissing his neck Cameron hummed Darian flicking his nipples .

CAMERON TURNED ROUND to face Darian they kissed again " Besides we have all afternoon " Cameron looked at Darian and shook his head " I have work to do " they kissed again Darian pushed Cameron against the tile lifted up both his hands kissing all the way down his chest licking his nipples until he got to his cock and took him in his mouth . Cameron leaned against the tile Darians head bobbing up and down Cameron holding onto his head working his way back up again kissing Cameron's chin and neck . " Turn round " Cameron turned round Darian kissing all down his back Cameron arched his back tingling spontaneous sex was good he thought Darian licked and kissed his bottom Cameron spread his legs . "Mmmso willing " Cameron painted it felt good even the little bit of kink they sometimes did was good too .

Darian stood up licked Cameron's ear again " Patience " Darian flicked a finger inside him kissing Cameron's neck he moaned Darian worked his way back down again kissing all the way . " Darian stop teasing " Darian moved back up facing Cameron " You love it " . Kissing Cameron's neck and licking the droplets of water off his neck .Cameron moaned while Darian carried on kissing his ear and neck. Cameron leaning against Darian again turned his head and they kissed again chasing each other's tongues .

DARIAN ENTERED CAMERON moving slowly kissing his neck Cameron held onto the tiles he was close to coming Darian still leaning into Cameron " I love you " Darian confessed pushing in again he grunted sliding his arm round teasing in and out of licking his ear . Darian stilled when he came kissing Cameron's neck again they faced each other . " Was that good baby " Darian asked Cameron, touching Darians face " Yes it was I love you " " .love you to " .Darian touched Cameron's face they kiss again then Cameron pushes Darian against the tile he smirks and goes to bend down looking up at Darian looking down at him .

Cameron licks up and down Darians shaft he hisses chewing his lip while Cameron takes Darians cock in his mouth fuck that's good Darian thought holding onto Cameron's head Cameron flicked a finger inside Darian he bit his lip of the intrusion opening his legs wider access .

" Cameron I'm " Darian comes into Cameron's mouth holy god he thought Darian leaning against the tile Cameron stands up wiping his mouth smiling Darian stares at him " Good " Cameron asks Darian grins Cameron coming nearer to him " What do you think " . Darian wraps his arms round Cameron and they kiss. Darian goes to touch Cameron's cock when he stops him Darian looks at Cameron . " Darian I have more chapters to write and you have to pick up Philip " Shit Darian forgot it was his turn to pick up Philip from school but that's not for at least two hours he thought looking at Cameron .

Cameron went to move getting out the shower followed by Darian he kissed Cameron's shoulder looking at each other in the mirror " I know what your thinking mister " Cameron giggled shaking his head " Ok ok I will behave " slapping Cameron's bottom on his way out to the bedroom that man Cameron thought but he wouldn't have him any other way .

DARIAN LEANED AGAINST the car waiting for Philip to come out, Frank sniffing around his feet and barking, Darian looked down at him and shook his head " He is coming " Darian said he knew what Frank wanted, a pupachino . For a treat Darian would take Philip to get an ice cream for being good and with starting school a guy came over to the school gates he hadn't seen before one of the dads he thought looked at his phone and backed up searching for the kids.

Then some of the other mothers arrived and dads then the kids came out of the building Philip walking with Jacob and Molly . Molly waved to the guy " You must be Darian " He looked round at a lady waiting " im cora Alicia's partner " .Cora smiled Darian nodded she seemed nice he thought .Not at all what he thought she would look like lipstick lesbians they say just like Alicia .Darian smiled not himself thinking like that not at all what he thought she would look like he thought .

" Pleased to meet you " " isn't it incredible that they have bonded" Darian couldn't believe it either how Philip got to school and made friends so quickly " Yes it is " . Cora looks over at the kids coming out of the school noticing coming out with Jacob Philip beside him .She was glad that Jacob and Philip bonded quickly too .

" MUMMY, " JACOB SHOUTED, going over to his mum. Frank barked, jumping up to Philip. He clapped him, giggling .The silly dog thought he was looking up at his dad watching him .Has Frank missed me to still giggling Darian watching him with the dog .

" Daddy that's my friends Philip and Jacob " Molly explains Going into the car her dad strapping her in " That's good honey " "Daddy " Michael looked at Molly before shutting the car door " What is it " " Can we go to the park " Micheal went into the driver's seat he looked round at Molly " Not today honey we're going to get mummy at her work ok " .Molly pouted Micheal looked round at her " Another day ok honey " " Ok daddy " .Molly sighed looking out the window Micheal looked at her in the mirror shaking his head she can't have her own way all the time Micheal thought driving off .

PHILIP GIGGLED AT FRANK licking his pupachino at the drive in Darian eating his ice cream. He shook his head at the two of them " Daddy he's so silly " " Did you have a good day at school " Philip sighed while eating his ice cream .Nodding his head while he ate his ice cream .

" Uh huh Mrs storey was asking what our mum's dad did for work " Darian nearly choked on his ice cream he looked at Philip " I said my three daddies have three jobs " That boy Darian thought he had no filter just gave away too much information. Darians phone rang a call from Aida Darian Connected the call " Darling thinking for your birthday what would you like " Darian huffed and looked round at Aida `` Haven't thought about it " licking his ice cream . His would really like to forget about it Darian thought I don't feel my age he thought that's what they all say apparently.

Philip leaned over taking the phone from Darian Aunty Aidy " "My boy are you ok"

" I'm good aunty Aidy having ice cream " Philip handed the phone back to Darian eating more his ice cream " Were at the drive in I'll call you back later " Darian disconnects the call from Aida Frank now lays down after finishing his pupachino and after finishing there ice creams Darian drives back home .

" Dont fuss " Tom scorned at Mae she sighed trying to fix his blanket he she shook her head Sam annoyed with him he had also brought some supplies for him " I need a fag " Mae looked at Sam not Mae thought " Tom you can't " .Sam shook his head Tom tutting again Mae looks at Sam shrugging her shoulders .What can we do Mae thought the nurses have insisted he don't smoke for now which was making Tom grumpy .

Tom huffed again. Why can't I? He thought it's my choice whether he wanted to smoke or not. He crossed his arms ``Dad the doctor said you need to try not to smoke because of your chest infection " Tom huffed again as he looked round at the bag of stuff Sam had brought . " Can at least get what's in the bag then " seriously he was like a grumpy child Sam handed him the bag .

Tom took out a chocolate bar and eat some off it " Tom we need to discuss the flat we have cleaned some off the mess " " whose we " Tom asked looking over at Mae and Sam they looked at each other " Geraint helped out " " Right so when am I gonna meet him and my granddaughter " Well that's an improvement he's interested to see Daisy Mae Sam looks at his Aunt she smiles at him and thought the same .

" WHEN YOU'RE WELL ENOUGH Dad " Tom grunted probably doesn't know about me he thought but that's my fault I should have been a bit more understanding maybe they wouldn't have been estranged and maybe got on more . Maybe Sam wouldn't have Taken drugs back then but it was his choice to take them but he had blamed himself it wasn't a good area that he lives in to many junkies and alcoholics around temptation .

" Sam " Sam looked up at his dad. He went over to him sitting on the chair beside his bed. " If it's ok I'd like to see Daisy Mae. " Sam looked over at his aunt again and Sam looked at his dad again . She smiled and nodded. He's trying to make an effort she thought was good.

Sam was pleased that his dad was making an effort now and now wants to meet Geraint and Daisy Mae and that was fine but he didn't want him to have an outburst in front of her and blow it; that's what he was scared of .

" I have another grandad " Daisy Mae asked when Sam and Geraint told her about Sam's dad after dinner while getting her ready for bed "You do honey but he's not very well at the moment " Daisy Mae cuddled into her blanket looked at her dad Geraint sitting at the end off the bed " what's wrong with him " .Sticking her thumb back into her mouth Sam thought of getting her to not suck her thumb anymore .

" He has a sad Heart " Geraint explained Daisy Mae scrunched her nose "Why " Sam thought that is a good way of explaining it looking at Geraint because he didn't know how to explain it to her .

" You see some people get ill if there Heart doesn't work right and right now grandad heart isn't " " Will he get better " Sam looked at Geraint and smiled he nodded " I hope so honey now it's time to sleep ok " "But daddy I'm not sleepy " Daisy Mae pouted snuggled into her blanky then yawning .Yea right Sam thought not sleepy .

SAM SNIGGERED AND SHOOK his head who is she kidding he thought she definitely is tired he stood up bent down and kissed Daisy mae's head Geraint came over and did the same they both looked round at her before they left the room " Do you think she understands " Geraint took Sam's hand he looked at Geraint.

" I'm sure she does babe c'mon let's go to bed " " Your amazing " Sam said Geraint lay his arm round Sam leading him to the bedroom he looked round at Sam "I know that Sam shook his head thinking will it go ok Daisy Mae meeting his dad . "You're overthinking again" Geraint wrapped his arms round Sam he looked up at Geraint " Sorry I know it's just " .

Geraint bends to kiss Sam they look at each other " C'mon you let's get to bed no more thinking ok " " Ok " .

" I hope he won't be mad. " Steven looked at Jordan while they waited on their luggage. Jordan lay his arm round Steven and squeezed " I'm sure he wont dont stress ok " Dont stress he thought looking down at his hand his wedding ring shining there . Steven smiled thinking back to their week in las vegas they had decided to elope and not tell anyone till they got back they would have a party soon they just didn't want a fuss or a big wedding . Just the two of them on their special day, maybe a party for their year anniversary and he hoped Cameron would understand.

" There is our bags Babe " Steven looked up at jordan smiling " I love you " Steven just melted " love you to " Steven texted Cameron they were on there way home he messaged back with a smiley face Steven smiled nodding hoping Cameron won't be to mad that they eloped they will have a blessing Cameron could be his best man for that .

MALCOLM WALKED ALONG the aisle with Philip getting some supply's he did insist that he wanted to bake a cake for School god knows why Malcolm thought and while they were in the supermarket might as well pick up some bits for the house even though they get a shop delivery every week . " Daddy, can we get pizza? "" Philip, it's on the shopping delivery " .Malcolm said sighing is that boy ever gonna stop asking questions Malcolm thought .

Philip pouted and Malcolm walked on. He smirked and thought he's gonna ask about sweets next " Daddy " " What now Philip " Malcolm looked down at him smiling up at his dad " Can I get a sweetie " How can he not refuse that cute little face he thought . " Ok you can " Philip jumped up and down Malcolm giggled. Philip can be so adorable at times he thought and demanding at the same time but he and Darian and Cameron were teaching him to compromise on things and not demand on getting things a lot .And they were trying not to spoil him too much but it's hard not to say no all the time .

As they were about to turn the corner they bumped into someone Malcolm looked up to and was surprised to see his ex Joe who he hadn't seen in a long time Joe smiled " Joe hi " " Hi surprise " yea it sure was Malcolm thought although they did keep in touch the old update from him . " Are you visiting your parents " Joe looked down and back up at Malcolm " I am mum's not too well at the moment her angina is bad " " sorry to hear that Nate is with you " .

" Daddy " Malcolm looked down at Philip hiding behind him Joe looked round at the little boy hiding behind his dad " Hello " Philip looked up at Malcolm " Are you my daddy's friend " Malcolm snorted and shook his head looking at Joe " Wow he's got so big " " I know and cheeky to " " Got them " Cameron announced coming round the corner and spotted Joe and Malcolm talking " Joe hi " " Hi Cameron " Philip goes over to Cameron and hides behind his legs to " How are you " " Good apart from mum she's not too well. At the moment her " Angina" " Sorry to hear that " .Cameron looks round at Malcolm and back at Joe Malcolm looked surprised he thought .

" THANKS, I'M HERE TEMPORARILY until she gets better " .

" I'll get you at the check out c'mon Philip " Cameron and Philip go off to the check out to pay leaving Joe and Malcolm to talk " He is cute " " Sometimes he can be a bit demanding at times " Joe looked round at Malcolm it was so good to see him he had thought about texting him he was in the county but didn't want to cause problems with Darian and Cameron . " You should come over for dinner " " wouldn't be a problem would it " .

Malcolm snorted and shook his head " No it wouldn't Joe besides Darians a teddy bear " Joe giggled with Malcolm's influence he would be they should definitely catch up while he is in the Uk .Joe had a pang of sadness he wished sometimes it worked out between them and he had never left for New Zealand but it was a good opportunity for him he didn't want to lose and working for his brother was good .

MALCOLM GOT INTO THE passenger side Cameron texting whoever it was he looked round at Philip engrossed in his comic " Steven and Jordan are back " " Already I thought it was tomorrow " Cameron looked at Malcolm he touched his knee Malcolm smiled and took his hand . " is it weird seeing Joe " " kinda but I've a feeling it's something else " Malcolm maybe thought he was overthinking it maybe not he hoped things with Joe and Nate were ok . And it would be good to catch up with him before he goes back to New Zealand. He did wish sometimes they would keep better contact but Joe had a better life in New Zealand now .Which pleased Malcolm he didn't regret not going with him to New Zealand one bit he was happy with his life in Scotland .

" YOU THINK SO " " MALCOLM looked at Cameron he lifted his hand up and kissed it Cameron smiled Philip screwed his face up " Eugh Dad " They both looked round at Philip " Philip what did we talk about " Malcolm scolded him he put his head down and pouted " Sorry " . Malcolm and Cameron looked at each other and shrugged their shoulders. " Does someone want pizza tonight? " Cameron asked, Philip's face lit up and nodded, grinning . Cameron started the car and drove off with the music on . To One of Philips favourite songs from Robbie Williams Angels the three of them sing to the lyrics .Cameron and Malcolm holding hands on the drive back home .

The Club was getting busy Claudia was sorting out the bar area for drinks Darian was getting ready to go home Claudia would be in charge tonight he came out to the bar noticed a few regulars had arrived since it was midweek some came to just drink or indulge in the rooms . " Claudia " "Yes Darian " Darian looked over at Darren Parker, a regular of the club " Can you remind Mr Parker about his membership again please ".

Claudia looked over at Darren Parker with a few people `` Will do " Darian left and was about to get into his car " Darian " he looked round to see who it was " Eric " Eric had been a regular off Darians a while back he hadn't been around for a while Darian leaned against the car Eric stood he felt awkward which hey shouldn't be he thought . " Is there something you want Eric " Eric huffed and stuck his hands in his pockets. What a welcome he thought Darians phone rang off he ignored it .He will call Cameron back What is up with Eric Darian thought looking at him .

" I saw you coming out the club just thought I'd say hi " " Right sorry I got to go pizza night "Darian looks up at Eric what does he want Darian thought they had parted in good terms when Darian decided he Cameron and Malcolm got together Darian moved off the car Eric watching him Darian was about to get back into his car .

" ARE YOU HAPPY DARIAN? " Darian glared at Eric. How dare he ask him that he has been faithful to Cameron and Malcolm for the past 6 years; he swore to Cameron he would never cheat again . "Yes I am, we have a good life. Excuse me, it was nice to see you I must go now Eric". Darian got into his car. Eric watched him drive off smiling, shaking his head. Who is he kidding? Eric thought of playing with happy families .He will slip up one day. That's for Sure Eric thought then what will happen with his happy family or am I just jealous of what Eric thought .Leaning against the wall thinking back the good times he and Darian had .

Darian rang back Cameron while driving hands free "Sorry I was getting into the car " " What kind of pizza do you want? " Cameron asked in the kitchen Malcolm sitting beside Philip with Frank beside him " Oh my usual you know " Cameron thought Darian sounded strange, maybe tired or the members being awkward again.Possibly tied to the club had been gruelling past while he hoped it wasn't anything too serious Cameron thought .

" Darian are you ok " Darian bit his lip was he ok he thought maybe just tired had been a long day " Yes 'm ok just tired I won't be long love you " " We love you to see you soon " Cameron disconnected the call Darian sighed why did Eric corner him like that he thought was he trying to prove something try not to think stupid things switching on the radio while driving Olly Murs comes on .

He did sound strange Cameron thought but he didn't have all the burden off the club now that he and Malcolm were co managers now " Cam " " Mmm" Cameron looked round at Malcolm holding the plates for the pizza . " What's wrong is Darian on his way " .

" Yes he is " " Cam " Cameron looked at Malcolm looking concerned. Cameron lay his arm round Malcolm and smiled " Let's sort the plates " . Malcolm looked at Cameron and was not telling him something Malcolm thought " Malcolm you're worrying over nothing ok Darians Fine " Thank god for that Malcolm thought . The man worry's to much Malcolm thought and he shouldn't .

" Hello, we're here. " Steven said hand in hand with Jordan. Finally, Cameron thought, even though they had to rest after their journey back from Las Vegas. "Uncle Steven " Philip ran to Steven and picked him up " Miss me" " Uh huh " . Steven ruffles Philip's hair and he giggles .I love this little guy someday he and Jordan will start a family he thought .Looking at Jordan thinking about how good a dad he would be in the future .

" You did what Cameron was shocked to hear that he and Jordan got married in Vegas without him and the family Cameron looked round at Malcolm` ` Cam was going to get a blessing. We just didn't want all the fuss right babe " .

Steven looking at Jordan taking his hand smiling at each other " I get that but a heads up Steven " " Will you be my best man for the blessing " .Cameron smiled of course he would do anything for his best friend he thought .And guessed that he is probably right they just didn't want a fuss with wedding arrangements .

" Of course I will. " The three of them hugged and patted each other's backs. Malcolm smiled at the interaction. Then when the front door opened Darian arrived home. He saw Steven and Jordan in the lounge kitchen when Cameron came over to him .Darian sliding his arm round Cameron's waist Darian kissed Cameron's cheek glad to be home .

" Those Two eloped " Wow Darian thought he didn't expect that good news for them though " Congratulations " Steven and Jordan's hand why not he thought if that's what they wanted to do and not have the expense for a big wedding .

" Thanks Darian " the doorbell rang. Malcolm went to get it which was their delivery just in time Darian thought " Daddy " Darian looked down at Philip looking up at him . " Yes buddy " " Will you help with baking a cake " . What does he want to bake a cake for Darian?

Darian looked up at Cameron and Malcolm. What's this for he wondered " He wants to bake a cake for his class " Malcolm announced that boy he's just too kind sometimes where he gets these ideas from Darian wondered if it was a good idea to do so for his class
.

" Yes, I'll help, " Philip smiled. Frank barked, painting beside them. He wanted some pizza. "Can't leave you out, can we Frank? " Malcolm picked up a slice and tore off some bits to put in Frank's bowl. Philip giggled at the silly dog he thought was Frank guzzling down the Pizza . Darian goes into the fridge and brings out the wine " Well I guess this calls for some wine " pouring some of the wine into glasses handing the glasses round to everyone .

" Congratulations to you both " Darian announces and everyone raises there glasses to Steven and Jordan the door chaps and in walks Sam with Geraint with Daisy Mae to join them " Did you smell the wine " Darian asks smiling " Congrats guys " Sam and Geraint both shake and hug Steven and Jordan pleased to hear about there news.

" Thanks guys " " it's all downhill from here " Geraint jokes laughing Sam punches his arm Jordan looks at Steven worried look on his face " Babe he's joking " Patting Jordan's leg " I hope so " .Jordan giggles shaking his head poor Steven his face .

" So what's next? " Malcolm asks. They didn't need to move, especially just living across the road from them now Steven and Jordan looked at each other and smiled " we're thinking about having kids " Steven announced Cameron was surprised he didn't think he and Jordan wanted to go down the kids route . "When did you decide this? " Cameron asked, smiling . Steven looked at him. " Ever since you guys had Philip and Daisy Mae, now we think it's the right time, right , Jordan ? "

" I've always wanted kids were gonna look into it the clinic you guys used sounds ok so we're gonna call for an appointment " " Are you gonna go the surrogacy route " Malcolm asked Steven and Jordan did think about surrogacy or adoption and maybe fostering to whatever options there are they will check it all out first to see what the best options for them to go through .

LATER THAT NIGHT AFTER everyone left Cameron put Philip to bed with his nighttime story he got up after he finished kissed Philips head " Night baby " " Night daddy " Cameron put off his bedside light looked round as Philip snuggled in slightly shut his door leaving the hallway light on .Malcolm came up the stairs and they both went into the bedroom where Darian was on his Laptop Cameron shook his head looked at Malcolm he shrugged his shoulders . Malcolm went into the bathroom to have a quick shower. Cameron sat on the side of the bed beside Darian and he looked at Cameron .

" What's worrying you " Darian shut the laptop he took Cameron's hand " Just memberships " Cameron shook his head and took Darians Laptop and sat it on the table beside his bed " Darian stop there is worse things worrying about membership ok your not losing any are we " .

" No course not I " " The business is making a profit right " Darian nodded Cameron leaned over to Darian they kissed and slid his hand inside Darians pj bottoms he hissed " Will this stop you worrying " Darian smirked as Cameron carried on what he was doing that's good Darian thought closing his eyes letting Cameron wank him off .Darian sighed they kissed mmm that's so good Darian taking his stress away they kissed .and yes he was right I shouldn't worry to much about the club and other stuff Darian thought .

" WHEN ARE WE " MALCOLM stopped mid sentence at the sight off Cameron giving Darian a blow job he smiled leaning against the bathroom door what a lovely sight he thought "Well i didn't even wait for me " Darian looked up at Malcolm and smiled Cameron sat up wiping his mouth sitting beside Darian he looked round at him . " Better " " Mmm Yes ' They kissed. Malcolm came beside them and kissed Darian and Cameron " mmm I like spontaneous' ' Darian snorted at what Malcolm said as Malcolm came over to Darian kissing him then Cameron .

Malcolm went to reach over to Cameron they kissed wrapping his arms around Cameron Malcolm went to straddle Cameron Darian rubbed Malcolms back then the three of them started kissing each other and helping each other to take their clothes off .

Malcolm felt Cameron's hardness against him Cameron kissed licked Malcolms ear he hummed Cameron kissed Darian feeling each other Cameron reached over for the lube while Darian bent to lick up and down Malcolm shaft while Cameron kissed and licked down Darians back .

Malcolm eased himself onto Cameron Darian watching them make love he smirked at the sight before cocking his head Darian started stroking himself while he watched Cameron and Malcolm Fuck .

Malcolm lay on his side. Cameron slid into him again Darian got up slid over to Cameron kissing his neck wrapping his arm around Cameron guiding himself inside Cameron having their threeway all together Malcolm bit into the pillow to stifle his moans .

The three of them got into a rhythm. The friction for Malcolm was amazing, he thought Malcolm stroked himself too Darian kissing licking his neck Cameron licking Darians ear he turned his head to kiss Cameron Malcolm wiggled his ass Darian impaled him again Malcolm cried out . Cameron pushed against Darian he groaned it was so good this way they thought getting into a rhythm .

It didn't take them long to come laying on the bed all three satisfied with their lovemaking " I can't feel my legs' ' Malcolm announced looking round at Darian and Cameron the three of them giggled snuggling into each other saying there Love yous . Darian kissed Malcolm's shoulder Cameron got up to go into the shower Darian grinned getting up Malcolm sat up watching Darian disappear into the bathroom he shook his head and lay back down .

Darian peels round at Malcolm he looks up at him grinning then disappears again Malcolm chews his lip then grins decides to get up going into the bathroom looks at Cameron and Darian making out in the shower Malcolm goes over to them and joins them for another make out session .

Chapter 3

Saturday came when Bill and Dean met up with Philip and Chloe. They went to the Wetherspoons in town for a meal and drinks. Dean seemed nice Philip thought down to earth, easy to chat to. Bill couldn't believe that Chloe and Philip were already married a year ago. It had gone so fast .And they seemed happy Bill thought which is good for them they deserved to be happy and he was glad they were .

" it's been a good year hasn't it love " Philip squeezed Chloe's arm she looked at him her face beaming Bill was glad they were happy " So glad you guys could come this night how did you guys meet " Dean sniggered and looked at Bill he blushed " What's funny " Chloe asked looking between the two them . Looking at Philip he shrugged his shoulders looking at Bill and Dean .

" At the club " Dean announced looking at Bill " I saw him from a distance and thought cute " Dean explains looking at Bill again " Just to clarify we haven't had sex yet " Bill says Dean blushes " Yet " Chloe looks at Philip and raises her eyebrows which she was surprised about . " Took us a while didn't it Philip " Chloe looked at Philip he nodded " it's getting to know the person right " Dean said he was right Bill thought .They both wanted to get to know each other first before they had sex it was only Six weeks since they have been dating .And Yes getting to know each other which is the main thing for the both them .

" More drinks anyone " Philip asked " I'll come help you " Bill got up to help Philip with the order Bill had noticed Chloe hadn't drunk any alcohol tonight was she on one of these diet things he thought they got back to the table . " We have news " Philip announced looking at Chloe she smiled and nodded " I'm pregnant " Chloe announced Philip taking Chloe's hand that brilliant news both Bill and Dean thought looking at each other .Someday they both wanted kids which they talked about when they got together they had talked loads before different things they both wanted to do in the future .

" What that's great guys " Philip looked at Chloe she was beaming " Thanks Bill and yes we're happy right hun " "We are " Philip squeezed Chloe's leg she leaned into Philip holding onto his arm she can't believe they are going to be parents Sydney couldn't wait to be an uncle and Ruth a granny again .Chloe wanted a family with Philip and so did he if it was a boy or girl he would like Chloe to name their child after his parents which they discussed before and Chloe was ok by that .

" How's the club going " Philip asked Bill he had heard that Darian was thinking of opening up a new one " Good it's good that Cameron and Malcolm have gone into business with Darian new input and fresh ideas too . Darian wants to expand the business to Glasgow " .

" THAT'S GOOD TO KNOW hope it won't be to much " Philip asks hopefully not Bill thought Chloe excused herself to go to the bathroom feeling sick Philip wondered if he should go see if she is ok this is the worst part of her pregnancy the docs did say after the three month mark the morning sickness should lessen. Chloe came back after a few minutes she did look a bit pale Bill thought " At this stage I don't know if a want to be sick or eat " They all giggled Philip laid his arm around her shoulder Chloe leaning into him kissing her head cute Dean

Joe came into Club Nero a couple days later Malcolm was waiting for him at the bar when he arrived he sitting beside Malcolm "What do you want to drink " "Beer thanks " jack one the bar men made up the drinks for them Joe looked around the club it was busy for a Saturday from what he could remember the weekends were always busy . " Busy tonight " Joe asked Malcolm, looking round the club and back at Joe " weekends are always the busiest " Joe took a sip of his beer and he noticed the bar man that served them kept looking over at them .Joe smirked still got it he thought and the guy was kinda cute to Joe thought .

" Cameron not here " " Gone to London on business Darians in the office Cams meeting his publicist and a possible sequel to the book which we hope will happen "

" Cool, I saw the highland fling was really good. I hope it does happen. Hopefully Malcolm thought it's what Cameron wants " He is also thinking of doing a memoir to " .

" What of " Joe asked sipping his beer " Darians life and ours " Sounded good Joe thought there have been a few actors doing that lately Books about there life in the limelight .Sounds interesting Joe thought and why not while they chatted away Joe thought about Nate for a second thinking is he missing him .

DARIAN WAS PUTTING away a file when he noticed on the cctv Malcolm and Joe talking he had mentioned Joe was back home visiting his parents Darian watched them for a second a pang of jealousy came over him stupid he thought why should he be jealous of an old ex he thought . A knock on the door Claudia came inside she went over to the safe for more money she looked up at Darian watching the cctv " Darian something wrong " Darian looked over at Claudia " No nothing wrong by the way the Richardson's haven't paid their membership this month " .Not another member with there late payments Claudia thought Darian was getting frustrated about it .And so was she this won't do There members were usually bang on time paying .

" I'll get on with everything else " " Not at the moment " Claudia left what's with everyone being late with their membership fees lately he thought this needs to be fixed soon not that he was losing members there were more wanting to join the club by word of mouth which was good he thought . They just need to pay for their membership .

" Joe how are you " Darian snaked his hand round Malcolm waist he looked up at Darian and looked over at Joe `` I'm good Darian you " " Very well excuse me " Darian squeezed Malcolm's waist before he left to go over to a regular Malcolm sniggered Joe looked at him what was that about . "What's up? " Joe asked Malcolm, " Oh nothing just Darian " they looked over at him chatting to regulars .Darian looked over at Malcolm and Joe while he chatted to some regulars .He had got to quit that Malcolm thought no need to be jealous of Joe that's for sure Malcolm thought .

" Malcolm " Malcolm looked round at Pam one the waitresses` ` Champagne from Darian up at the vip " wow Malcolm thought how kind off Darian he thought " Thanks Pam " Jesus Joe thought that's kind of Darian but a bit much though so he isn't jealous that he is here to see Malcolm after all .

Darian was chatting with other regulars in the vip when Malcolm and Joe came over Malcolm sat beside Darian he whispered to him " Thank you " Darian touched his face and lightly kissed his cheek .Malcolm leaned into Darians touch noticed by Joe they are definitely affectionate towards each other Joe notices .

" Joe how is your mother " " Getting better thanks Darian " Joes phone rang off he got it out and excused himself to take the call Malcolm looked round at Darian " He is being weird regarding Nate " Darian touched Malcolm's knee " He will tell you in his own time don't stress " Malcolm nodded and sipped his Champagne one off the regulars passed the vip looking over at them Malcolm recognised him from before when Darian slept with him a long while ago .What is his problem Malcolm thought he had noticed David and Eric being weird around him lately and wondered why is it to do with Darian he thought .

Darian looked over at David he nodded back at Darian then moved away just as Joe came back " Sorry about that my dad with an update on mum " " How is she " Darian asked holding Malcolm's hand rubbing it Malcolm looked at him and smiled " Improving " . Malcolms phone rang . Cameron on facetime connects the call. Cameron's face appears " Hey " " Hi say hello to Joe " Malcolm turns the phone towards Joe he waves Darian takes Malcolm's phone and he goes off to chat to Cameron .

Joe thought it was a bit weird off him doing that Malcolm looked at him " We have no secrets Joe " Joe looked at Malcolm and nodded he picked at the label off his beer bottle " Joe is there something wrong " " Nate and I are having problems " Joe looks up at Malcolm he sighs and sits back " What kinda problems " . This doesn't sound good. Malcolm thought he did think Joe was being weird about Nate before .

" He cheated on me some months back said it didn't mean anything but I'm not convinced " " Oh Joe that's not good " Darian came back and handed Malcolm his phone back he sat beside him he sensed tension there was giggling and a whoop from over at the far corner off the vip area they looked over at the 4 couples drinking and kissing. Darian grinned good on them he thought, shaking his head. I expect they will want a room soon . Malcolm looked over to Joe " You should come over for dinner Joe " Darian asked Malcolm looked at Joe " Thank you that will be great " .

MALCOLM WAITED OUTSIDE with Joe while they waited for the Taxi Malcolm felt for him especially what's happening with his mum and the problems he's having with Nate Malcolm had thought he was doing ok in New Zealand "When do you go back " " Not sure gonna wait to see how mum's first " Joe looked at Malcolm and up at the building "You guys have a good relationship Joe looks round at Malcolm he is happy he can see that " We do and trust each other we made a pact no one else just the three of us " .

Wow Joe thought especially with Darian owning a sex club and his reputation Joe stuck his hands in his pockets `` That's good Malcolm " A car horn beeps the arrival of the taxi Joe looked round at Malcolm before he went into the taxi . "See you soon" Joe got into the taxi he waved as it drove off . He was a good guy Malcolm thought it's sad that he has a lot to deal with just now Malcolm looks up at the building smiling into himself thinking back to when he and Darian meet and him being a bit of a brat then .

MALCOLM WENT BACK INSIDE the Club Darian stood at the top off the stairs waiting for him Malcolm smiled and cocked his head Darian held out his hand for Malcolm to go to him Darian snaked his arm round Malcolms waist as he got a touch of the green eyed monster Malcolm thought .Malcolm kissed Darians cheek smiling at him Darian leaned into Macklemore squeezing him .

" I want you " Darian whispered, kissing Malcolms cheek as they looked at each other Darian took Malcolm's hand. He stopped . Darian looked round at Malcolm "What " " Not the office " Darian smiled and nodded he knew what Malcolm meant .Darian took Malcolm's hand kissing it licking his finger Darian looks at him when he does that . It makes Malcolm hard and it's really hot to Malcolm chews his lip Darian touches Malcolm's mouth .Oh the things I could do with that mouth Darian thought they kissed bumping heads Darian moved Malcolm to the wall his hardness against him leaving Malcolm breathless .

Malcolm stood in the middle of the room looking over at the bed. The smell from the fragrance burner smelled amazing; he had always got ones with a nice fragrance in the past Malcolm thought . Darian was over at the drawer for the essentials. He looked over at Malcolm going over to the bed. He sat down looking over at Darian biting his lip again watching Darian .He is teasing Darian though Malcolm is cocking his head grinning at Darian .

Darian leaned over Malcolm they kissed Darian slid his hand down Malcolm's chest about to unbutton his jeans Malcolm stopped him Darian looked at him going for Darians zip looking up at him they kissed again . Malcolm slid his hand inside Darians jeans he hissed as Malcolm tugged at him " Not yet " Darian said lifting Malcolm's chin bending to kiss him .Malcolm groaned Darian hovering over him Darian took Malcolm's hand placing it on his crotch Yep he was definitely hard Malcolm thought squeezing him .

Darian leaned over Malcolm while on his front massaging the oil on his back he had his shirt off his jeans opened and hanging on his hips Malcolm butt naked on the bed what a glorious sight he thought as Darian carried on massaging his shoulders Malcolm moaning Darian leaned over and licked Malcolm's ear . " Mmm " was all Malcolm could say Darian lightly kissed licking down Malcolm's back he nipped at his butt Malcolm arched up Darian slightly smacked him .Malcolm groaned Darian slightly smacked his butt again then massaging him.

" Darian " Malcolm looked round Darian standing watching him " What is the safe word Malcolm " Malcolm smiled he turned to face Darian Darian came over to him with the cuffs " Blue " Darian looked at Malcolm he smirked shaking his head Darian lifted one arm and cuffed it to the bed " Wrong answer " .He is teasing again

Darian thought he will only get punished again if he gives him the wrong answer .

"Yellow " Darian huffed he's teasing now he thought he leaned down they kissed Darian lifting up the other arm and cuffing it to the other side off the bed Darian got off the bed and went over to the drawer bringing out a vibrator and a leather feather he looked over at Malcolm watching him .Lust in his eyes he will have to be patient Darian thought and no teasing either Malcolm chewed his lip again

.

Darian rolled down the Vibrator on Malcolm's chest on a low level he squirmed it tickled a little till Darian flicked the vibrator around his cock he moaned Darian bent over Malcolm as he carried on doing the same rotation " Tell me that's good " " it's good " Then Darian flicked the vibrator at his entrance teasing him with it just at the edge Darian looked up at Malcolm his eyes closed his face in ecstasy Darian loved the look on Malcolm's face .Whenever he gave him pleasure Darian repeated what he was doing with the vibrator a couple times and licking Malcolm's ear after him groaning .

Darian bent down and took him in his mouth while using the vibrator Malcolm tugged at the cuffs again The sensation was amazing tingling up his back Darian sat up taking off his jeans Malcolm looking at him he licked his lips at the sight of him all in his glory .Darian crawled up to Malcolm licking and sucking his nipple he looked up at Malcolm " Mine " Malcolm whimpered as Darian licked down his chest and back up at him " What are you " " Yours " Malcolm whispered Darian flicked on the vibrator again .Fucking hell Malcolm thought I'm gonna cum soon sweat glistening on his chest .

" Just fuck me " Darian looked down at Malcolm scowling he cocked his head " Patience Love " Darian bent down they kissed Darian easing the vibrator inside Malcolm Darian flicked to a higher setting Malcolm squeeled his head going back and forth shouting no more Darian switched off the vibrator .Malcolm looked up at him isnt he gonna finish he thought " Darian " Darian pulled up his jeans no underwear he looked round at Malcolm as he tugged at his cuffs Darian tried to stifle a laugh he went over to Malcolm took off the cuffs he rubbed His wrists . Mad at Darian he was just about to cum asshole he thought staring at Darian I will get him back for that .

" Darian that's not fair " Darian looked round smirking Malcolm scooted to the edge off the bed Darian came over to him leaned over Malcolm " Do You think i'd not let you finish my boy " Malcolm glared at Darian what is he playing at the thought Malcom shook his head stop this game he thought .Malcolm shaking his head Darian leaned over him lifting his chin up sticking a finger inside his mouth Malcolm sucking on it .

Darian pulled Malcolm down helping him to the top the bed turned him onto his front he took off his jeans `` This will be quick " Darian whispered entering him Malcolm hisses at the invasion as Darian pounded into him holding Malcolm's hands . Darian lifted up Malcolm. Slightly entering him again wrapping his arm round his chest getting into a again it didn't take them long they both came and collapsed onto the bed .Fuck that was amazing Malcolm thought I can't move while lying face down Darian licking his ear .

" I can't feel my legs " Malcolm announced Darian pulled Malcolm close to him " I love you " Darian said to Malcolm he sat up leaning on his arm " love you to " Looking up at Darian they kissed Darian pulled Malcolm closer to him kissing his head . Boy he had shown his dominance tonight Malcolm thought but that ok it's there thing a little kink now again is good .Malcolm snuggled into Darian he kissed Malcolm's head " Better " Malcolm asked looking up at Darian he bent to kiss Malcolm " Mmm " .

AFTERWARDS WHEN COMING out of the room they bumped into a member on his way to have a fun threesome with a member who Darian had slept with " Mr Renwick " He turned round to face Darian David looked over at Darian . " Can you make an appointment regarding your membership ".Mr Renwick looked between Darian and his friends blushing .Shit now Mr Renwick thought damn probably to do with my membership he thought.

" Of course I'll get on that "Mr Renwick was about to leave with his two friends Darian turned to " Please do enjoy your night officer Renwick" Malcolm sniggered into himself as Mr Renwick looked at them and his friends .

Mr Renwick scowled. Then the three of them went into their room David scowled at them before they disappeared into the room to see what Malcolm thought . " Babe that was harsh " Darian looked at Malcolm he snaked his arm around his waist " Was i " Darian asked raising his eyebrows shrugging his shoulders I don't think so Darian thought .

Malcolm cocked his head and shook his head " Anyway if he wants to be discreet because of his job he should be on time with his payments " " i love it when you're being " Darian smiled he kissed Malcolm " Let's go home " Malcolm asked Darian nodded Yes good idea Darian thought time to go home " You are a beast Darian Longstrom " Darian smirked slapped Malcolm's bottom " You love it " Darian whispers to Malcolm .Darian laid his arm round Malcolm on there way out time for some chill time now Darian was thinking about when he gets home .

MALCOLM SLIGHTLY OPENED the bedroom door to check on Philip he was asleep sucking his thumb snuggled into his teddy Malcolm smiled he was just to cute he thought Darian came behind him looked in on Philip " it's late let's go to bed " Darian announced it was after 2 now they had stayed at the club longer than they had wanted to they were only going for a couple hours tonight . But with their unexpected love making at the club they had been longer which was ok it was fun .

DARIAN LAY HIS ARM out for Malcolm to come to him leaning his head against Darians shoulder Darian kissing his head the door creaks open and a little person appeared Darian and Malcolm sit up look at each other then Philip who comes over to them " What's wrong Son "Malcolm asks Philip coming nearer the bed " I heard noises papa " holding his blankie he had probably heard them coming home and it woke him up .

" C'MON LET'S GO BACK to bed " Darian goes to get up " Can I sleep here " Darian looks at Malcolm he nods Darian opens the cover for Philip to get in he goes in the middle between Darian and Malcolm sometimes Philip sleeps in the bed with the three of them . They don't encourage it all the time;just in case he got used to it too much but sometimes as a treat they would top n tail they both kiss Philip's head and all three snuggle in falling asleep.

Chapter 4

Another grampa " Daisy Mae asked her dads when they mentioned about Tom her dads dad and explained that they hadn't seen each other in a while Sam left out the other explanation Daisy Mae looked between her dads " I can make him a card couldn't I " Sam smiled looked at Geraint and back at Daisy Mae " That would be great honey " She is so sweet Sam thought he looks at Geraint he squeezed Sam's hand he is amazing Sam thought .

Daisy Mae got up and went over to her box of crayons and paper and brought them over to the table and started drawing Sam and Geraint looked at each other and smiled. They were going to take her to the hospital with them today and Geraint will also meet Tom for the first time also . Sam was nervous about this Geraint had reassured him last night that it would be fine and not be anxious about it too much .And if they didn't think it would go ok they would just leave then maybe think of another suggestion on how to handle Tom.

Tom looked better Mae thought when she visited that afternoon his physio was helping to strengthen his muscles on his bad side although he had complained each time whenever the physio came around . When Sam came inside he now had his own room which he liked better than being out in the ward. Tom looked up at him with another person, a tall black hair leather jacket and black jeans with a tear at the knees. A little girl with curly blonde hair hid behind Sam holding onto her dads knee Geraint holding her hand .

" Whose this then " Sam bent down to Daisy Mae he whispered something to her they looked over at Tom Sam took her hand and they went closer to Tom " Hello what's your name " Daisy Mae looked up at her dad he nodded she looked over at Tom " I'm Daisy Mae grandpa Tom " " pleased to meet you Daisy Mae " Daisy Mae giggled and scrunched her nose she handed Tom a picture he took it " What is it " Tom asked Daisy Mae sighed Tom looked at her " it's a sun silly " .

Sam sniggered Tom thought she's a feisty one "Ahh I see now thank you " Daisy Mae looked up at her dads standing watching " Well are you gonna stand there all day then " Geraint got the chairs Daisy Mae sitting on Geraint's knee Tom reached for his sweets "Do you want a sweetie " Daisy Mae shook her head "My dads said I not to take from strangers " Tom looked at Sam he's taught her well he thought " Honey it's ok you can take one from grandpa Tom " .

Daisy Mae got up went over to Tom she picked out a sweetie and said thank you " Very good manners " " My dads said to be polite " Mae felt her heart burst at the interaction so cute she thought Tom looked up at Geraint " So what do you do for work Geraint " " I work in construction my dad owns a building business " .Tom nodded Daisy Mae came back over to her dads " Good good " " Baby why don't you go with Aunt Mae and get a drink " .

Daisy Maes face lit up Mae got up went over to Daisy Mae took her hand and they went off to get the drinks "You have a good kid there son " Sam looked at Geraint he smiled Geraint nodded " Dad about the house " " Och your aunty told me " Sam sighed Geraint squeezed Sam's leg he nodded . "How are you gonna cope in the house dad " .

" Like I've always done " Tom said looking at Sam he sighed looking at Geraint shaking his head " Dad you need help in the house " " No a don't " Tom rummaging through his bag for something he tutted Sam went to help Tom batted him away . " I can do it. " Tom huffed. Sam took a deep breath and went closer to Tom. " Dad please just listen to what we suggest for Daisy Mae's sake ."

" Are you guilt tripping me now " " No dad " Sam got up Geraint took his arm Sam shook his head and went outside Geraint let him go he knew to let him have a moment to himself " He is a bit like me stubborn " Tom explains Geraint looks at him " I know that " Tom looks over at Geraint still rummaging through the bag . " Would you mind " Geraint got up and went over to Tom " What do you need " "My phone " Geraint took the bag and went into it bringing out Tom's phone handing it to him .

" I'm not want to be difficult, ya know we well ya know " Tom did feel bad about his outburst with Sam but he didn't want all the fuss because he knew he did need help with things. Geraint seemed nice, which he didn't think he would be and the kid was cute . Hopefully things will get better .

SAM LEANED AGAINST the wall outside the room Aunt Mae came around the corner with Daisy Mae saw him outside the room when she got closer "Daddy I got a drink for grandpa Tom " " That's great honey you go in first ok Aunt Mae and I can talk " Daisy Mae went inside Sam moved to the window he turned to his aunt . "Why can't he just cooperate? " Mae put her hand on his shoulder and Sam placed his hand on hers . " I know I've been trying to even suggest he come stay with me " .

Sam snorted was she serious he thought he would drive her crazy Sam looked down at his feet Mae came closer to Sam he looked up at her " " Just give him time he will come round " " I know " They went back inside Daisy Mae was up n the bed Tom interacting with him while drawing wow Sam though. He wouldn't have thought she would have taken to him so quickly. same with his dad Geraint looked round at Sam and Mae came in .

" LOOK DADDY GRANDPA Tom drawed a picture " Sam looked down and smiled cute he thought " Its drew Daisy Mae " Geraint corrected her Tom tutted and shook his head kids sometimes get words wrong he thought but it was good they try to get her to say the proper pronunciation. But it was good that they were correcting her on how to say things the proper way .Daisy Mae lifted up the drawing to show Tom which was him sitting on his hospital bed. She stared at him and looked down at the drawing . " Is that me " " Uh huh " Daisy Mae looks at her dads Sam looks at Geraint watching them their interaction " Grampa you can put it up on your bed " " Ahh Thanks " .

MALCOLM FIST PUMPED Philip on his way into school he giggled then set off in with Jacob beside him Malcolm smiled he was growing too quick he thought " Malcolm " Malcolm looked round at Carrie one of the mums coming over to him she went into her bag and brought out an envelope handing it to him . " invitation to Molly's party a week on Saturday " .

" Great thanks Cam will be back then the three off I mean 4 of us will be there " Carrie giggled at Malcolm corrected himself he looked round at the kids waving before they went inside " Proper little threesome aren't they " Malcolm nodded and grinned certainly were he thought " They sure are " .And hopefully still be good friends when they are older he thought .

" Micheal will be home that weekend " Malcolm looked round at Carrie while they walked to their cars he works away " Yes he's offshore 3 weeks away at a time" Malcolm sensed a sadness in her voice regarding Micheal working away it must be hard for her . Even Malcolm found it weird with Cameron having to go to London for business too .But that wasn't all the time just when he needed to go for his publisher.And sort out book deals etc whenever he went to London .

Before Malcolm started the car his phone went off. It was Sam who connected the call to him "Hey " " you wanna come to the hospital to see dad " Malcolm snorted remembering back when they. Were kids they had sneaked in alcohol.Also nearly getting caught having Sex in Sam dads house Sam's dad found out about the drinking alcohol at 15 they got told off for that " Sure how's he doing " " Well he seems to be improving " .

" THAT'S NOT TOO BAD right " "Yea if he just agrees to having carers come into him to help " Sam sounded exasperated the way his dad is at the moment he really felt for him right now " Sam it's not all on you Aunt Mae is there for him right now " " I know I gotta go take Daisy Mae to nursery text later " They disconnected the call at least he had reconciled with his dad Malcolm thought . After many years of not talking Sam had tried Getting his dad to stay sober but failed . And getting Tom to accept that Sam is Gay and that wouldn't change either .Malcolm remembered that time back then when Sam told his dad his sexuality Tom didn't take it too well then and avoided each other sometimes .

CAMERON WAS IN THE kitchen making himself a sandwich and Frank one to he was patiently waiting at his side Cameron sniggered looking down at him that dog is so spoiled he thought Frank barked knowing what was coming " I know patience boy and I missed you to " Darian came into the kitchen he stood at the door off Cameron and Franks interaction . " So did everyone else " Cameron looked round at Darian coming over to him they embraced and looked at each other " I should go away more " " Please don't "

Cameron cocked his head kissed Darians Cheek Frank barked they both looked down at him .That bloody dog Darian thought always inpatient .

Cameron tore off some off the bread sandwich he made and put it in Franks bowl Darian pinched Cameron's bottom he yelped and looked up at Darian " You behave " Darian pointed to himself and smirked Cameron stood up and snakes his arms round Darians waist they kissed someone clears their throat they looked over at ingrid coming into the kitchen with the laundry. Cameron and Darian looked at each other and giggled " Sorry Ingride "She nodded and carried on with sorting the basket off washing .Many a time she had caught the three of them cuddling and kissing in the kitchen she was used to it now before Darian moved to the house whenever he had company over at the flat .

" I'm just gonna sort out a couple emails " Cameron announced Darian took his arm and shook his head Cameron smirked and shook his head he whispered to Cameron he looked at Darian and they both ran upstairs ingrid shook her head they won't be seen in the next hour or so she thought .Since Cameron was away on business in London Ingrid sniggered shaking her head .Smiling into herself carrying on with her chores while Frank lay on his bed .

THEY WERE KISSING CLOTHES were discarded when they got to the bedroom they stood facing each other like it was the first time again Darian went closer to Cameron he bent down liked up his thigh Cameron looked down tinges up his leg from Darian licking inside his thigh Darian looked up at him Cameron bit his lip . Darian stood up feeling Cameron's mouth " When you do that it turns me on " Cameron bent down and did the same licking the inside off Darians leg Darian held onto Cameron's head it also tingled .

Cameron stood up turning Darian round kissing his neck as he held onto the bed post Cameron worked his way down a Darians back and up again licking his ear " Did you miss our little threesome " " mmm " Cameron worked his way back down again nipping at Darians bottom he gave it a little slap Darian flopped his head forward a little whimper came out . Cameron went into the drawer and brought out the lube he went back over to Darian he squirted some on his hand and rubbed it inside Darian . "Fuck " Cameron flicked in and out kissing Darians neck Cameron held Darians hand while he was wanking off helping him smooth strokes . Darian turned his head to Cameron they kissed then Cameron slicked himself with the lube held onto Darians back entering him Darian bowed his head as Cameron got into a steady rhythm .

Cameron holding onto his back Darian groaned Cameron moved nearer to Darian kissing his ear getting into a rhythm again Darian swore in Italian Cameron slapped his bottom .

Darian bit into the pillow coming Cameron spilled into him they fell onto the bed Darian scooted over to Camerom "You didn't give me a chance " Darian complaining leaning on his arm feeling Cameron's chest he sniggered " Darian Longstrom are you complaining " Darian sat up he bent down to kiss Cameron `` never with you my Love " Darian got up Cameron watched him Darian looked over at Cameron `` Shower " Darian asked as he was about to get into the bathroom Cameron got up and. They both raced to the shower for another make out session this time Darian taking the lead

.

Both Cameron's and Darians phones went off after another from the school which they didn't hear when they got into the shower. Their phones were on silent then the school left voicemails for them

.

CAMERON CAME OUT TO the car to fetch Philip who looked pale Malcolm picked up his and Philips bag from the back off the car Darian was at the door waiting for them "My poor boy what happened " " He had a slight temp the school said " Cmon buddy let's get you to bed " Malcolm looked at Darian and Cameron before he took Philip upstairs to bed Igriide had put a hot water bottle in his bed to keep it warm for him . Darian took Malcolm's arm he looked at Darian ` ` What is wrong "Darian asked Cameron to take Philip up to bed " I had an important meeting Darian " Malcolm was furious that his meeting had to be cut short for him to collect Philip from school .Because them having a make out session could have waited Malcolm thought .

SHIT DARIAN THOUGHT one off the outreach kids he probably thought " Sorry I'll get him a drink " Darian disappears into the kitchen maybe he was a little cross with Darian Malcolm thought well they did have an agreement if the other is not around and in the mood Malcolm shook his head even though he had rescheduled his meeting for next week for the outreach kids .But that wasn't the point the poor kid had to get sorted and into a programme soon it was a little embarrassing.

CAMERON SAT BESIDE Philip in his bed he had stopped being sick when he got home there were also a couple kids at school took unwell to he temp was coming down now Darian came into the room with medicine for him " I know it tastes horrible but if you don't take it you won't get better that right dad " Cameron explains looking up at Darian handing Cameron the bottle .Philip made a face while he took the medicine horrible he thought but his dad s were right take the medicine to get better .

Malcolm comes into the room after he had chatted with the locum doctor and Mollys mum she also comes down with a viral thing to": Docs said there is a viral thing going around just keep an eye on him Carrie said Mollys feeling the same"

" MR DARIAN MISS CLAUDIA on the Phone " Darian left to take the call Malcolm sat on the bed beside Philip he looked kinda pissed off Cameron thought he went to take Malcolm's hand he looked up at Cameron " I'm ok Cam as long he is to " Looking down at Philip now asleep Malcolm smiled Cameron took his hand again "Don't worry it's just a bug " .

" I know I just overreacted " Malcolm smiled at Cameron taking his hand Cameron kissing it he knows Philip will be ok in a few days Malcolm worries too much sometimes.

Cameron and Malcolm got changed into their track bottoms Cameron checked on Philip who was still asleep poor wee soul he thought he wouldn't be going to school the rest of the week he thought he heard Darian come up the stairs while on the phone .

Darian sighed and rubbed between his eyes Cameron looked at him Malcolm came out the bedroom " Claudia is sick too as well as Ed and Julia Malcolm looked at Cameron and back at Darian . "Can you shut the club tonight " Cameron asked as they went into the bedroom Darian sat on the bed "Can't im going to have to go in now its s/m night remember " .

Darian did some theme nights every two weeks which was going well since reopening after the fire Darian got up to go into the closet to get changed "Do you need us there? " Malcolm asked Darian to look round at him Darian went over to Malcolm wrapped his arms around his shoulders. " You don't have to, there are spare staff that are coming in " .

" I'm sorry, " Darian cocked his head. What was Malcolm sorry for? He thought Cameron was overreacting regarding Philip. Darian huffed and touched Malcolm's face and kissed his cheek . " No need to be sorry my boy " Darian gave Malcolm a quick kiss and looked in on Philip before he left to go to the club.

Darian was grateful for the staff and security he had all teamed together to get the club ready for opening he thanked the staff for helping out at short notice and making sure everything was ready he had the staff he could rely on they had the old grumbles but it got ironed out most of the time . Cameron texted Philip had managed some soup and kept it down which was good to hear. He was glad their boy was feeling better as he sat at the end of the bar . The club was getting busy with members arriving for S/M night all mingling together in various get ups for the night Darian sipped his red wine looking around the room as the members greeted him when they arrived .Couples singles and couples that often meet up at the club too.

A YOUNG MAN WITH BLONDE hair who he hadn't seen before at the end of the bar slim looked like he worked out a bit of leather jacket t shirt leather trousers looking at him he nodded at Darian he nodded back at him . " Boss " Darian looked at Dean one the bouncers `` Vips have arrived " " Thanks Dean show them where to go I'll be there in a minute " Dean left Darian got up as the young guy came over to him " Darian right " Darian looked at him he looked round the room and back at Darian `` Yes that's me " . The young man smirked, leaning against the bar. What did Darian think?

" Right great place you have here to talk of the town " " Are you new here " He huffed and stuck his hands in his pockets " I hope so you have quite the reputation Darian Longstrom " So he's heard from other people about him Darian thought and the club hopefully good things . " Right and you are " " Elliot " Elliot stuck out his hand which Darian didn't take " Please excuse me I have things to attend to enjoy your night .Darian was about to move Elliot stepped in front of Darian , Darian sighed and looked at Elliot .

" I intend to I hope " Elliot smirked again and watched Darian walk off over to the vip area then another guy caught his attention talking to people cute Elliot thought going over to him to chat .Ellot looks over at the vip area where Darian is he is really is Interesting Elliot thought while he chatted to the guy .Seems intense Elliot thought he also heard he has two boyfriends and a kid .

Later that night Darian sat in his office sitting back on his chair, legs crossed enjoying his whiskey and the CCTV in front of him off the bar area . When people are in the rooms CCTV is turned off but still recording in case Darian needs evidence of any complaints the door chapped Mel one of the waitresses came inside with a file .

" Boss the file you asked for " " Thank you Mel " Mel sat on the chair at the table giving Darian the file the door chapped again Bill comes inside and goes over to the filing cabinet . " Boss, should we be worried? " Mel asked Bill, looking round and back to the filing cabinet. His staff were worrying over nothing he thought which they didn't need to be .

Darian huffed, "Does she think she is going to lose her job or the club in jeopardy? ` Mel relax, your jobs are safe and we're not going anywhere " .

" Sorry had to ask " " We just need to check members info and their payments Mel " Good to know Mel thought if the business was in jeopardy she would have to look for another job but she loved working for Darian . He was a good boss and paid well even though he was a stickler for the regime but that was ok .

After Darian went back to the bar to check on things at the bar which was winding down Elliot was at the bar chatting and drinking he noticed Darian had come back. Elliot and his friend started kissing, noticed by Darian. What is he trying to prove? Darian thought, shaking his head. Is he trying to make him jealous? Darian thought that it wasn't .

" Sandy, can you wind down everything with the others i'm going to head home " sure boss "Before Darian left he went back into the office to collect a couple things he came out of the office bumping into Elliot .

Elliot smiled as he leaned against the wall he cocked his head staring at Darian" Going so soon " Darian locked the office door he looked at Elliot "Yes i have a family to get back to " Elliot nodded he did notice the ring on his wedding finger . " Ahh yes your throuple relationship cool "

Bill appeared to take Darian home and noticed the exchange between him and the guy Darian looked up " i'll be there in a minute Bill " Bill left Darian went closer to Elliot " I suggest opening a membership it's our policy " Darian smiled Elliot grinned. Oh now maybe I should Elliot because I like what I see so far .

" Got it " Darian walked up the steps he looked round at Elliot " Also the boss is off limits to " Elliot pouted " Shame cause i like what i see " Darian shook his head in the old days he wouldn't have had second thoughts and had Elliot taking him to one the rooms .Giving him pleasure showing him his dominance .

" Elliot " Elliot looked round at Darian " You don't want to mess with me " and at that Darian left wow Elliot thought that was blunt and straight to the point Elliot smiled an arm came round his shoulder Elliot looked over at Dan the guy he was chatting to . " Ready , we're getting an uber " " Great let's go " .

While Bill drove Darian home he sniggered into himself and Elliot reminded him off Malcolm when they first met he sure has some balls. The young lad Darian thought my family is everything to me. I would never dare start again; they would never forgive me .

Darian stood in the bedroom at the sight before him Philip in the middle of Cameron and Malcolm he smiled at his little family Darian went over to Cameron and gently shook him, waking him he looked over at Darian . " Hey you " "What time is it? " .

" After 2 Philip ok " Cameron looked round at Philip and Malcolm asleep " He seems fine " Cameron got up they both went downstairs to the lounge kitchen Cameron made himself a hot chocolate Darian sat on the stool and wiped his face Cameron looked over at him he looked tired . " You want one " Cameron asked Darian he shook his head Cameron went over to him wrapping his arms round Darians shoulders . " Tired " Darian looked up at Cameron into his blue eyes he kissed his nose " Not to bad just got to sort out the memberships there's something I've been thinking about we could go over with discuss it with Claudia when she's Better "

" Sure we can do that " " Daddy " they looked round at Philip standing at the kitchen door Darian went over to him and bent down to his level " Hows my boy " Darian felt his head a little warm " Do you want a drink buddy " Philip nodded his head footsteps on the stairs Malcolm appeared hair a mess and bleary eyed .

" What's going on? " Darian sniggered and shook his head at his family. He looked over at Cameron with Philip getting him a drink. " You just got in. " " Yes, let's go to bed. " " Philip, ok " " seems okay. " Darian lay his arm round Malcolm's shoulder kissing his head Malcolm looks up at Darian still sleepy he looks beautiful Darian thought at that moment .

" Daddy can I sleep in your bed again " " Philip asked Cameron" Sure buddy c'mon let's go back to bed " Philip held Darians hand going upstairs to the bedroom Philip running over to the bed jumping on it Darian sniggers watching him my beautiful boy he thought we are so Thankful to have him .

Philip went in the middle between Darian and Malcolm Cameron on Darians side Philip snuggled into Darian sucking his thumb Darian looked round at him he smiled at his little champion he thought this is my family no one can break it . And if they try to, well there will be hell to pay if they do . Philip snuggles into Darian sucking his thumb Darian lying awake thinking he looks round at Malcolm and Cameron he smiles Malcolm lays his arm round Darians stomach Darian holds his hand then eventually drifts off to sleep .

Chapter 5

The day off Mollys birthday party that Darian , Malcolm and Cameron were invited to also Sam and Geraint with Daisy Mae the kids played in the Garden at Carrie and Michaels home while the parents sat outside on the patio since the weather was warming up and nearly the end of May .The food was inside in the kitchen for everyone to take when they wanted so it didn't get spoiled by the flys good company Carrie thought while the conversation flowed .

Micheal was inside getting food and drinks sorted Carrie came inside to help Michael's Phone beeped Carrie looked over at him ignoring his phone " Can you bring the wine out Micheal " "Sure " .Carrie sighed looking at Micheal while he sorted the drinks out .

Carrie shook her head and sighed again then left to go outside. Micheal took a deep breath holding onto the sink before he went outside. Shaking his head he was not much in the mood for all this today but it's for Molly he thought it's her birthday he just wished he could sort things with Carrie they had to talk about things .

" What is it you do Darian " Stella Alice's wife asked Malcolm tried not to laugh Cameron dunted him " I own a club in town " " Which one " Darian looked at Cameron and back at Stella " Club Nero " " " We should visit it Hun " Malcolm snorted everyone looked at him what's funny Carrie thought when she came over with the food and drinks . "Did I say something wrong? "" Stella, it's a membership club, " Darian said, smirking. Stella still didn't understand.Looking at Alice she shrugged her shoulders not knowing either .

" A men's club do you mean " ". Women can go with or without a partner. It's a sex club called " . Carrie nearly choked on her drink. Micheal came over what's going on he thought just as one the other mothers came out from being. In the bathroom. " What have I missed? " Joanna asked everyone. " Joanna looked round at everyone and at her husband Chris ." Wow really is that how you guys meet " Stella asked Chris whispered to Joanne what happened she was wide eyed . " NO " Chris nodded, grinning .

" I knew Darian first before Cam came along " Malcolm announced looking at Darian and Cameron " So you guys dated first then " Carrie asked looking at Micheal and back at Darian " Not exactly " Malcolm said " More friends with benefits thing for a while " Darian announced fascinating Stella thought looking at Carrie she smiled at her wife taking her hand . " What " Stella shook her head Carrie did notice some tension between Carrie and Micheal would talk to her later about it .Maybe she needed girls to talk about stuff .

" I WAS INTRODUCED TO the club by a friend. That's how we met," Cameron said looking at Darian and Malcolm. " We did meet in the toilet at the club. " Malcolm giggled. "Wow, everyone thought in a toilet " Not like I was cleaning it at the time " . Cameron grinned looking at Malcolm. He did think back at that time how cute Malcolm was. Malcolm smiled at Cameron and noticed by Darian my boys were eyeballing each other he thought sipping his wine .

" So how much is the membership then " Carrie asked Micheal glared at her what a thing to ask he thought " it's 2 grand a year " Darian explained " No way really " Stella asked that's pricey she thought looking at Alice `` We are thinking off extending right

Darian " Malcolm looking at Darian he nodded " Were to " Michael asked looking up at them oh he can speak now Carrie thought after being silent for the past half hour . " Looking at property in Edinburgh and Glasgow "

"DADDY I NEED THE TOILET " Philip asked Darian he got up and off they went inside the house " He's quite intense isn't he " Carrie mentioned to Cameron " He is a pussycat really " " Darian can be intense sometimes if he's not sure about people right babe " Malcolm explained looking at Cameron and back at Carrie " I get that " .Carrie said once get to know people Cameron, Malcolm and Darian are nice people she thought . She did notice before Darian was intense but she guessed that's the Italian in him .

" UNCLE ELLIOT " Molly shouted when she spotted her uncle coming into the garden she raced over to him he bent down to pick her up and swung her round Carrie sighed and shook her head Micheal looked round Malcolm and Cameron senses tension " My little brother and he's late " Carrie got up and went over to Elliot taking him inside to chat . She didn't sound pleased that Malcolm thought they did not get on at all .

DARIAN CAME DOWNSTAIRS after helping Philip in the toilet he got a shock when he saw Elliot from the club in Carrie's kitchen "Daddy can I get a drink " " Sure buddy " Darian looks at Elliot while Philip gets his drink. What is he doing here Darian thought.

" DAD I'M HUNGRY TO " Darian got a plate and piled some sandwiches on them for Philip also helping himself to some crisps

" Darian my brother Elliot , Elliot Darian " " Pleased to meet you " Darian nodded gave Philip his plate he went outside to Cameron and Malcolm "Thats Cameron and Malcolm there in a throuple relationship " .Carrie explains to Elliot he looks out to the garden a throuple they are in nice he thought smiling to himself .

" Wow cool " Elliot smiled Darian smiled and nodded " More wine Darian red or white " " Red please " Carrie poured Darian more wine as Elliot went into the fridge for a beer " Elliot's at college doing engineering " Darian hummed thinking holy shit what age is he Darian thought he picked up a sandwich listening while eating Carrie explaining that Elliot was in his second year at college .

"MUM CAN WE GET OUT the karaoke please " Carries son jack asked oh god she thought there gonna be at this all afternoon " Ok come on then " Carrie and jack disappeared into the lounge to get the karaoke machine leaving Darian and Elliot in the kitchen " Small l world " Elliot looking outside at Malcolm and Cameron with Philip Malcolm looked over at Darian in the kitchen with Carries brother .

" Our policy is you have to be 21 to join the club " Elliot snorted he knew that the security should have checked that he thought" damn I have 2 years to wait " taking a drink off his beer looking over at Darian " karaokes starting soon " Malcolm announced coming into the kitchen he came over to Darian he shakes his arm through Darians looking at Elliot . " Hi I'm Malcolm" he and Elliot shook hands " The throuple couple I've been hearing about " Malcolm looked at Darian and back at Elliot `` Thats us and that's Philip our kid " Malcolm pointed to Elliot looked over cute kid he thought sitting with his other dad .

" Cool " then the karaoke started Molly singing first Elliot sniggered that kid he thought they got the kids the karaoke machine for Christmas "Uncle Elliot come sing " Molly came into the kitchen and dragged Elliot outside .Elliot looked round at Darian and Malcolm smiling when he got over to Mollys karaoke machine .Malcolm seemed nice he was yet to speak to Cameron he had heard that they were a tight bunch it looked like it he thought from what he had seen .

Malcolm looked at Darian and smiled " Babe pour me a glass wine im going to the bathroom " Darian sighed and shook his head Malcolm had already had 3 glasses he was flushed he pinched Darians bottom and whispers " Don't sigh with the attitude " kissing Darians Cheek " oh and Cam wants another glass to " Bossy Darian thought shaking his head while he poured the wine .

Malcolm went upstairs to the toilet Darian went back to Cameron and handed him his glass wine " Whats up "Cameron asked Darian touching his knee noticed by Elliot " Nothing love " Darian looked over at Philip jumping on the trampoline Cameron looked over to he sniggered he's gonna be one hyper boy when he gets home .But he was having fun with his friends which was a good thing Cameron thought .

" Kids huh " Carrie said sitting down next to them looking over at her brother with Molly "How do you manage it " Darian and Cameron looked over at Carrie what did she mean as they sipped their wine chatting ." What do you mean? " Cameron asked Malcolm, who came back outside and went over to Sam and Geraint who were talking to Elliot, noticed by Darian.

" Parenting with the three off you " " it just came naturally i guess right Darian " Darian nodded and smiled " We compromise on stuff we each take turns on the school run , bedtime routine etc also helps we have a nanny to " " We wouldn't get anything done if we didn't " Darian announced Cameron looks at him that's true Cameron thought .

" That's so great you guys " " He also understands about us three to nothing fazes him now we don't hide anything from him " Darian explains that's the way they were going to approach it at first and it's not harming him in any way Cameron thought .

The others thought that was great and Alice and her partner were the same with Jacob. People were always curious who the mum was. It wasn't their business unless they asked questions which was fine just don't be weird about it . It's happening all the time same sex couples or single people having families just other people have got to accept that if they didn't like it that was their problem .

Later when they got home Malcolm had a little too much to drink Sam helped him upstairs to the bedroom Philip thought it was funny the boy was a tad to hyper Darian thought to much sugar intake for one day " Daddy's drunk " Cameron tried to keep a straight face by the comment Sam.came back downstairs into the lounge . " I've left him on the bed " " Thanks Sam " .Darian tutted Malcolm should have known not to drink so much he will definitely suffer in the morning .j

" No problem Cameron see you guys tomorrow " Sam left Darian to put the kettle on to make coffee for him and Cameron ` ` I'm not tired daddy " Darian heard Philip complaining he shook his head that boy he fights every time . " Go get your jammies then and you can sit up for a bit " Philips face lit up and he ran upstairs to his room.and brought down his jammies to put on Darian made him a drink .Philip sitting beside Cameron snuggling into his blankie Cameron lay his arm around Philip while they watched a bit of tv before bed .

Darian shook his head when he got upstairs to see to Malcolm he was laying sprawled out on the bed he went over to him standing over him shaking his head " Malcolm you need to change " Darian leaned over to help Malcolm groaned and held onto Darian. Going to kiss him the smell of alcohol off him .

" You are the the best "Malcolm says holding onto Darian " Yes yes i know c'mon lets get you changed " Darian went to help to take off his shirt Malcolm grabbed him " Are you trying to seduce me old man " .Malcolm grinning at Darian tearing at his shirt trying to take off Darians shirt . " Malcolm no c'mon " Malcolm pouted laying down on the bed " Spoilsport " Malcolm huffed, shaking his finger at him .

Darian stood up and thought it best to leave him. He can be very tetchy when he has had alcohol. He laid the blanket around him and went back downstairs. Cameron is sitting in the lounge with Philip reading a story to him. He looked up at Darian coming into the room going over to them . " Malcolm ok " " He's fine, fell asleep " .

Micheal had read Molly her bedtime story he left her bedroom door slightly opened she was exhausted after her party he went downstairs he heard Carrie and Elliot talking in the kitchen she was having a go at Elliot about his promiscuity over the past couple months Micheal shook his head he was young still and still had a lot to learn but she was right in a way . Micheal cleared his throat and went into the kitchen " Micheal please talk some sense into him " " Sis I'm being careful you shouldn't need to worry about me " Micheal stood at the table listening to them bicker it's really not my place to tell Elliot what to do all we have to do is support him .

Carrie sighed she did worry about him she thought all she wanted was for Elliot to find someone to love since Leyton passed away he hasn't shown any interest in anyone else since just sleeping around lately which has got to stop Carrie thought .All she wanted for Elliot is to be happy but he didn't seem happy lately she thought and wondered what she could do to help him through a tough time .

Darian is in the office a couple days later at the club going over the plans for the new possible club for Glasgow that Cameron and Malcolm will go over to . Frank Sydney's friend had come across two possible venues for Darian to check over Frank had also Emailed Darian regarding the second site for him . The location sounded good in the west end of Glasgow the busier side off Glasgow Darian had thought about extending the club years ago but didn't do anything about it till now .He had wanted the club in Edinburgh to be a success which I has been thankfully he was also thankful for the great staff he has to .

Darian sat down at his desk checking out the plans the door chapped, possibly his staff arriving for their shift they normally popped their head in whenever they arrived . " Come in " Darian looked up as the door opened. Elliot's face appears smiling Darian sighs and shakes his head at this kid he thought entering his office . He sure has some balls, that's for sure he thought I have no time for his games Darian thought .

" I'm busy what do you want " Elliot huffs what a nice greeting he thought noticing the table with papers looks like plans Elliot thought Darian looks up cocks his head "What's this " " Nosey Aren't you " Darian stands up gathering up the papers rude Elliot thought " "If you must know they are plans for a new venture " " Cool " Elliot sits on the couch Darian looks over at him as he has made himself comfy on his couch Darian sighed getting annoyed with Elliot .

Elliot notices Darians annoyance and what's up with him Elliot thought is it my presence or does he not want his husbands to know I'm here Elliot smirked Darian staring at him calm down Elliot thought .

" Malcolm and Cameron will be here soon " Elliot looks up at Darian he smirks again what's he scared off Elliot thought Darians phone pings off a text he checks it which is from Cameron on his way over " what's the problem old man " Darian scowls at Elliot again shakes his head . The door chaps again " Come in " Julia appears and notices the young man from the. Other night Elliot nods . " Boss Ed's here and spencer to "

" Good Claudia will be a little late when the others come in check the rooms Carlos the Dj will be here soon to set up " Julia leaves " I'm looking for a job "

" Look somewhere else Elliot " Elliot pouts Darian looking up at him Darian gets up goes over to the door and opens it gesturing for Elliot to go he gets up goes over to Darian leaning into him . " Do you know you're pretty hot when you're angry? " Darian shakes his head. Elliot leaves the sniggers going out of the office. Darian watches him. Darian swears in Italian, shutting his office door and calming himself don't get angry, he thought .

Cameron is coming down the steps as Elliot is coming up them. What's he doing here Cameron thought " Elliot " " Hey we meet again oh Darian asked me to come along for an application form to fill in for bar work " Funny Darian didn't mention that he probably forgot Cameron thought . Elliot went off Cameron going into the club Malcolm had noticed the exchange between Cameron and Elliot when he drove up to the club and also wondered why Elliot was here too.This guy had no shame he thought what is his game Malcolm wanted to know .

Darian kissed Cameron's cheek when he came into the office the door chapped again Malcolm came inside coming over to Darian " why was Elliot here " " That's what i was wondering to Cameron and Malcolm looking at Darian he huffed those two are being silly he thought . " Carrie thought a job in the club would be good for him bar work " Darian explains to Cameron and Malcolm .

Malcolm looked over at Cameron and back at Darian " is there something you want to tell us " " Mal " Cameron said Malcolm sniggers Darian huffs again Malcolm pats Darians back " Your face "

Darian huffs he has to stop teasing me like that Darian thought . The door chaps and opens Claudia appears she looks kinda pale Darian thought " Claudia are you ok " .

" fine nothing to worry about i'll go check on the others "

" Babe is Claudia ok " Malcolm asked looking at Cameron`` Not sure " Darian hoped she was ok for a while Claudia wasn't being herself lately and he hoped it wasn't anything too serious or to do with her boyfriend Nick who she has been with for seven years now he was a lovely chap Darian liked him he and Claudia were good together and had been in a long term relationship for seven years now .

They looked at the plans for the new potential building in Glasgow Darian called Frank to arrange the meeting to check out the buildings Anna Called Cameron after picking up Philip from school and they were on there way to the club after the three of them went out to the bar everyone was setting up for tonight Carlos the regular Dj has just arrived to set up . He was reliable which was good and if he wasn't able to help out then his work partner helped out with the Dj sets .

CLAUDIA WAS CHECKING out the drinks when Darian came over to her she looked at him " Claudia I have known you long enough to know something is wrong " " Not here " Darian nodded and they both went into the office Darian leaned against the table Claudia standing in front of him she chewed her lip feeling nervous " You know Nick and I have been together a long time " "He hasn't cheated on you has he ". He better not or I will have words with him Darian thought he had a good lady in Claudia .

Claudia snorted and shook her head looking up at Darian `` No he wouldn't dare it's nothing serious apart from in 7 months your gonna have to hire a new co manager "What did she mean Darian thought are Claudia and Nick planning on leaving he hoped not Claudia went into her bag and handed him an envelope he looked at her . " This better not be a resignation letter " Claudia giggled at the silly man she thought "Definitely not Darian look at it " Darian opened the envelope and it was a scan picture surely not Darian looked at Claudia she nodded Darian smiled . Wow Darian thought staring at the scan photo looking at Claudia grinning and nodding .

" Your pregnant " Claudia nodded tears forming Darian went to her they hugged just as Malcolm and Cameron were coming inside they looked at each other " what's going on " Darian and Claudia looked over at them " Claudia is with Child " Oh wow Cameron thought that's brilliant news he and Malcolm going over to Claudia congratulating her . " We didn't want to jinx it before I'm sorry I didn't mention it before " " That's ok I'm happy you're ok " .All three of them hugged all happy with Claudias news. It's what she had wanted for some time now Darian thought she would be a great mother .

Philip arrived bursting through the door running over to Darian he bent down to pick him up looking over at Claudia " it's the best feeling in the world " Darian pinching Philips cheek " Except for the sleepless nights " Malcolm announced Claudia giggled that wouldn't matter she thought she had always wanted children and now it's going to happen . She couldn't wait, it didn't matter boy or girl and she could see Darian dotted on Philip as well as Cameron and Malcolm.

"Daddy can I get a cola ":"Off course you can aunty Claudia can take you " Philip went over to Claudia he took her hand she bent down going into her pocket bringing out a pound Philips face lit up " Thanks Aunty Claudia " .

OFF THE TWO OF THEM went into the bar for Philip to get a drink sitting on the stool at the bar area Cameron sat on Darians chair Malcolm on the couch Everything ok Anna " " Fne there's a letter something about a school trip out " Anna handed Malcolm the letter opening it he read it an outing for next month to the zoo and a picnic after That's good he thought Philip would like that he loves the zoo whenever they get a chance to go .

Bill was engrossed in his phone over at the seating area when Darian and the others came out to the bar he didn't look too happy Darian thought he hoped it wasn't relationship problems Malcolm sat beside Philip on his stool while sipping his cola . Malcolm got out his phone scrolling for one of Philips programmes for him to watch while they waited Claudia fussing over Philip Malcolm thought she would be a great mother to her own kid .And Philip liked her which was good she was good with him whenever they brought Philip to the club .

Dean Bill's boyfriend appeared Darian noticed going over to Bill sitting beside him taking his hand " Darian " He looked round at Cameron and back at Bill " What is it " " Not sure " Cameron looked over at Bill with Dean talking Bill wiping his eyes Dean laying his arms around him .They have definitely had a fight Darian thought hopefully they will work it out Darian thought .If he wants to talk to him about it he knows he can .

" Who is hungry " Darian announced Philip beams Darian ruffles his hair and kisses his head " You are always hungry little man " Darian tickles him Philip yelps "Daddy stop " Cameron giggles that boy he thought Malcolm s phone rings he sighs and checks caller ID his work colleague Joanne he excuses himself to take the call .Cameron wonders sometimes Malcolm can't get a break but he knew what he was getting himself into with the job he enjoyed doing .

" Everything ok " Darian asks Bill and Dean they look up at him and at each other " Fine nothing to worry about Darian " Bill explains taking Dean's hand Dean is looking at him while he is kidding Darian though there is definitely something not right with them . " Darian " Darian looks round at Malcolm as he is on the phone dialling someone . "Sorry emergency I've gotta go into work " Darian sighs it's such a shame whenever Malcolm clocks off he sometimes has to go back in . " Joanne's coming for me " Darian lays his arm round Malcolm walking off to the door .

" That's ok we will see you later " Malcolm kisses both Darian and Cameron and kisses Philip's head before he leaves. He hates this part of trying to intervene for people but it's part of his job he has to do .The intervention part was hard on them and the person especially when they are sometimes in denial about the situation they are in .

Chapter 6

❝ It's not too bad right dad " Sam looking out the window off the rehabilitation centre that Tom got transferred to a week later Tom looks round the place it'll do he guessed sitting in his wheelchair Geraint sits down his bag on the bed " I suppose so " Sam looked round he looked up at Geraint he shrugged his shoulders them one the nurses came into the room to check on things to take some notes and emergency No's then left .

":Do you want to go outside for some air daddy?yh " " Not at the moment. Tom sighs and looks out the window of the Garden . He thought Sam and Geraint looked at each other shrugging their shoulders .

Sam got out some off his dads things while Tom looks out the window again Sam looks round and at Geraint he winks at Sam " Daisy Mae had started dancing lessons Tom " Geraint said Tom grunted Geraint looks at Sam the nurse comes back inside with a note for Toms belongings then leaves for Sam and Geraint to do .And to let them know when it's done for his file .

" Does she like it? " Tom asked, sighing , still looking out the window. " She does even ask if you want to come along one day. " Sam exclaims, Tom hums his answer and he seems interested . " Why is she not here that day? Tom asks Geraint who leans against the window .

" My mum will be picking her up at Nursery, we will bring her soon " Tom hums again to the other granny. He thought to the

Nursery " Do you want me to pick up more toiletries Dad " " Ok thanks " .

The door chaps the arrival of his Aunt Mae Laiden with shopping for Tom he doesn't look very happy Mae thought while she handed him his chocolate " Can I get a fag " Sam sighed god forgive me he thought if he asks that one more time . " I think they have a smoking area here. " Mae announced looking at Sam, he seemed annoyed at Tom . Understandably she thought he did constantly ask if he could have a smoke. She would speak to the nurse about that later while she left out Tom's supplies .

Darian , Cameron and Malcolm got out of the car and looked up at the building of the potential new club. They looked at each other. Malcolm thought will see what it looks like inside Frank and Lucy arrived a few minutes later. It was good to see them, Darian thought ." The caretaker Mr Johnson is inside waiting for us " Frank explains as they all go inside Paul the caretaker is waiting for them at the entrance . " Good to meet you Mr Longstrom ":" You to this is Malcolm and Cameron my partners " .

" Hello so what do you think as you see it's in the middle of the west end busy area around here there are the theatres " Paul explains the features off the club Darian nodding his head listening on the way round Malcolm looking at Cameron now and again hoping he will like the place it does look a tad run down Cameron thought probably needs a lot work done to and thought hopefully not to much work .And it was in a busy area to like Paul had mentioned with bars restaurants the theatres around .

" Interesting place but my concern is the work it needs done and why it's not selling " Darian asks Paul looks at Frank for advice " Darian I know but it has potential right "Frank says looking around everyone . They all nodded and Paul looked at Frank again hoping that Darian would agree to take on the place .And make it into something else that might interest new customers .

" Cam , Malcolm what do you think " " Well my thought is why don't we look at the other place then crunch no's right " Cameron says looking at Malcolm Darian nods and hums while taking a walk around Paul looks nervous Malcolm thought poor guy he probably need reassurance " Don't worry Paul he's thinking and taking it in " " Right ok " Paul looking over at Darian talking to Frank .Yea Malcolm's right he does seem engrossed and listening and he seems a bit intense to that's probably the way he is .

After the first visit they go to the second sight where they meet Deanna the other caretaker off the sight which didn't look as bad as the last one they looked at he looked a little more interested in this one Cameron and Malcolm thought and yea it does seem different from the other place while doing the walk round interaction with Deanna the caretaker .

Darian thought the site looked better than the last one; he liked the feel of it and it looked like they didn't need to do a lot of construction like the last one although they do need it inspected first before they go ahead and do alterations but yes definitely Darian thought and of course he Cameron and Malcolm would have to talk about it first before going ahead .

Elliot came into Club Nero he looked round the staff were busy getting ready for opening he went over to the bar where Julia was she looked up at him "Hey i'm Elliot " "Ahh Claudia mentioned you would be starting give me a sec ill call her " I think I'm gonna like working here Elliot thought and wondered if Darian would give him a full time position he thought .

Julia went over to one the phones dialled the no for the office Elliot looked round was Darian not here he thought " Claudia is coming " " Cool thanks " .He looks around the room again noticed by Julia who thinks he is wondering if Darian is around .

Julia went back to setting up Elliot and sat on the stool " Darians in Glasgow " Julia announced Elliot looked over at her in Glasgow what is he doing there for he wondered " Elliot " he looked round at Claudia standing beside him he got up Claudia gave a faint smile " Let's go into the office " .

Elliots uniform was there to pick up Claudia went over to the table, picked up an envelope to hand to Elliot " Your bank details , And Nda to sign " Elliot screwed up his face why an Nda to sign he thought opening the envelope. "Why an Nda " Also a copy of his employment agreement " It's a must for all employees our policy Darian doesn't want employees to talk about the club outside or to any other club or bar " Understandable Elliot thought but a bit extreme to he thought to .

Elliot signed it and handed it to Claudia. The door chapped Bailey and one of the other employees came in. " For tonight you and Bailey help each other get to know the ropes . " " Sure." . Bailey smiled and nodded Claudia sat at Darians chair she had hoped Elliot would do ok as long as he keeps out of trouble then Darian will be happy .

BAILEY AND ELLIOT SORTED out the tables in the bar for opening which was in an hour Bailey seemed ok as well as the other staff Elliot was starting to get a feel of the place " Hey Bailey what's with the Nda thing about " " Well the boss doesn't want us spouting things to other people " Yea understandable Elliot thought which he wouldn't do the others seemed ok to Elliot thought wouldn't be so bad working here thanks to Darian . "How long you worked here " " 5 years " wow Elliot thought he must like his job to stay for so long .

" What's Darian doing in Glasgow " " Your asking a lot questions Elliot " Claudia overhearing Their Conversation when she passed to go over to the bar Shit Elliot thought he didn't realise he had " Sorry didn't mean to pry " Before he went on to his next job Claudia pulled him to the side "Just remember he was good enough to give you this job for your sisters sake and I know you didn't mean to ask so many questions " . Elliot nodded no I don't want to fuck it up I need this job he thought and Claudia was right .

Claudia was right Elliot thought Carrie was good enough to asking Darian about a job while he was doing his course "You will do ok Elliot just keep your head down and you will get to know everyone " Elliot nodded yes I'm being a bit big headed he thought I should tone it down maybe thanks to Claudia advice . Just curious about everything Elliot thought and excited, maybe a tad too excited . He thought and maybe toned it down .

A COUPLE HOURS PASSED and the club got busy with the regulars Elliot helping out Bailey with the drink orders and taking champagne up to the vip area and leaving drinks outside the rooms to some the members seemed ok he quickly got to know who tipped and who didn't . And who was with who and some singles just at the club to drink and get to know people too.

SAM AND GERAINT CAME into the club Sam noticed Elliot so Darian gave him a job then he thought Geraint notice to " so little fanboy working here now " Geraint joked Sam looked round at him he shook his head Geraint sniggered they went over to one off the tables Claudia came over with there drinks . " How's he doing? " Sam asked. They looked over at Elliot taking a tray of drinks over to the vip area. " Not too bad at least he's taking it all in which is good " " That's good how you " Claudia looked down at her stomach and rubbed it she smiled looking at Sam and Geraint .

" Were good just got to keep down food " " it'll be worth it in the end believe me " Geraint said they knew when there surrogate had terrible sickness with the pregnancy " Need anything else " Claudia asked before moving on " We are good " Sam checked his phone for any updates from Aunt Mae . Geraint wished he wouldn't stress so much he thought he took Sam's hand he looked up at Geraint `` Babe your stressing again " " Sorry I know do you think he likes it there " Geraint moved closer to Sam lay his arm around his shoulder " Just stop we're here to chill out " Geraint kissed Sam they bumped heads `` I know sorry " " I know a good stress reliever " .Geraint cocked his head grinning at Sam .

Sam smiled he touched Geraint's face it had been a busy week with work his dad Daisy Mae her dance practice they had barely time for themselves Geraint moved closer "Babe let me take care off you tonight " Sam blushed he looked down at their hands intertwined Sam smiled looking up at Geraint he nodded Geraint got up going over to Sam pinching his bum and kissed Sam's cheek . " I'll go get the key " Sam nodded so good to him he thought as he watched Geraint go up to Claudia they chatted for a few minutes she smiled and nodded looking over at Sam smiling face at him .

SAM AND GERAINT WALKED into the room holding hands Sam walked over to the bed he sat down folded his legs and smiled at Geraint standing watching him Geraint goes over to the drawers he looks round at Sam watching him he smiles Geraint goes into the drawer bringing out a couple feathers a mask for over Sam's eyes and a vibrator . He goes into the other drawer for the cuffs " Babe not the cuffs " Geraint looks round at Sam at the top of the bed butt naked oh wow Geraint thought he loved the sight of his husband Naked and so willing Nice he thought .Sam smirking chewing his lip fuck me Geraint thought when he does that his cock went hard .

Geraint takes off his shirt unbuttons his jeans and crawls up the bed to Sam they kiss Geraint feels Sam's hardness against his leg very keen he thought Geraint lifted the mask and put it over Sam's eyes and lifting the feather gliding it down Sam's torso and giving light kisses after Geraint looks up at Sam his mouth open . Geraint repeated the same he did before this time licking Sam's ear and whispered " Is that good " " Mmm " is all Sam could say they kissed again grinding into each other .Geraint flicking on the vibrator rolling it down Sam's chest he wiggled at the vibration and hummed until he got to his cock rolling the vibrator over his groyne Sam moaning .Geraint loving the sound of Sam while giving him pleasure it was turning him on to especially Sam's little whimpers whenever he used the vibrator .

" How does that feel " Geraint whispers to Sam ``G ..good "
Geraint bends down and takes Sam in his mouth while rolling the
vibrator round his groyne it was intense Sam thought but good to
Geraint moved the vibrator inside Sam while they kissed tingles
down his back . Sam thought he was gonna come soon as Geraint
repeated the motion Sam bit into his hand as Geraint lifted me
off Sam's legs and entering him Sam lifted his arms onto Geraint's
shoulders Geraint pounding into him .Geraint kissing Sam stifling
his scream pounding into Sam again both sweaty Geraint holding
onto Sam's hand .

" Geraint so good " Geraint kissed Sam down his chin to his
chest flicking the vibrator up down Sam's chest again it tingles Sam
thought Geraint sat the vibrator down and lifted up Sam's leg
guiding himself in Sam hissed Geraint held Sam's hand getting into
a rhythm again.

They both collapsed onto the bed Sam took off the mask
snuggling into Geraint " Ok " " mmm yes " They kissed Sam leaned
on his arm his other hand on Geraint chest looking down at Geraint
groyne Sam licked his lips " Babe " " Mmm " Sam looked up " I'm
good you don't have to " Sam sat up leaning into Geraint " Let me
take care of you to " .Sam asked grinning Geraint lay back touching
Sam's face Sam looks down oh my he thought he is very willing again
licking his lips .

Sam kissed Geraint then slid kissing all the way down his chest
Geraint held onto Sam's head when he took him in his mouth
Geraint closed his eyes letting Sam do his thing while Sam took
the vibrator doing the same to Geraint in slow circles fuck Geraint
thought so good . Sam reaches up to kiss Geraint still the vibrator
on circling it over his cock " Shit Sam " .Man that's intense Geraint
thought but pleasurable he thought .

Sam giggled, trailing the vibrator inside Geraint teasing at his
entrance, Geraint bucked at the intrusion, Sam bent down taking

His cock in his mouth,Good Geraint thought going with the sensation Geraint came quickly, Sam looked up at Geraint, his face flushed, Sam wiping his mouth, grinning . He reaches back up to Geraint " Baby that was good " Good " .Sam kisses Geraint then leaning his head on Geraint's chest Geraint bending to kiss Sam's cheek just what they both needed Geraint thought no distractions tonight just them.

Elliot was taking a tray of drinks and champagne to one the rooms when Sam and Geraint came out one of the rooms arm in arm giggling Elliot smiled well aren't they lucky tonight he thought they both nodded at him passing arms round each other .

" lucky sods " Elliot muttered Sam looked round " Elliot " Elliot looked round at them " A bit of etiquette when entering the play rooms " Elliot blushed Sam looked at Geraint and back at Elliot " Sorry i didn't " .i've done it again Elliot thought I can't keep my mouth shut .Is this job really for me he thought .

" Just keep your nose clean ok " And when Elliot disappeared round the corner Geraint sniggered and Sam looked at him." That told him " Sam slid his arm round Geraints' ' He kinda reminds me of Malcolm a bit " .Sam said mind you Geraint thought he did a bit but the kid had a lot to learn he guessed .But he seemed ok just needed to curb his curiosity a bit .

DARIAN WAS SITTING on the chair in the hotel room still looking at the plans for the new club he was in his robe he sighed again chewing his lip thinking . Cameron looked round at him and shook his head while he dried his hair. What is up with him now Cameron thought while carrying on doing his hair . Philip came running into the bedroom followed by Malcolm. He was already ready for bed. He went over to Darian and picked up Philip onto his knee.

" What's that daddy? " Philip pointed to the plans " A new venture." Philip screwed up his face. Darian tickled him. Philip screamed as Cameron and Malcolm laughed. " Daddies and I are possibly buying a new place " To live " .Philip asked, snuggling into Darian, sucking his thumb .

" No baby , A new bar like the other one " Malcolm explained Malcolm could tell his little mind was ticking over " Why " Darian looked at Cameron and Malcolm " well we " thought it was a good idea and a new venture " .Philip screwed up his face Darian duffles his hair Philip giggling .

" Philip, your hot chocolate is ready, " Anna shouted from the other room. He jumped down and looked at Darian. " Daddy, What is a throuple " Malcolm nearly choked on his drink, looking between Cameron and Darian where did he hear that from they thought .Possibly school again the things they hear these days .

" It's something like double of everything, go on go get your hot chocolate " off he went into the other room Darian shaking his head " i think we will have to watch what we say when he's near " Darian asks Malcolm comes over to Darian and leans on his chair true he thought or he might have heard it from the other kids .

CAMERON READS PHILIP his bedtime story from the book he brought with him snuggling into his dad sucking his thumb "Dad " " Yes buddy " " Can we go to soft play tomorrow " .Philip looks up at Cameron snuggling into him .He does like going to the soft play but Darian hated it to many germs around he complains constantly about it several times but they still took him .

" Yes we can after daddy Darian has his meeting then we can go " " Ok " .Philip sighs and yawns sucking his thumb again Cameron shakes his head he will soon stop sucking his thumb they hoped .

Cameron shuts the adjoining door and locks it; he looks over at Darian still looking over the plans while Malcolm is texting Cameron goes over to Darian and takes the paper off him Looking up at Cameron " Leave it for tonight " Darian sighs tutting Nope I need to check " But " .

" Cams right you have been staring at it for too long " Is " Cameron holds his hand against Darians Hand he looks up at him again " No shop talk us time " Cameron takes his hand away Darian smiles looks over at Malcolm who gets up coming over to the two of them . Darian goes to get up, Cameron stops him and bends down, looks up at Darian " Let me take care of you " .

Joe came into the club he went to the bar and ordering a drink Claudia saw him from the Vip area he was alone she noticed Sam and Geraint had not long left she excused herself and went over to him " Joe how are you " Joe looks round at Claudia and thought has he missed Sam and Geraint he thought " Sam and Geraint just left " "Yes they mentioned they would be here Shame I missed them " Elliot noticed the good looking guy that just arrived at the club nice leather jacket he thought he was kinda his type to Claudia left to go back up to the vip area Joe drank his beer checking his phone when Elliot came over to the bar .

Joe looked up new guy he noticed he smiled then came over to Joe " Another drink " " Thank I'm ok you're new "Joe asked he hadn't noticed him.before he thought " Elliot just started tonight " Elliot smiled sorting out the drinks and nibbles Joe watching Elliot thinking naughty thoughts no i shouldn't think that he thought smiling into himself .But it doesn't hurt to look right Joe thought to himself while he drank his beer a few people at the bar getting there orders

ELLIOT LOOKS OVER AT the bar again he is cute Elliot thought shit he thought now I have a boner while he serves the drinks at the tables to customers Joe looks round at Elliot while he is serving the tables and notices his cute dimple stop staring Joe thought giving himself a pep talk shaking his head .

ELLIOT SAT UP IN BED he looked round at Joe asleep beside him and smiled thinking back about last night pretty good night he thought Elliot stretched his back hurting from last nights sex session he looked over at the bedside table the two used condoms Elliot got up picked up his clothes from the floor and went into the bathroom to get dressed . He checked his phone and his sister had texted asking where he was since he had let her know he wouldn't be home till the next day Elliot came out the bathroom Joe was awake sitting up in bed he looked round at Elliot coming out the bathroom. Already dressed, Joe thought and did not let him know .

" I gotta go " " So soon I was gonna make breakfast " Awkward Elliot thought breakfast no other one night stand wanted to make breakfast he just left after Joe cocked his head " Thanks anyway and it was fun " .Elliot smiled while fixing himself .Joe sniggers What is wrong with him is he feeling awkward Joe thought.

" Sure Elliot " " Yea " Joe got up went over to Elliot he looked up at Joe " I guess we both needed someone last night " " Yea " And at that Elliot left he leaned against the door shut his eyes for a second yea he guessed he did need someone last night hopefully no one would find out he slept with a customer he would be on big trouble but it was a fun night he liked Joe he got a good Vibe from him .

Chapter 7

" Daddy i want that one " Philip pointed to the superman pop figure Cameron looked up at the one he pointed to Malcolm over at the other side looking at the other figures in the forbidden planet store Darian couldn't figure out what the fascinating was for them .Although they did like the superhero movies and you would like not want " Malcolm sniggered he so sounded like Darian telling Philip the proper pronunciation " Daddy Mickey to " .

CAMERON BENT DOWN IN front of Philip " Philip what did we talk about " " Ok just the one then " Malcolm came over and bent down to and handed Philip the Mickey pop figure Philips face brightened "But since you have been good you can get two today " Cameron looked at Malcolm he shook his head Malcolm always gave into him sometimes but he's got to learn he can't get everything all the time and not spoil Philip to much .

" Have we decided then " Darian asked Philip, looking up at him and going over to him "Daddy two today " Philip holding up the figures Darian nodded he looked over at Cameron and Malcolm they shrugged their shoulders he guessed he would be paying for them . Cameron got his wallet out and Philip went to the till to pay for them while Malcolm still looked " Have you decided yet " Darian asked, sounding bored Malcolm looked at him " A couple I'm gonna get " .What is up with him Malcolm thought he is so impatient today .Malcolm looks round at Darian checking his phone for the thousandth time Seriously he had got to get out of work mood .

AFTER THEY WENT TO get food Philip sat his figures beside him after their dinner they went to the car Philip holding onto Malcolm's hand and noticing a couple people in shop doors " Daddy " " Yes buddy " Malcolm asked looking down at him " Why are those people sitting there have they not got homes " Malcolm looked over at the beggar at the shop door how does he explain it to Philip .But no sugar coating it he has to learn sometime why people don't have homes .Malcolm looks over at Darian and Cameron watching them while Malcolm tries to explain to Philip about the homeless man .

" PHILIP SOMETIMES PEOPLE don't have homes to stay in " Philip looked up at his dad Darian stood at the car with Cameron while Malcolm explained why people beg and circumstances at home could be difficult they both went over to the beggar and bent down Malcolm gave the man a ten pound note Philip hugging into his dad while they chatted to the beggar . " Bless you, thank you " .Philip leaned onto his dad while he spoke to the man .

" It's for food ok here is our card so you can come along for shelter when you need it " The man took the card to the place Malcolm worked for homeless people " What's the kiddies name " Malcolm slid his arm round Philips waist he leaned into his dad . " This is Philip " " Have you somewhere to stay tonight? " Darian asked Malcolm, looking up at him and back at the man. " I do the hostel but it's not very nice, weirdos of all sorts. " Understood Malcolm thought because there were people who took advantage of it .Maybe that's why he is sleeping outdoors .

" Sorry to hear that " Darian gave the man a twenty pound note. He looked surprised " For food ok " " Thanks mister " Wow Malcolm thought that was very generous he did hope the beggar wouldn't squander it and get food or something hot Darian can be generous sometimes and he was glad that he acknowledged the homeless man

.

They got back into the car Malcolm buckled Philip into his seat kissed his head and got into the other side Cameron was driving back to the Hotel Malcolm sat forward " Thanks you didn't need to " Darian looked round he smiled at Malcolm `` As long he gets food " "Daddy Robbie " Darian groaned not Robbie Williams again he rolled his eyes Malcolm sniggered Cameron put on the Cd and Angels came on . Malcolm tickled Philip he squealed "Daddy stop it tickles " Philip giggling .

The song "Let me entertain you came on " Philip punched the air on one his favourite songs. Darian shook his head. Cameron looked round at him and he reached for Darians hand ." You can have your classics later " " Oh great " They both laughed Darian looked round at Philip and Malcolm doing the actions off Robbie Williams . " Daddy, can we meet Robbie Williams one day? Darian sniggered where his imagination came from, he thought ."And that's a possibility someday to take Philip to one of Robbies concerts ." Maybe if you are good and do good at school and possibly get pocket money with doing some chores " " Really " Darian nodded Cameron grinned while driving Yea they could take him to a concert one day he thought .

SAM SAT THE CLEANING products in the kitchen cupboard. He looked round the flat and looked so much better he thought once his dad was up and about better he would be getting home. He and his aunt suggested he go into a sheltered housing but he

wasn't having any off that he wanted back home . " Hello only me "
His aunt shouted when she arrived in the kitchen "Smells so much
better doesn't it " His aunt said Sam sat on the chair in the kitchen
his aunt put on the kettle and leaned against the sink . "What are
you thinking? "" Nothing really, just that I wish he would consider
sheltered housing " .

Mae sat on the other side of the table. She brought out some
sandwiches for them. She handed a packet to Sam. " We can try again
Sam. " He hoped it would be so much better but his dad was strong
willed and would chat to his dad again about it soon .Besides there
were wardens at the sheltered housing and they could think about
getting him a carer or a befriender to help out whenever he and his
Aunt were not around .

Later that day Malcolm came with Sam to the rehab place to
visit his dad Sam warned him not to take any notice of what he says
Malcolm was used to his ways before which didn't worry him . Tom
was surprised to see Malcolm as Sam had mentioned how he was
doing lately and about Philip . Sam went to get the coffees leaving
Malcolm with his dad Malcolm thought Tom was looking not too
bad Sam did say he was doing better .Still his grumpy self Malcolm
noticed which Sam had mentioned before .

" You doing ok then " Tom asked Malcolm looked up at him "
I'm doing good Tom " Tom nodded and wished he could have a fag
also Malcolm got out his phone for a photo of Philip he handed the
phone to Tom he at it the little blonde blue eyed boy Tom smiled .
" Cute kiddie just like Daisy Mae " She is definitely a daddy's girl "
.Malcolm sniggered Yep she definitely a daddy's girl but Sam was a
good father to Daisy Mae .

" You two were right tearaways " Malcolm huffed thinking back
to the time he and Sam raised a riot back then they were young and
didn't know any better " I kinda thought you two would get married
or something " Malcolm huffed again and Sam married Malcolm

shook his head . " I care about him a lot. He's my best friend. I fell in love with two people who know what would have happened to Tom " .

Sam listened into the conversation outside he smiled he couldn't never be without Malcolm they had been through a lot when they were younger and the bond between them was strong and since that time away in Blackpool it got more stronger then and that would be between them . Sam took a deep breath and went back into the room with the coffees Malcolm looks at him and Winks Sam handing him his Coffee and his dad one too.

Later walking to there cars Sam patted Malcolm s back " Thanks Mate l " Malcolm looked round at him he repeated the same " Your welcome your ok right " Sam leaned against the car stuck his hands in his pockets " I'm ok you know what he's like " Malcolm snorted he cocked his head " I know hang in there he will come round " Sam nodded Malcolm checked the time on his phone shit he's gonna be late for Joe he thought .

" Talk soon I'm late to see Joe " " How is he? " That's what Malcolm wanted to know. He sounded sad when he talked to him the other day. Maybe he just wants a chat.Or maybe missing Nate who knows " Not sure " they both hugged and said they love yous and parted arranging to come over soon .

JOE CHECKED THE TIME for the hundredth time Malcolm had texted letting him know he would be running late. Joe sipped his coffee, his knee bouncing. He bit his nail again and sighed a pat on his back. He looked round at Malcolm, smiling down at him . " Alright " " I am now " Malcolm ordered two more coffees and a toastie for himself Joe seemed anxious Malcolm thought what is up with him Joe leaned forward looking down at his hands Jesus Malcolm thought will he just tell him what had happened .

" Joe whatever it is spit it out " " I feel bad but it was good now I feel guilty " Malcolm screwed his face he sipped his coffee how many did Joe have he thought " I went to the club the other night missed Sam and Geraint , I guess we just needed each other get over Nate cheating on me " . Malcolm smiled listening to Joe rant about his one night stand " .Well i guess it was what he needed and why not Malcolm thought .But now regrets it if that's what he is meaning .

"Am I a bad person Malcolm " " No joe you're not was it good " Joe snorted was it good he thought thinking back seven nights ago his one night stand with Elliot " That good huh " Joe nodded he bit his lip " Mal don't tell Darian please " " Joe don't be silly why would I want to tell Darian you had a one night stand " .

" it was one his employees " oh shit Malcolm thought one off the policy's that Darian made none the employee have sexual relations with any off the members " Joe I won't tell but " " I know it was stupid but we got talking and I wanted to make him breakfast next morning " Malcolm giggled Joe trying to explain things and thought who from the club who he would sleep with . " Joe honestly don't beat yourself up about it, we all make mistakes right, have you seen him again " .

Joe shook his head and he dared not to repeat what happened. " I've talked it out with Nate and told him what happened. He was ok about it, surprising "" That's good right he understood, especially he did the same " . That is good Malcolm thought they were talking. I hope they try to forgive each other .

Joe took another sip of his coffee now he felt much lighter talking it out with Malcolm " Nate's coming in a couple days so we can sort things out I can't forgive him yet but I can't let him go either does that sound sense " " It does especially if you still live with each other " .

That was good to hear Malcolm thought Joe and Nate had to talk it out and try not give up on their relationship. Maybe compromise in things he thought " So how the new place coming along " Joe asked. Hopefully they could start the renovations soon Malcolm thought maybe that will not stress Darian anymore .He was being a nightmare lately and if anything isn't right it had to be perfect .If it's not perfect well everyone gets it the sooner they get things going the better .

" Darians stress about it but I think we made the right choice in the building. The location is good so here's hoping it's a success like the club "" I hope so too " .Joe meant that for Darian to have the success of a new Club and hopefully it will work .He likes Darian and he could see Malcolm was happy to a nice little family unit they have maybe he and Nate will have kids someday in the future that's something they can chat about .

After they hugged their goodbyes and made arrangements to meet when Nate arrived Joe beeped as he drove off Malcolm got into his car to pick up Philip from school .Shaking his head about Joe and his one night stand he will not mention it to Darian unless Joe says something about it .

CLAUDIA HAD GIVEN ELLIOT a good report back to Darian Julia and Bailey had given him good praise regarding his time keeping and keeping his nose clean Darian hoped he would keep it up . Darian had given Claudia the night off he would host the next couple nights she had done well since he had been away in Glasgow. Darian sat at the edge of the bar going over rotas for the next month. The club was getting busy with members, some coming for a good time, some just to hang out with friends having drinks and Chatting.

" Hey " Cameron pinched Darians bottom. He looked up and smiled. Cameron leaned on the bar facing Darian " Taking a break " Darian asked Cameron had been writing in the office editing and adding new to his book . " U huh i wanted to see your face " Darian shook his head and huffed . " You see enough of me love " Darian gave Cameron a peck on the nose they hugged .

Elliot was going round the tables collecting glasses and bringing members their drinks. " Elliot " He looked round at one of the members calling him.he went over to him " You want another drink " "Yea and the inside scoop " handed Elliot a packet of something under his tray then stuffed it in his pocket . " Ok " . Is it bad of me that I took it? Elliot thought he looked round hoping that no one saw them looking at the guy nodding at him .

" Julia cover for me pee break " .

ELLIOT SNORTED THE coke up both nostrils he wiped his nose and sat on the toilet seat letting the effects off the coke come over him good stuff he thought feeling euphoric after a few minutes Elliot cleaned up the remants off the coke he flushed the opened the cubicle door he got a fright Darian standing against the sink fuck Elliot thought busted did he notice earlier Elliot thought .

" Boss " Elliot waved his hand " I would give that a minute " Elliot looking at Darian he was looking furious shit Elliot thought he thought he was being discreet seemingly not .Elliot went over to the sink to wash his hands Darian watching him .

" My office now " fuck Elliot thought maybe he shouldn't have took the coke after all did Darian see him with Will I have fucked it up haven't I now dammit Elliot you idiot following Darian to the office .

Cameron sat on the other side off the couch Darian was fuming shouting at Elliot saying how could he be so stupid and trusting him giving him the job after Carrie asking if he could give him a job Elliot looked so small sitting on the couch Darian was right at what he was saying to him . The door chapped Ron once the security came inside with Will Ron stayed with them Will looked down at Elliot he looked like he was about to cry .

" Mr Matthews what's our policy in this club " Darian asked Will looked down at his feet and looked back up at Darian " No drug taking Darian I do apologise I didn't mean " Will looked at Elliot what could he say he made a mistake " You are suspended for a month "What the hell " Will thought a month that's harsh "your lucky your not barred Will " Cameron announced looking at Darian which he thought he needed to calm down it has been s stressful few days he thought now having to deal with this .

" Ok I accept that my poor judgement " " Ron will see you out " Darian sighed pinching the bridge of his nose. I don't need this, he thought , not in my club . I will not have drug taking in my club. I will have to speak to the staff about it, he thought .Also the security needs to have more check members before coming into the club .

Will walked up the steps as Carrie arrived Julia saw her arrive before she also went into the office looking round at everyone what was going on Julia thought Elliot looked upset " Julia will you let members know we're closing at 11 " " sure boss " . Must be serious if Darian is closing early he looks really pissed too .

Carrie shook her head shocked to hear what happened between Will and Elliot. He was doing so well going to college doing his shifts at the club she thought he was on the right path this time Carrie took Elliot's hand he looked at her Carrie sighed . " We really have to have a good talk when we get home Elliot " Elliot nodded and looked up at Darian and Cameron " Two weeks suspension you're lucky it's not a month like Will " . Darian says it's got to be done. He is lucky he didn't fire him but I'm doing Carrie a favour and give Elliot a chance to sort himself out .

" Ok accept that I am sorry " Elliot was relieved that he was to keep his job, his head pounding from the effects of the coke he liked working at the club The people and boy Darian ran in ship shape taking no shit from anyone .Which is a good thing Elliot thought his staff were definitely loyal to him he could see that .

Malcolm arrived at the Club and went into the bar. He could tell everyone was tense and doing their best to keep busy after his call from Darian letting him know what happened ." Hey Julia how bad is it " " Bad Malcolm he's suspended Will for a month " Shit Malcolm thought that is bad the security should have been more thorough in checking this kind of thing didn't happen before he thought . " He had decided to close early "understandable Malcolm thought after what had happened .

While driving back home Elliot wiped his eyes blew his nose while on a come down from the effects off the coke he took Carrie looked over at him Elliot looked out the window "I miss him " Carrie looked over and back at the road she nodded she knew exactly what he meant " Your bound to Elliot how long has it Been " . Carrie did feel bad for Elliot. He was really upset; she knew exactly how he was feeling but what could she do to help him out .

" Two years sis i'm sorry i really am " Carrie sighed she went to take Elliots hand then he started crying oh god Carrie thought he's really feeling it now " C'mon now its ok " They will have to talk more and about Leyton Elliot's boyfriend that died two years ago now .She should have known how he was feeling Elliot shouldn't have kept it to himself .

"Thanks Lauren for looking after the kids " Lauren touched Carrie's shoulder Elliot was exhausted he went up to bed Carrie sat at the table she was exhausted too . " No problem, the kids are fine there sleeping " .

Thank god for that Carrie thought she didn't have the energy to deal with them right now .As well as Elliot she will have to talk to Micheal tomorrow when he calls from offshore and text him later with an update and things will have to change around here Carrie thought her and Micheal will need a good proper chat about it .

ED, RON AND MAX THE security stood in front off Darian in his office Bill sat on the couch " Sorry boss " Ed said Darian shook his head "Guys we need to be more careful in future especially new members they know the policy and i trust you guys you have been here the longest " The guys understood Darian was a good boss a firm but fair boss regarding the club and of course they would be more vigilant next time .

" He was really upset Micheal " Carried said to him over there Skype call they did every couple days whenever he worked away from home " I could be doing with you here right now Micheal " Carrie sat back in her chair yawning " I know you do honey I know your exhausted just hang in there ok "

Carrie huffed and hung in there she thought it's a lot to deal with at once " Michael I don't want to fight I honestly don't but you're not here and when you are you don't want to be " " Carrie that's not true I do you guys are my world " . Carrie wanted to believe what they could do to sort it, she thought . " Then prove it Micheal " Carrie was right there were things they had to work on in their marriage and working away didn't help either . With Elliot living with them didn't help much either but Carrie didn't want him to move out she wanted to keep an eye on him but many a time Micheal had said he wasn't a child and adult and decided for himself if he wanted to move out .

ELLIOT LAY IN BED SCROLLING through photos off his late boyfriend Leyton the good times they had his first boyfriend the love his life the plans they were going to make when they left school Elliot thought back if only they hadn't gone to that rave everyone was going on about and the bad ecstasy tablet Leyton took which cost him his life . Elliot wipes his eyes he thought he had moved on but it had hit him like a lightning bolt thinking about Leyton and what their life would have been like Elliot giving his sister a hard time. Maybe he should look for his own place now like he had always wanted to do .

The door chapped Carrie came inside with hot chocolate for him she sat at the edge off the bed she looked tired and signs she had been crying " You always made the best hot chocolate sis " Carrie smiled and patted his knee she went to get up looked round " Is Micheal mad " " Just a tad " Carrie looked over at a photo off Elliot and

Leyton Elliot looked over at the photo to . " It's his birthday soon, " Elliot exclaims. Carrie nods, " I was gonna visit " " You want me to come with you " .

Elliot shakes his head he would rather go himself this time it had been at least a couple months since he visited Leytons grave " I'm gonna go to bed now Micheal will be home next week we can all talk about stuff then ok " " Sis I was thinking about getting my own place " .He has been thinking about moving out for a while Carrie thought maybe it be a good thing maybe .

" Elliot it's up to you I could help you out wouldn't it be too much with your college fees " " Just an idea " Elliot lay his head on Carrie's shoulder she patted his head it had been a rough night for both of them he just needs to sleep it off now Carrie thought .

MALCOLM THOUGHT CARRIE didn't look happy while they waited on the kids coming out. It had been a couple days since the incident at the club Carrie sighed Malcolm looked round at her . " Carrie whats up " she looked round "How do you guys manage it" Manage what " " Philip your own time together "

Malcolm sniggered and shook his head. Carrie looked round at him " How is Elliot and we schedule things " Carrie looked round at Malcolm shedule stuff she thought " Sometimes we don't have to ".

" Elliots fine now at college today Micheal and I need to get back to what we were before you know" we definitely need to have us time she thought because there wasn't much of that lately .When Micheal is home he often goes golfing with friends or they are busy with the kids which is full on .

" Daddy " Philip came running over to Malcolm followed by Molly and Jacob Alice came over to Carrie and Malcolm she could tell Carrie wasn't happy they exchanged words as Malcolm put Philip in the car he looked up at Carrie and Alice hugged before they got into their own cars. Alice hoped it wasn't anything too serious she thought because if.she wanted to chat she was more than welcome to.

ELLIOT PLACED THE FLOWERS on leytons grave he noticed a fresh bunch laying there and still the teddy that Elliot had left the last time Elliot bent down in front off leytons grave " Hey you you like the flowers " Elliot touched leytons grave stone and bowed his head sniffing Elliot wiped his nose . " I'm trying to move on to Leyton but it's hard you know " Elliot places the flowers beside the stone " College is going ok I got a part time job nearly botched that i think but the owner well he is something else Leyton " .

Elliot stood up wiped his eyes he was aware off someone behind him he looked round and was surprised to see Darian standing how did he know he would be here he thought his sister maybe " Boss " I " hope you don't mind " Darian came closer to Elliot handing him the flowers he nodded Darian placed them beside the stone they look at each other a silent understanding . What a kind thing to do Elliot thought he looked over at Darian and smiled and looked at Leytons grave again taking a deep breath Jesus Leyton is wishing you were still here .

" He was my first love " Darian looked at Elliot he looked at Darian "You never get over your first " Darian exclaimed Elliot looked at him so did he have heartbreak to he thought " What happened " " His name was Zeke he also passed away " Shit Elliot thought he's also lost someone he cared about to Darian put his hands in his pockets and sighed Eliot cocked his head . " Have I still got a job then? " Darian huffed and shook his head "smiled at Elliot "Of course you have " .

Elliot smiled moving closer to Darian he placed his hand on Darians chest he looked up at Darian "Good to know " Darian took

Elliot's hand away from his chest " Not a good idea like i said before Elliot " " God I'm sorry shit " Elliot turned his back from Darian misread again Elliot thought when will I ever get it right he thought " You will find love again Elliot " Elliot wiped his nose and eyes looking round at leytons grave . "Do you think so " " I do " .

Elliot looked round at Darian would he find love like he did with his partners ``Let me drive you home " Elliot huffed why was he being so kind to him he thought as they walked to Darians car nice Elliot thought inspecting the sports car Darian watching him . "It's new Cameron thinks I'm going through as they say a mid life crisis " Elliot looked up and laughed mid life crisis so funny it certainly did seem he was .

While driving along Darians phone rang he turned on the phone by his earpiece Malcolm's voice Darian smiled Elliot looked at him " You get him " " I did love taking Elliot home now " Darian looking at Elliot while he's looking out the window " He ok " Malcolm asked Darian looking over at Elliot " Seem so " .

" Good " Malcolm looking over at the door of his office at the family that just arrived for mediation " Love you " Malcolm said Darian smiled " Love you to " Elliot looked over at Darian after he said it and smiled they must have a really special bond he thought .which is ok he guessed he is a catch and he is italian and all italians must be this good looking Elliot thought. And probably good lovers as he expects .

CARRIE HANDED DARIAN his coffee while Mabel, their cat, sniffed about Darians feet. Carrie picked her up and sat her on her knee stroking her, the cat purring away Darian Dogs Cats were weird . There were some photos on the mantelpiece and table Darian noticed one photo of Carrie , Elliot with a lady Carrie noticed him looking curious to know who they were .

Carrie picked up the photo "My mum is in a nursing home unfortunately she has Huntington's syndrome " " Sorry to hear that " Thats sad to hear Darian thought there must be a lot for Carrie to deal with does it run in the family Darian thought.

Carrie nodded as she picked up the plate of biscuits handing them ro Darian " Thanks " " Elliot was only ten when she was diagnosed Micheal and i were engaged at the time " Ahh Darian thought Carrie became both mother and sister then that must've been hard for them at the time.

Noises coming from the garden the arrival of Carrie's children Elliot had gone to pick them both up from school they came into the living room they noticed Darian sitting there Elliot came into the lounge with the kids bags . " Guys go and get changed ok uncle Elliot will help ok " Elliot looked at Darian he nodded then took the kids upstairs to get changed Carrie watched them go smiling .

" HOW DO YOU THINK he is " Carrie asked Darian letting Mabel down and she scarpered off of to the kitchen " Probably needs to talk to a professional how he's feeling " Carrie nodded maybe Darians right she thought he had been keeping stuff from him ever since Leyton died and didn't date much after his death .Darian looks at his watch he should get going soon " I've kept you long enough Darian sorry " .

" it's ok not to worry, I do have to get going soon " .

Darian gets up the same with Carrie Darian notices another picture with Carrie and Elliot with another person then it becomes clear who it is " That's our other brother he died " Carrie explains when she noticed the picture Julius long lost sister and brother when was it taken he wondered . " Long story " Darian. Nodded and smiling Jesus in his head thinking about Julius , Elliot came into the lounge watching Darian leave. Carrie looked round at him while talking to Darian before he got into the car ." He is a lovely person once you get to know him " Carrie said looking at Elliot they looked at each other Elliot nods about to go upstairs.

" Elliot he has a family " He knows that Elliot thought and had turned him down several times " Carrie I know besides I wouldn't do that well I kinda made a pass at him twice " Carrie was shocked to hear that he did possibly just a crush she hoped Elliot goes up to his room sitting on the bed and looks over at Leytons picture .Picking up the picture looking at it Elliot lays on his bed with Leytons picture on his chest thinking about stuff .

WHILE DRIVING BACK home Darian dialled Lyle his friend and private eye Lyle answered on the second ring " Darian what can I do for you " " Lyle I think I may have found Julius estranged family Carrie Mathews can you have a dig for me."

" Sure I can do that, send me the details " . " Will Do "

" DADDY " PHILIP SHOUTED when Darian came into the kitchen he picked him up and gave him a kiss on the cheek Cameron came into the kitchen Malcolm was already there sorting out dinner with ingrid Darian gave Cameron a kiss on the cheek and pinched his bum he sniggered shaking his head . Darian went over to Malcolm giving him a hug which Darian thought was a bit cold he didn't want to acknowledge was Malcolm in the huff with him he thought maybe to do with Elliot Malcolm gives Darian a faint smile acknowledging him .

" IS ELLIOT OK? " CAMERON asked Darian, sitting down on the stool beside him." I think Carrie said he was visiting his late boyfriend's grave. Malcolm looked round at them when Elliot's boyfriend died Darian looked round at Malcolm and back at Cameron . " He died two years ago from a bad ecstasy tablet he took at a rave " Not great Malcolm thought that is a lot to deal with Malcolm thought especially not his fault his late boyfriend dying because of a dodgy ecstasy tablet.

" That's not good " Malcolm came over to the table leaning on it. That's bad he thought poor guy he must've been devastated at that time. " Do we need to have a conversation? Malcolm asked Cameron and Darian looked round at him. He did look across, Darian thought .Maybe I've overstepped regarding Elliot he thought and that's why Malcolm is cross with him .He and Cameron both know that he would never do anything with anyone again since the last time .

" About what "Malcolm sighed, stood up, crossed his arms and stood. In front of Darian and Cameron "C'mon Darian isn't it obvious Elliot has a thing for you "" Mal " Cameron scolded, shaking his head Darian sighed, not remotely interested in anyone else Darian thought he went to take Malcolm's hand he pulled away .He is definitely cross with him the way he is behaving towards Darian .

"Didn't we have a pact if anyone was interested in anyone we would talk about it " " Malcolm I am not interested in anyone else I have told Elliot how it is please believe me you two are all I need forever we swore on it didn't we " Cameron lay his hand on Malcolm's shoulder he looked at Cameron and back at Darian .He needs to calm down Cameron thought it's obvious that Elliot just has a crush on Darian .

" Please believe me i have learned my lesson " laying his hand on Cameron's shoulder Cameron smiled and laid his hand on Darians a silent understanding he knew Darian wouldnt cheat ever again . "

Are you happy with us Darian? Malcolm asked Darian and Cameron looked at Malcolm, shocked at what he said .Why would he ask that he had the family that he has always wanted, a son who he adores and two men who he loves equally .Off course I am happy with our little unit Malcolm's just pissed at me .

Darian reached for Malcolm he went closer to him " You two and Philip are my world you guys are more than enough " Darian looked between Cameron and Malcolm the three of them hugging . Philip came into the kitchen and saw his dads hugging. He ran over to them and went in the middle, all four moving closer to each other. Cameron picked up Philip. The three of them kissed their son's cheek Philip giggled.screwing his face up .My Daddies are being weird again Philip thought they parted Darian touched Malcolm's face he leaned into his touch . " I love you both please believe that "

Malcolm nodded, maybe he was a bit harsh regarding Elliot and maybe it is just a crush he has and maybe they should all talk to Elliot about it he thought .

Chapter 8

S am listened to Malcolm rant when he came over to chat. He really let rip about Elliot while Geraint did the dishes Daisy Mae was drawing .Sam felt for him after what they had been through to be together over the years and Darian cheating on Cameron then regretted it after . "Am I being unreasonable " " No Mal your not I would be the same to at least you know he wouldn't right "

" What about you have a foursome " Geraint suggested he looked round from washing the dishes Sam Glared at him " Definitely not " " Just suggesting " Geraint went over to Daisy Mae kissed her head she screwed up her face at him " I'm gonna go run her bath " Geraint announced leaving Sam and Malcolm to talk Malcolm's phone beeped of a text he checked it which was from Darian .

Malcolm huffed probably wants to sweet talk him I'm not giving in Malcolm thought make him sweat a bit checking the text .

Darian " I miss you ❤ ❤ ☺" Malcolm smiled Darian had gone to the club to check on things his phone beeped again Again Malcolm checked the text sweet talker he thought .

Darian " I love you so much ❤❤"

" Smooth Talker " Malcolm whispered Sam looked up what's he on about he thought Malcolm looks up at Sam " Darian texting me " Malcolm got up said his goodbyes to Sam they hugged before leaving then went home Cameron was in the office Malcolm slid the door open Cameron looked round at Malcolm standing there he smiled and lay out his arms for Malcolm to come to him .

Malcolm bent down and lay his head on Cameron's knee " Vent over " Malcolm looked up and nodded. Cameron smiled "Good then you have nothing to worry about ok " Malcolm stood up and brought the other chair over to sit on . " I know and saying Elliot needs help with a couple things it just brought it back when he helped me " .Cameron touched Malcolm's face he leaned into Cameron's touch . " Please don't worry too much, ok " Malcolm nodded. Yea he just feels stupid now he thought .overreacting to the situation .If Darian strayed again he would cut his balls off sniggering into himself shaking his head silly bugger .

DARIAN IS IN HIS OFFICE Lyle had checked out some stuff for him while he was going over his hunch . Carrie and Elliot are Julius siblings he wanted to make sure first before he said something to Cameron and Malcolm the door chaps Darian puts the envelope in the drawer Malcolm appears . Darian smiles and Malcolm comes over to him and they hug " I'm sorry for overreacting " " I know it's ok " . Darian smiles cocking his head Malcolm standing at the door then comes over to Darian he looks up at Malcolm leaning over him .

  " I love you to " Darian sniggers he's come over to the club to tell him that he could've just texted it Malcolm gets up goes over to the door and locks it Darian smirks " Make up " You bet Darian thought he gets up goes over to Malcolm they kiss while stripping Darian pins Malcolm against the wall grinding into him .kissing then clothes were discarded .

  Malcolm leans over Darian on the couch sliding his hand down to Darians crotch Darian hisses Malcolm kisses Darians neck " This is mine no one else's right " Malcolm looks up at Darian scowling " You understand right " " Yes yes of course " Good Malcolm thought smirking Darian went to wrap his arms round Malcolm's waist he lifted up Darians arms pinning them to the couch and wiggles his bum . " No teasing " .

Claudia walks along the corridor to go to Darians office with his coffee she chaps the door goes to open it which is locked and hears noises oh my she thought and blushes and smiles well I guess he doesn't want his coffee now she giggles into herself and decides to leave his coffee outside the office .He will probably want it later when they are finished .

JOE WAITS AT THE ARRIVALS for Nate to arrive. He was nervous and excited at the same time his mother was getting better now and he and Nate had to talk it out and Joe maybe decided to go back to New Zealand . Some people started coming through the arrivals gate. After a few people arrived Nate came through the gate Joe waved and they met halfway and embraced " I'm so happy to see you " Nate said Joe nodded tears in his eyes Nate wiped them away "Happy your here c'mon let's go " .

They held hands all the way to the parking lot. They stopped at the car looking at each other. Joe goes to open the car but Nate takes his hand again. They look at each other again. " Baby steps Nate ok " " I know I came didn't I " .Joe comes over to Nate they look at each other Joe goes to hug Nate .

" I have missed you " That's good Nate thought he had to Nate patting Joe's back " Right let's get to my dads " Joe wipes his eyes going over to the drivers side and they drive back to his parents house .Baby steps Joe thought they needed to get back to what they had before Nate cheated and why Joe thought Nate reached for joe's hand he looks round at Nate smiling at him Joe takes his hand on the drive back to his parents .

Chapter 9

D arian is checking out the drinks orders a couple days later t with Paul while Claudia is checking out the other orders at the club. The renovations for the new club in Glasgow are going great and going to plan, Darian and the others will meet with Lucy and Frank to go over more plans for the colour scheme . Darian asked Sam to come up with the sign for the club which will be Nero's instead of club Nero this time .So not to confuse people and everyone else thought it was a good name too .

" Boss " Darian looked up at Bill he also noticed Micheal Carries husband he was looking around the club " Mr Mathews wants to talk to you " Bill looks round at Micheal who is over at the seating area I wonder why he is here Darian thought thanking Bill .He doesn't look to happy Darian thought is it to do with Elliot maybe..

DARIAN TAKES MICHEAL into his office Darian leans against the table Micheal looks nervous he thought Darian gets up goes over to Micheal puts his hand on his shoulder " Spit it out Micheal " Darian goes round to his chair at the desk Micheal sitting down at the chair at the desk " I don't know how to say this but I was wondering if you could help Carrie and me " " What with " An unusual request Darian thought but ok .

Shit Micheal thought wringing his hands Carrie and him talked two nights before they had a good sex life before the kids came along and with him working away off shore it depleted a bit. Maybe the odd quickly at bed time were both frustrating . " It's been about 2 and a half months since Carrie and I had you know good sex " Darian snorted. Wow, he thought he hadn't had someone come to him regarding this before . " Sorry I didn't mean to laugh, go on " .

" it's ok you see we used to have a good sex live you know she's stressed because of her mum and Elliot the way he's been " Darian nodded Elliot seems to be doing ok he thought keeping his nose clean Darian sat forward thinking how he could help "What you both need is a night out no kids overnight at a hotel " .Maybe that would help Darian thought sometimes he Cameron and Malcolm did that to .

" Could we book a room here " " You can I'll even give you it for free " Wow Micheal thought that was generous of him he wasn't so bad after all Micheal nodded he will need to plan it out though . " Can i ask whose more dominant do you like a bit kink toys " Micheal snorted they did use toys before kink dominance no but wouldn't rule that out he guessed he would try anything new as long as Carrie went along with it too .

" Toys yes but maybe a little kink " Darian went into his drawer and got out his pad off phone no's he would need he knew the two people that could help he wrote down the no's on the other pad and went to put the file into the drawer the file he had about Julius family still there . " Darian " he looked up Micheal looking concerned " Yes sorry I was just thinking i have a madam and Dom that come in to do workshops there names are madam Venus and Dom Nico they are a couple " .

" Oh i ..maybe Carrie and i could come along to check it out " Darian smiled. Maybe it would be a good thing if they did that there had been a mixture of couples coming to the workshop who wanted to learn more about s/m . Bdsm and kink since some were new to the scene .And wanted to try out new things that could work for them .

"THE NEXT WORKSHOP WE have is in a week's time please come along I will let madam and Dom Nico know " " Thank you so much Darian " " No problem " He is ok after all Micheal thought a bit intense still but Darian understood what people's needs were .

" You're not so bad after all " Micheal announces "I'm not that bad" Darian thought maybe a little intimidating at first with people he didn't know he expected.

After Micheal left Darian went back into the drawer and brought out the file which he had meant to take home and let Cameron and Malcolm know about Julius family the door chapped Claudia came inside " Its nearly two Darian " " Thanks Claudia " Darian stuffed the file back into the drawer he looked over at Claudia her stomach starting to show he smiled . Thinking back to when Philip was due " What are you gonna call the pup" " Not sure yet " Darians phone rang he sighed it was Malcolm he connected the call " I'm leaving now " .

Malcolm looked over at Cameron who was waiting at the car " He's just leaving " Malcolm shouted Cameron shook his head and then helped Philip into the car with Frank . What has kept him Cameron thought he did say he would be here when they were picking up the puppy .As usual work keeping him back again Cameron thought Malcolm just worries too much .

WHILE DRIVING ALONG Frank secured in the back seat Philip clapping him " Daddy " " Yes buddy " " What will we call him and will Frank like him " " We can name him anything you want " Cameron pipes up while Malcolm drove along he shook his head that boy " Frank already likes him remember from the last times " Malcolm explains " Dumbledor " Philip suggests Cameron looks at Malcolm " it's a girl Philip " .

" But girls can have boys' names right " he's probably right Malcolm thought boys and girls do have boys names these days " Luna Harry's friend " They all giggled at the suggestion of the girls name for their new puppy. Cameron liked the name to sound ok, he thought why not it may suit the new dog .

DARIAN WAS ALREADY at the breeder waiting for Malcolm and Cameron to arrive while he chatted to the couple Mhiari and Ed who ran the breeder farm where they got a good report from friends . They heard the car coming up the drive Malcolm parked the car Darian met them at the car while Cameron let out Philip and Frank he took the lead . " That was quick " Malcolm asked Darian he better not have been speeding he thought .

" Don't worry I wasn't speeding and I have something interesting to tell you later " oh Malcolm thought a bit of juicy news he thought Mhairi and Ed took them inside to see their puppy they were taking their daughter Hannah was with the other pups and their dog was separated so they could interact with her .

They kept Frank on his lead so not to frighten the pups the puppy was a border collie it was 2 months old and ready to be rehomed Malcolm went to her first her licking his face he giggled " I know I like you to " Philip stood beside Darian holding his hand not sure about the puppy maybe a bit overwhelmed Darian thought .Hopefully he will be ok he wasn't like that with Frank in the past they had him first before they had Philip he will eventually be ok Cameron thought all puppy's get excited .

Frank barked excitedly to see the puppy said to let them greet each other Darian bent down to Philip `` What is wrong buddy " " Will Frank like him? " Darian looked over at Malcolm with Frank interacting with the pup he smiled as Cameron watched on . " Look he likes her already " Cameron lays out his hand to Philip he goes to his dad Darian stands up watching them . Cameron looks over at Darian watching them and he cocks his head . " What's up? " Cameron asks Darian. He looks at Cameron. "Nothing love, I'm ok, look at them." They look over at Philip and Malcolm with Frank and the puppy running around . That's good progress they thought Frank seems ok with her which is good and Philip isn't too fazed by it .

Cameron slides his arm round Darians waist and they look at each other "We will be a family of five soon " Cameron says Darian nods " C'mon let's pick a name for her "For The Past couple days they had been picking out names for the new puppy but was still to pick one .Each giving out silly fun names for her which everyone thought was just to silly .

" WHAT ABOUT THIS ONE " Darian asks when they stop off at the pet shop for new stuff for the pup he picked out a new crate for her " Yea that should do for Luna " Malcolm looking round the crate Philip pouted noticed by Cameron he shook his head " Do you not you like the name now " " Not sure now Philip pouts hanging onto Cameron " Malcolm bent down in front off Philip pinched his cheek " We can call her anything you want buddy " Philip smiled nodding his head looking up at Cameron I think maybe he is a bit overwhelmed by it all Cameron thought " Ok " .

" Let's get some balls ok " Malcolm took Philip's hand while they headed to the toys section watched by Cameron and Darian " Micheal came to the club today " " What for " Cameron asked surprised " " To help him and Carrie get their sex life back " .Cameron looks at Darian again that's surprising he thought .But at least he came to Darian asking for advice he liked them .

" Wow really " Malcolm and Philip came back with the new toys and doggy treats for Frank they would be picking up Luna ? Next week to take her home with them " A decided on her name " The three of them looked at Philip " Luna is that ok " They were all in agreement at last the puppy will be called Luna thank god Darian thought .Because he couldn't go another day picking Dog names all day .

" WERE GOING ON A DATE " Carrie asked when Micheal suggested he and Carrie go on a night out just the two of them well that's a surprise she thought what's got into him since he got home it was nice though " Who is looking after the kids"

" Elliot I've asked him he's ok about it and I've warned him to " Carrie reached over to Micheal touching his face " I love you " Micheal announced Carrie blushed it had been a long time she heard him say that " I love you to " " You two get a room " Elliot laughing coming into the lounge they both looked over at him he had just come back from college . " How was college? " Carrie asked, getting up, picking up the washing basket, " Fine, same, I'm gonna crash for a bit, " And then Elliot left to go up to his room, while Micheal watched him go upstairs.

Micheal goes over to Carrie wrapping his arms round round Carrie's waist she leaned into him he kissed her cheek " I do wanna sort this Carrie " Carrie looks up at him and nods at me she taught .Me to we need time away to be together for a night .We need a night off to have some fun for a change get our groove back Carrie thought .

THAT NIGHT ELLIOT WORKED at Club Neros and was checking Me Lionel's card which was coming back declined twice " Mr Lionel your card has declined " Elliot had checked the members card Mr Lionel looked at Elliot " Are you sure can you check again " Elliot did the same with the card came back declined again " I don't understand " Mr Lionel going into his pocket bringing out his wallet .Checking his other cards how embarrassing he thought .

Malcolm was sitting at the end of the bar going over orders for the club when Elliot came over to him " Malcolm Mr Lionel's card had declined twice " Malcolm looked up at Elliot looking over at Mr Lionel flapping his card shaking his head at his friend trying to calm him down . Malcolm sighed this had been happening a lot with members he thought " Thanks leave it with me " Elliot went off to get more orders in Malcolm dial's the office to let Darian know what's going on with Mr Lionel .

" MR LIONEL COME TO my office," Darian asked him. Mr Lionel tutted what a carry on this is he thought following Darian to his office while Cameron was there sitting on the couch Mr Lionel sat at the chair at the desk Darian sat round the other side . " I don't understand Darian, my card has been working fine " Darian looks at a bit of paper and looks over at Cameron . " Mr Lionel you have been spending a lot on champagne and using the vip perks which is now over your limit " Darian looks at Mr Lionel handing him the inventory Mr Lionel taking it .

" Really oh my I didn't realise I do Like my champs " " it's 150 quid a bottle Mr Lionel " Cameron exclaims Mr Lionel the estimates off what he had been spending on Mr Luonel looked at it looking up at Darian . " Oh gosh it's a lot I will go over when I get home I am so sorry " . I really hope so, Darian thought, because his fees are not cheap he thought . " Mr Lionel if you could sort that Asap please " Darian asks before Mr Lionel leaves .

After Mr Lionel went out well that kinda went ok Darian thought he looked over Cameron " I was calm right " Cameron looks at him he smiles as Darian gets up " Yes you were calm babe " Darian comes over to Cameron he bends over him Cameron looks up at him smiling Darian cocks his head Cameron moves forward to kiss Darian . " Not right now Stud " Cameron smirks and sits back raising his arms along the back of the couch as he teases Darian and shakes his head . Oh he's teasing is he Darian thought shaking his head that won't do now .

" HEY YOU GUYS GOOD " Malcolm asked Joe and Nate who had just arrived at the club they both looked at each other and smiled "We had a good talk didn't we " Joe said Nate nodded "Mums doing better I'm gonna go back to New Zealand next week " " " That's great guys I'm pleased " Elliot looked over at Joe with another guy who was it he thought while they chatted to Malcolm Joe did mention another guy back in New Zealand could it be him Elliot thought .

WHILE MALCOLM GOT THEM drinks Joe looked round the club showing Nate where everything was. Joe noticed Elliot clearing tables; he hadn't seen him since their one night stand last week. Malcolm noticed Joe staring at Elliot while he and Nate chatted. Was he the one night stand Joe told him about he never said who it was with but it wasn't his business it was between Joe and Nate .

DARIAN AND CAMERON lay along the couch kissing both had hardons their shirts open the door chapped Darian had locked it dammit Darian thought what is it now he got up fixing themselves Cameron picked up the cushion holding at his crotch Jesus bad timing . Darian unlocked the door and opened it to Malcolm, smirking at Joe standing behind him with another guy . " We have visitors, " Malcolm announced, coming into the office. He looked over at Cameron on the couch looking flushed. " Darian , Nate, " Joe announced as they shook hands . Wow Nate thought he is handsome indeed like Joe had mentioned those eyes to and he seemed intense like Joe mentioned .

" Welcome lovely to see you " "Thanks Joe has told me a lot about you guys and the club I'm very impressed " " " Thank you "

Darian looks round at Cameron he gets up and goes over to the drinks cabinet " Drink anyone " " Thanks whiskey for me " Nate announces Cameron pours them all the drinks . Then handed everyone their drinks .

" I'M HEADING BACK TO New Zealand next week mums doing much better now " " that's good Joe please to hear that " Cameron says handing him his drink " you will miss Darians Birthday celebrations " Cameron says looking at Darian grinning at him .

Darian sighed sitting back on his chair Malcolm looked round at him Darian trying to forget he will be 80 soon 50 for others " Sorry about that what's the plans " " working on that " Malcolm looking at Cameron both them had something planned and Darian had thought about having his birthday celebrations at the club a theme night he had thought maybe an 80s theme .

JOE WENT TO THE BATHROOM just as Elliot came out of the stalls. They looked at each other. Joe smiled. Elliot washed his hands. " You good. " Joe asked. Elliot looked up at Joe. " Yeah you " " My boyfriend Nate and I'm going back to New Zealand next week. Joe nodded so he made up with his boyfriend, which was good for him, he thought at least they had sorted out their problems.

" That's great I better get back " Elliot left Joe did his business and went back to the office afterwards Malcolm walked Joe and Nate out to the taxi Nate waited at the taxi while Joe and Malcolm chatted .

" Joe " he looked up at Malcolm and looked round at Nate " it's Elliot isn't it " Joe nodded Malcolm shook his head and tutted " Mal I " Malcolm held up his hand and shook his head " How did you guess " "Intuition don't worry I won't say anything " .Malcolm grinned .

" Thanks Nate knows I slept with someone else but not who it was' ' They hugged then Joe and Nate went into the taxi they both waved as the taxi moved away Malcolm guessed Joe needed someone to get over Nate's infidelity .And they will definitely try and keep in touch more .

LATER THAT NIGHT WHILE Sam and Geraint slept Who the hell was calling at 2.30 in the morning when the ringing woke him up Sam sat up in bed and checked his phone the rehab centre " Sam " Geraint asked he looked round at him " It's the rehab place " Sam got up and went out to the landing to call them back what's going on he thought especially at this time at night .

" Hello it's Sam " " Sam there's no other way to say this but your dad has passed away " All the air got sucked out of Sam he dropped his phone and fell to the floor his hands on his hair he couldn't talk Geraint ran to him and took his phone from the floor to talk to the nurse . How can he be dead? He was ok the other day they went to see him. They had just reconciled that there were all these things Daisy Mae had wanted to do with her and Tom.

This can't be happening I'm not ready for this Sam thought Geraint picked up Sam from the floor taking him into the bedroom, tears running down Sam's face Geraint lay his arm round Sam comforting him giving him words of comfort while Sam sobbed in his arms " Why Geraint it's not fair " .

" THANKS CAMERON FOR taking Daisy Mae " Geraint had Called them regarding Sam's dad Malcolm bent down to talk to Sam he was so pale from the shock about his dad " It's no problem " Darian came to the door he looked over at Sam and Malcolm Cameron looked at him "She is asleep " .Good Sam thought its gonna be hard to talk to her about Grandpa but first they had to the rehab place .

MALCOLM LOOKED IN ON Daisy Mae in the spare guest room she was cuddling into her teddy poor Sam he thought so suddenly Cameron lay his hand on Malcolm's shoulder Malcolm looked round at him he lay his head against his shoulder . " c'mon let's go back to bed " Malcolm nodded Darian was already in bed he stretched out his arms for Malcolm to go to him Darian patted his back Malcolm sobbing it isn't fair he thought Tom was doing so well he thought .He felt bad for Sam they had just reconciled after all the years they didn't speak poor Daisy Mae to .

THE STAFF WERE SO NICE Sam thought of taking him and Geraint into the office to wait for his aunt to arrive Mel made them tea Geraint held Sam's hand he had been so quiet on the drive to the rehab Mel handed them their tea . " He was doing so well that's what I don't understand " Sam looked at Geraint while they held hands " it happens a lot Sam your dad isn't the only one we have lost with heart problems ":.Mel explained she was used to that in her job .

" Tell me he didn't suffer " " He didn't I promise Roland was doing his checks your dad was already gone " Sam nodded the door chapped Mae came into the room she went over to Sam and Geraint they embraced the door chapped again Lauren came inside . " Do you want to see him? " Mel asked if Sam thought it would help him, maybe for some comfort in himself. Sam wasn't sure if he did want to see his dad, maybe remembering how he was or maybe it would help him in his grieving .

They stood outside his dads room, Sam willing himself to go inside taking a deep breath before he went into the room Geraint took his hand Sam looked at him " I'm here it's ok " Sam looked at his aunt Mae he reached out his hand for her and then they went inside . Sam took another deep breath while the three of them held hands looking at the bed his dad was laying there .

Sam stared Mae took Tom's hand talking to him while Sam stood back and watched Mae look round at Sam. She reached out her hand for him to come forward which he did . He didn't look too bad . Sam thought it was like he was sleeping. He didn't see his mum when she died so he didn't know what a dead person was like . " You couldn't wait then you old sod " Sam said Mae sniggered and shook her head he was right Mae lay her arm round Sam's shoulder . While Geraint stood back letting them do their thing he was being brave Geraint thought it was good it will take time to process and grieve for his dad and Geraint will be there whenever he needed him .

" Don't you worry now Tom I will look after these two " Mae said holding Sam's hand he nodded he looked round at Geraint laying out his hand for Geraint to come to him which he did . " Ok " Geraint asked Sam nodded Mae turned to the two of them ." I'm here whenever you need me ok " Mae said Sam nodded and all three of them hugged .

TEARS RAN DOWN DAISY Meas face Geraint held her hand after they told her about grandpa Tom Sam touched her face wiping her tears away she was so brave he thought which was good " Daddy why did he have to die " God Sam thought how can I explain this he thought he looked at Geraint for reassurance " Grampa Tom Heart was sick " Geraint explained Daisy Mae nodded she looked up at her dads " he will be ok in heaven won't he " .

"Yes honey he will be ok in heaven " Daisy Mae went to hug Sam Geraint, touched her head she was being good and trying to understand. " Who will look after Grandpa Tom " Daisy Mae asked, sitting between her dads looking between them . " Well I guess lots of people will look after Grandpa Tom " Geraint explains as she screws up her face then stands up . " Will I make a picture for Grandpa Tom " God she is so cute Sam thought he looked at Geraint " Yes you can make a picture for Grandpa Tom " .

Chapter 10

Malcolm went into the office to get Darians Filofax to take to Glasgow. They did think about not going to help out Sam but he did insist they go. It would only be a couple days before they would be there to meet with Frank and Lucy . Malcolm went into the Drawer to get the he noticed a folder in there and wondered what it was .Maybe Darian forgot he had it in there maybe to do with meetings or orders he thought .

" Got it, " Cameron asked at the door. Malcolm looked up at him, looked down at the drawer, and shut the drawer.He looked round at the desk before leaving curiosity getting to him . Malcolm got into the car, handing Darian the Filofax while on the phone . Malcolm's phone beeped of a text from Sam thanking him for looking after Daisy Mae telling him she was upset but accepted it asking questions and that they were meeting his aunt to go over funeral arrangements.Thats good he thought he really felt for Sam and understood how he would be feeling at this time . Especially with his own parents' death many years ago it still hurts some days that they are not here .

" Sam ok " Cameron asked Malcolm, humming his answer while he sat at the back of the car while Cameron drove Darian in the front seat. They looked at each other and Malcolm was sad for Sam they both thought maybe he should have stayed back to help but Malcolm insisted that Sam would be ok .

LUCY OPENED THE SWATCHES of the colour schemes that Darian, Malcolm and Cameron looked at before while Darian and Frank took a walk around the club off new improvements that had been done the past couple weeks which were looking better they thought Lucy looking through the swatches Darian had suggested purple red and other colours but didn't decide on them yet .

" What were the colours we decided on? Lucy asked Malcolm, sighed , noticed by Cameron while they looked through the notes " Burgundy red. I think " Malcolm announced, sounding exasperated, he excuses himself to go to the bathroom, watched by Cameron. Darian watches him to look over at Cameron. He is still upset regarding Tom Darian's thought but he didn't need to be disinterested in Darian 's thought .

" Is he ok? " Lucy asks. They did hear about Sam's dad when they arrived. " Just upset about Sam. " Malcolm came back and they carried on with the plans and took a walk around the club and afterwards lunch at one the local pubs in town to go over some plans too .Sam had let Malcolm know about what plans were so far each time he had texted Malcolm .

SAM AND HIS AUNT CHATTED to the undertaker his dads wishes he wanted to be cremated. His Aunt Mae found his dads will. They looked at some of the coffins. I hate this part Sam thought while the undertaker went over the payment plans and which type of coffin . Sam thought does it really matter what coffin is the best . Afterwards he and his aunt went for a coffee Sam's head pounding after chatting with the the undertakers Mae took Sam's hand he looks at her " I know it's hard right now Sam I'm here if you need me ok " Sam nodded his Aunt was so kind Daisy Mae loved visiting her whenever they went to her home .And she had spoiled her rotten most the time .

" I know thanks, it just brings it back for Mum's funeral " .

Malcolm lay in the bath his head back against the tile eyes shut Sam had texted regarding the funeral arrangements which still to set a date he was overthinking about parents funeral back then . A chap at the bathroom door Malcolm looked up at Darian coming inside and sat on the toilet he looked over at Malcolm. " How do you fancy an Indian? " Malcolm moved forward in the bath. " Yea take away be good " .Malcolm scrubbed and he looked up at Darian watching him .

" i thought we could go out to the place " " Darian i'm tired " . Malcolm scrubbed his face.want to chill a bit . He didn't want to go out. All he wanted was just to stay in, get a take away and with his two favourite people can't Darian understand what he thought .

Darian got up and bent down taking Malcolm's hand he looked at Darian " Takeaway " "Mmm " . Malcolm smiled and Darian touched Malcolm's face,facing him leaning into his touch kissing Darians hand .

"Take away it is " Cameron chapped the door, they both looked up at him standing at the door " Indian is it then " " Sure " Malcolm said then Cameron left to make the order Darian looks round at Malcolm again Darian cocks his head .

Darian reached over to kiss Malcolm bumping heads " Love you " Darian says first they kissed " Love you to " Darian touches Malcolm's face again he leans into Darians touch he just wanted there then to take his sadness away he was also sad for Sam too and would help out if needed .

Darian moved his hand down Malcolm took his hand " Not now Darian " Darian nodded " Are you sure " Malcolm nodded Darian kissed his head he stood up and looked round at Malcolm before leaving the bathroom " i'll leave you to it " .i just want to take his sadness away Darian thought leaving Malcolm to have time to himself .

Malcolm lay back down in the bath, closing his eyes thinking about stuff and the envelope in the office drawer that Darian has not mentioned yet. He better not keep things from them he hoped again. Maybe I am overthinking about that .

CARRIE LOOKED UP AT the club building Micheal was taking her on date night to the club he said it would be a surprise in the past he did surprise her for date nights Elliot was looking after the kids and was warned by Micheal any upsets he wouldn't be doing it again Elliot promised he would be ok with them .And best behaviour to especially with the kids he promised he would and get them to bed at a reasonable time .

":Carrie " "Mmm" Carrie looked round at Micheal he held out his hand for her to take it which she did and they walked into the club which was filling up with couples `` Keep an open mind ok " Micheal said Carrie nodded as they walked along to get to there seat . Carrie looked around, not so bad she thought of a sex club " Drink sir Madam " one of the waiters asked if they both took their drinks looking around then Carrie noticed Alice and Nora. That's surprising, she thought, smiling. They were a lovely couple and they got on well with both of them .

" Micheal over there " Micheal looked over at who Carrie was pointing to, he smiled and they went over to where Alice and Nora were. Carrie tapped Alice's shoulder and they looked round " Surprise " Alice was gobsmacked to see her and Micheal for the workshop . " I'm just as surprised about you two " Carrie said Alice looked at Nora they blushed . Carrie waved her hand and said she thought "Hey it's your business " .Carrie and Micheal sat behind Alice and Nora Micheal took her hand Carrie smiled at him .

" Evening everyone " two people came out a man and woman both dressed in leather Carrie liked the bask the woman wore they introduced themselves and that they were a couple who had been together ten years and had taught workshops for quite some time Carrie looked at Micheal, he looked down at her and smiled kissing Carries hand he is so sweet she thought ..

" If you're a beginner don't worry about any questions please come to us after any regulars that have been before we have some new techniques to show you to " .

The lady mistress Selena brought out some toys and gadgets for everyone to look at as well as a brochure on what toys gadgets to check out there were also feathers, lotions and paddles for any hardcore bondage for others who are into different styles of s/m .

" Anyone familiar with the rampant rabbit " mistress Selena brought out oh my quite big Carrie thought Micheal shifted in his seat " This one is quite popular also butt plugs I know not for everyone " Definitely not for me Carrie thought she didn't understand why people would find that pleasurable.

A few giggles in the audience about that while the staff stood and watched the workshop Micheal looked at Carrie she looked engrossed in the workshop he reached for her hand again Carrie looked at him and smiled Micheal winked .Carrie blushed looking away and watching the workshop she bit her lip while they chatted about vibrators other different kinds and lube different kinds to use to .

The couple brought out a paddle explaining what it's used for can give you pleasure in different ways whatever your kink is .Oh Don't think I would be into that Carrie thought .But kudos to those who were into that stuff though.

Afterwards on the drive home Carrie thought back to the workshop she smiled into herself thinking about the couple doing the workshop display in front of people that was something else she thought not that she would ever want to do that in public .Micheal reaches for Carries hand looking over at her she looks over at him " Honey what are you thinking ". " It was just an interesting night " Micheal thought about the workshop exhibition .He nodded yes, some things looked good and some things not he and Carrie could explore .

" Micheal " "Hmm " Micheal looked over at Carrie she bit her lip and smiled " We don't have to hurry back do we " hell no he thought until they came across a parking space beside a stream with no other cars around . Micheal reached over to Carrie they kissed then she moved over to his side. . No room they wangled their way into the back giggling Micheal slid down his jeans . " Carrie wait they said not to rush it " Carrie snorted looking down at Michaels hard on .Chewing her lip licking her lips yes indeed she thought .

" Bugger that " Carrie slid down her pants and mounted Micheal " Shit honey wait " Carrie sliding inside Micheal they kissed his shirt hanging off. Carries dress half open " I can't wait " " shit fuck honey your so beautiful " while Carrie fucked him Cartie licked Michaels fingers he touched her breasts .She was flushed he loved the sight of his wife on top .

" Are you there yet " Micheal asked he was close to Carrie could feel her orgasm looming " uh huh " Micheal lay Carrie on her back he entered her lifting one leg up pounding into her kissing her breasts "Shit I'm coming " Micheal shouted out of breath holding onto Carrie . Micheal looked up at her. Theyboth giggled and realised no wet wipes wipes. The Giggled again. were they both thought .I can't move Carrie thought and we have no damn we wipes though giggling funny he thought Carrie looked at Micheal . " No wet wipes " damn

Micheal held onto Carrie and she looked over at him. They were both soaked with Micheals cum oh god Carrie thought definitely of a shower when they got home Micheal kissed her cheek . " I Love you " Micheal said Carrie snuggled into him " Love you to " .All sticky that will be a bit uncomfortable she thought But was fun Micheal moving to sort himself .

ELLIOT WAS WATCHING TV. He had just checked on the kids. It was after 11 no college. In the morning since it was the weekend thankfully he had a shift at the club at the weekend. HE heard the front door open and giggling they must've had fun Elliot thought lucky Sods he got up went into the hallway. As Carrie and Micheal ran upstairs a cough stopped. They looked round at Elliot standing at the door . " Kids ok " Carrie asked looking at Micheal " kids are fine" .Elliot grinning they have had sex he thought .

" Great " they ran upstairs into the bedroom. Wow Elliot thought must've.been a good night he thought i think i need to get some action Elliot went into the lounge and opened up Grindr for a look for anyone up for a good time .It had been about a month since he met up with anyone .

Micheal and Carrie collapsed onto the bed after their second sex session Micheal looked over at Carrie getting her breath back Micheal moved over to her side lying his arm around her . "OK " Micheal asks Carrie, looking round smiling " U huh " Micheal leans over to kiss Carrie again he moves her closer to him Carrie snuggled into him ." Love you " " Love you to " .

" WANNA GO AGAIN " CARRIE giggles and bats him away " Are you trying to kill me " Carrie giggles Micheal giggles Carrie lifts up the covers Micheal snuggles into her kissing her neck Carrie laying her arm on his stomach well definitely the dry spell is over Carrie thought .

Chapter 11

Malcolm is in the office at the club looking through the filing cabinet. He looks over at the table. He thought it's probably nothing but his curiosity was killing him. He chewed his lip and decided to go and check the drawer. Is it bad of me wanting to find out what Malcolm thought?.

He opens the drawer and the file is still there. He brings it out. There are photos and information regarding Carrie , Elliot and Micheal and another photo, an old one in which he recognised the person with another woman ." Julius " Malcolm whispers . The door opens Malcolm quickly shuts the drawer as Darian comes inside shit Malcolm thought nearly got caught composing himself .Looking down at the ground has he lost something Darian thought .

" Find it " He asks Malcolm, checking the filing cabinet he looks over at Darian " Still looking " Darian comes over to Malcolm laying his arm around his waist " Ok " Malcolm looks at Darian it's getting annoying now Darian asking him the same questions " Darian stop asking I'm fine " Darian looks at him nodding he's just concerned that's all Darian thought .He thinks Malcolm is being weird with him is it to do with Sam he thought .

" I know " Malcolm wasn't looking forward to Sam's dads funeral. He hated them. It reminded him of his parents one many years ago. Darian kisses Malcolm cheek then leaves the office Malcolm lets out a breath he was keeping in . Malcolm quickly goes over to the drawer and brings out the file and stuffs it in his bag has Darian known all along about Carrie and Elliot he thought that's what he wants to find out no secrets between them he thought .Why isn't he saying anything about it Malcolm wondered I will ask him about it and why he had kept it to himself .

THAT NIGHT AT HOME Darian looked at the file Malcolm threw on the kitchen table Cameron picked it up opening the contents and was surprised to see what it was " I can explain " Darian said getting up Malcolm stepped away shaking his head " Are Julius and Carrie siblings " Darian sighed he looked down at his feet "When i went to visit Carries home after taking Elliot home i saw the old picture off the 4 off them with Carrie's mother ."

" That was two and a half weeks ago Darian, why didn't you say anything? " Malcolm shouted. Cameron thought the same to " Look didn't know till then that's why I asked lyle to check it out I was going to tell you both but with the plans for the club I completely forgot " .They both look mad Darian thought I did intend to tell them and not keep it from them.

" Darian you should have said something once you found out " Cameron tutted looking over the contents of the file " I am sorry please believe me what with the new club i should have please believe me i wanted us all to talk to Carrie and Elliot about it together " .Malcolm was furious looking at Cameron checking over the file this won't do he thought looking back at Darian .

" Your fan boy needs to be told Darian " Malcolm says angry Cameron thinks so Darian sighs and shakes his head . " Malcolm is writing to Darian " " I have already told him please believe me " Darian took Cameron and Malcolms hands Malcolm pulled away . " Malcolm " Malcolm gets up and takes his backpack " I need a bit of space " .Stomping Off Darian sighs Looking at Cameron .He is mad to don't let us fall out over this Darian thinks Cameron tuts gets up going over to the sink to wash his cup Darian watching him willing himself to say something .

Malcolm goes up to the granny flat just as steven and jordan arrive " Let him.cool off ok " " What's up with him " Steven asks looking between Darian and Cameron " Just a slight disagreement " Cameron glared at Darian Steven had to know about this to he thought .They definitely have had a fight .

" Anyway the blessing next month here is your invite " Steven handed Cameron their invite Darian got up and put the kettle on " Loch Lomond " Cameron looked up at Steven and Jordan they looked at each other " Yep the little cabins beside the hotel everyone can stay in whoever can come " .Steven looks at Jordan it's

" LOVELY I'VE HEARD it's a nice place to stay " Darian asked he had heard from other people about it " I'm all ready " Philip announced coming into the kitchen in his pjs coming over to his two dads and wondered where papa Malcolm was " Dad is on a call buddy " Cameron explains Steven and Jordan look at each other and smile noticed by Cameron . " What's going on? Cameron asks, looking between Steven and Jordan " Just the clinic regarding the surrogate " .Steven says smiling looks at Jordan beaming at each other .

" My friend Rose, she wants to carry our baby. " Wow Cameron thought that's great news and asked Jordan's friend to give them a special gift. Cameron was pleased about that . " Daddy the gruffalo tonight " Philip asked Darian he got up and took Philip's hand Cameron kissed his head " and an extra kiss from daddy Mal " .

" Ok what's with the tension " Steven asked sitting up on the stool Jordan sitting beside him "Just a slight disagreement that's all don't worry " " He can be a bit intense " Jordan announced Steven sniggered yea Darian can be intense sometimes but that was just him and Cameron liked it that way or he wouldn't be with him . " Sorry I didn't mean to " Cameron waved his hand and laughed " It's fine Jordan that's just Darian he's a pussycat really " .They all laughed yea they could believe that .

MALCOLM CAME OUT THE shower and dried off and on his robe he was sorting his hair when Darian appeared standing watching him Malcolm shook his head Darian cocked his head Malcolm looked in the mirror watching him he's not getting away with that look he thought standing his ground . Ignoring Darian, I will not give into him, Malcolm thought .

Darian came over to Malcolm he lifted his chin Darian pouted rubbing his back looking at him again oh no he doesn't Malcolm thought Darian lifting the robe off his shoulders revealing his skin and kissing it looking at him in the mirror again " Darian no " Darian looked up Malcolm started and was about to move when Darian stopped him they kissed Malcolm scrunching his shirt . Darian turned Malcolm to the sink lifting up the robe and sticking a finger inside him Malcolm hissed as Darian licked and nipped at his shoulder while fingering him from the back. Fuck sake Malcolm thought why do i give in leaning into Darian .

Malcolm arched up whimpering Darian licking his ear then bending down licking and nipping at Malcolm's backside Cameron entered the bathroom and saw them he watched for a second his cock straining at his jeans Darian and Malcolm looked round at him smiling . Cameron went over and the three of them kissed Darian in the middle, Malcolm kissing his neck while Cameron and Darian kissed. Is this making up now Cameron thought .

DARIAN HELD ONTO THE sink while Cameron and Malcolm sucked him off kissing each other same time fuck that was good he thought he felt his orgasm looming " Oh my god " Malcolm stood up while Cameron carried on sucking Darian off he and Darian kissed " You won't keep anything from us again right " " Yes love I won't shit " Malcolm tugged at Darian show him he thought Malcolm bent back down and took Darian in his mouth again while Darian stuck his hand down Cameron's jeans wanking him off kissing each other .

After they all came together they fell to the floor in a heap laughing Malcolm sat up looked round at Cameron and Darian " I mean it Darian " " I know " Malcolm straddled Darian which surprised him " swear it "leaning closer to Darian pinching his nipple Malcolm smirked " I swear ok " Malcolm gave Darian a peek got up held out his hand for Darian and Cameron to get up .

" I'm dirty again " Malcolm smiled looking round at the both of them and getting into the shower for another make out session taking turns again on there make out session .

IT WAS A GOOD TURN out for His Dads funeral Sam thought a few friends he had kept in touch with also all had come to the crematorium as well as Sam's cousins to later they would go to the tea at the local community centre his dad frequented before. To remember him by which he and his Aunt would be a nice gesture for his dads sake .

Sam's uncle Dan, his aunt's husband, did the eulogy that he and his aunt did together with a couple of poems . Frank Sinatra going in and for the arrival of the coffin and another Frank Sinatra song for the committal . Sam and Geraint held hands the whole way through and Daisy Mae insisted she wanted to be there.For her Grampa funeral which her dads were ok with it after his aunt Mae said to let her go She drew a sunflower for her grampa which sat on top of the

coffin with a real sunflower which everyone thought was a nice touch
.

A FEW PEOPLE CAME TO the community centre for the tea
and to pay their respects to Tom and whoever couldn't make the
crematorium came to the centre which Sam was pleased about .
Malcolm was getting drinks at the bar for him Darian and Cameron
Sam came over to him.They had been his rock as well as Geraint
helping him through with stuff which he was so appreciative of his
friends rallying round for him .

" Alrite " Sam asked as they looked over at Darian and Cameron
chatting to Lorna Sam's cousin " Yea we kinda made it up " Sam
shook his head Darian looked up at them both chatting .Cameron
also looked over at the both of them .Malcolm couldn't be mad at
Darian for long when he got his way some the time.

" Sam , Malcolm " they both look round at one off Toms friends
Mr McLaughlin who lived two doors up from Tom " Mr
McLaughlin how are you thanks for coming " Sam shook his hand
he look tears eyed Sam thought " Gone too soon son " " I know
" Malcolm noticed his uncle Mick arrive with his aunt Tom had
frequented Bennett's why wasn't he at the crematorium Malcolm
thought .Malcolm had thought he would have been there .

Darian noticed Malcolm's uncle Mick arriving when Cameron
touched his leg he looked at Cameron " What " " Not today babe "
Darian snorted as if he thought he and Mick had never got on over
the years but for today he would .He had also thought why wasn't
Mick at the cremation.

" Sam how you holding up " Mick asked when he approached
them " it's been tough but it's gone ok hasn't it Mal " " It has " Daisy
Mae came over to Sam he picked her up and she cuddled into her dad
Malcolm giggled that girl isn't shy he thought . " She's gotten big, "

Malcolm's aunt Flora asked .Malcolm nodded, Malcolm sticking out his tongue at Daisy Mae .

" Honey, aren't you gonna say hi? " Daisy Mae shook her head, still a little upset about today Geraint came over to take her and let Sam talk. " It was only a short time but they kinda bonded, " Sam explained about Daisy Mae and Tom . Malcolm, bought his aunt and uncle a drink they looked well he thought " How is the pub " " Fine there some changes which you should come and see "

" I will uncle Mick " " Mick , Flora nice to see you " Darian announced they looked round at him don't start anything Malcolm thought " Darian how are you " Flora asked sipping there drinks " Good and you both " looking between everyone Malcolm glared at Darian he needs to relax i won't start anything .

" Good I hear you're looking into new property " News travels fast Darian thought looking at Cameron and back at Mick .Had Malcolm mentioned anything about the new venture Darian thought .

"Mick , Flora help yourself to the buffet " Sam comes over to them as others tuck into the buffet Mick and Flora go over to the buffet where Malcolm is Malcolm hugging his aunt and uncle it was good to see them .

" How are things? " Mick asks Malcolm, looking round at Darian and Cameron and back at his uncle. " Good uncle Mick, just the new venture taking up our time just now but we are hopeful of no other problems " . That's good Mick thought he did sense tension maybe to do with the new venture .

" Uncle Mick you don't need to worry its all good " " Good " Mick patted Malcolm back noticed by Darian and Cameron over at the bar " Darian " He looks over at Cameron " You're staring again " was i he thought he slid his arm round Cameron's waist " i wasn't " . Who is he kidding Cameron thought Malcolm is fine he shouldn't worry too much .

SAM COLLAPSES ONTO the couch when they get home. What a day he thought the worst part was over now the flat to sort out and when the ashes are free to pick up and decide where to scatter them . " I'm beat " Geraint sits beside Sam he takes his hand Sam looks up at him and smiles he's been his rock all through this Sam taught "Me to " Aunt Mae comes in with Daisy Mae who had fallen asleep in the car " I'll take her " Geraint gets up and takes her off Mae he goes upstairs to sort her out .

"Well it was a good turn out wasn't it " "" it was surprising " Sam takes off his jacket and tie gets up and goes over to put the kettle on uncle Dan sits on the couch and opens a bottle whiskey pours a fair amount for him Sam , Mae and Geraint " To Tom " they al, down there glass . " Aunt Mae I was thinking of his clothes and stuff we could donate to charity " .

" I was thinking same love let's wait a few days then tackle it ok " " I know and thanks"

THAT NIGHT LYING IN bed beside each other Sam thinking back to when he was younger his sister she would be 30 soon what would have happened if she was still alive he thought a squeak of the door and a little face appeared before them . " Daddy sleeps with you tonight " Geraint sighs he opens his covers and Daisy Mae jumps in beside them in the middle .Daisy Mae lays in the middle Geraint and Sam snuggling into her Daisy Mae sucking her thumb before falling asleep. Sam thought she was missing her Grandpa Tom. It's been a tough day for everyone. At least you are at peace now dad .

A FEW DAYS LATER MALCOLM comes through to the bar Sam and Darian are talking Darian lays his arm round Sam's shoulder Malcolm stood watching for a second to watch Darian guiding him Sam nodding what's wrong Malcolm thought he was holding something Sam looking down at what he was holding ." Alrite " Sam looks over at Malcolm red eyed siting the box on the bar he looks at it . " My Dads ashes " Shit Malcolm thought that's what he is upset about ." It just feels weird I went on my own Geraint is at work I thought I would be ok then I ended up here "

Malcolm goes over to Sam. They hug poor Sam. Darian thought he felt for him " I know but I wanted to do it on my own then when I got in the car and there just sitting there you guys were here ,Am I being stupid " . He looks over at Malcolm and Darian .

" No Sam , you're not being stupid here, take this to calm yourself " Darian poured him a glass of whiskey . He felt so stupid now his phone rang off. It was Geraint who connected the call " Babe are you ok " " I am now I just came to the club Mal and Darians here " .

" Do you need me I'll be there soon " " I need you " Sam thought he could handle it on his own but he needed his husband he disconnected the call he sat on the stool Darian and Malcolm watching him " Tell me it gets easier " Malcolm looked at Darian then at Sam he lay his hand on his shoulder Sam looked up at them . " It will be in time for Sam " Sam nodded even though his dad was not on speaking terms over the years he still cared about him and with their recent reunion he thought they had more time but sadly no . Darian slid his arm round Malcolm he leaned into Darian they looked at each other Malcolm couldn't bear to think how he would feel if Darian wasn't here .

SAM AND GERAINT HELD hands on the way home Geraint looked over at Sam holding the box ":Sam " Sam looked up at

Geraint " Put him in the bag " he was right Sam thought and stopped wallowing he thought " Sorry ..I "" I know " . Geraint squeezed Sam's hand on their way home Geraint put on some music to lighten the mood Adele Hello came on they both liked the song .Sam had thought about his dads ashes and where he could lay them .

Chapter 12

M alcolm is at work a day later and on his computer checking emails and visit schedules for the next week and a scheduled meet for a soup kitchen a chap at the door he looks round at Michelle his work colleague standing at the door " Malcolm and Elliot here to see you " what's he doing here he thought he sighs shuts off the computer " He looks upset " Michelle says looking out at reception yes he did look upset Malcolm thought when he looked out he looked like he had been crying to . " Thanks Michelle " " If you need me " . Michelle asked Malcolm to shake his head going over to Elliot god he looks awful Malcolm thought .

" Elliot " Elliot looked round at Malcolm standing watching him Elliot wiped his nose and eyes hugging into himself " Sorry I .. ahh " Malcolm went over to Elliot sitting beside him as he came down he thought Elliot looked at Malcolm then looked down at his hands . " I know it's bad that I came here but what could I do? I can't talk to Carrie or mum `` .Elliot was shaking Malcolm could see what had happened he thought .

" ELLIOT ARE YOU ON a come down " Elliot looks at Malcolm shakes his head Malcolm nods " Come into my office " They both get up and they go into his office Elliot looks round the office while Malcolm makes him tea " Here drink this " Elliot takes the tea and takes a couple sips which is quite refreshing Elliot thought Malcolm waited till Elliot calmed a little letting him take his time . " Why are you being so nice to me? " Malcolm sniggers and shakes his head looking at Elliot . " You're not so bad " .Which he isn't Malcolm had just overreacted thinking Elliot was after Darian and his money which he wasn't .Just a silly crush it was mind you most people in the club had a crush on Darian .

ELLIOT TOOK A DEEP breath he bit his lip he took a hankie and blew his nose and threw it in the bin " I went on a Grindr date the other night he seemed really nice a bit older 5 years I think we had drinks bit dinner which I unusual what do you think " Malcolm shrugged his shoulders and smiled not that unusual most Grindr dates are just sex or just want to go out on a date . "Not that unusual Elliot " .

" After he suggested we go to his place I was feeling it going with it I kinda liked him so I thought " tears ran down Elliot's face he bowed his head Malcolm went closer to him took his hand "Take your time no rush " " Malcolm I can't " Michelle looked in at the window she chapped on it Malcolm gave a thumbs up he was dealing with it .If he needed her he would let Michelle know but at the moment no .

" I said no " Elliot mumbled punching the chair he looked up at Malcolm " I think he drugged me I vaguely remember another person in the room I said no Malcolm " Jesus Malcolm thought he had dealt with many cases in different circumstances but hearing what Elliot was saying " Elliot you have to go to the police you need to report it " . Elliot shook his head. How can I? He thought I'm scared, sucking in a breath of tears running down his face .

" How I don't know how I kept the clothes, how do I get over this " Malcolm took Elliot's hands again looking into his eyes " Listen to me you will someday Elliot believe me you will " . What does he mean? Elliot thought, shaking his head .

Elliot bowed his head holding his head Malcolm sent a quick text to Michelle to come into the room the door opened after a few minutes Malcolm looked up at Michelle coming inside .Elliot looks up why is she here Elliot thought " Elliot Michelle needs to be here to for confidentiality "

Michelle went over to Elliot, tears running down his face, she bent down in front of him taking his hand " Everything you say to us Elliot is all confidential ok " Elliot nods looking at Malcolm he also nods " Ok i understand what do I do now " .

CARRIE CAME INTO THE centre she said her name at reception the receptionist called Malcolm he came out his office a few minutes later " Malcolm what's going on " " Elliot has something to tel, you Carrie ": Elliot looked up at the door when Carrie arrived he looked terrible she thought and had been crying Malcolm shut the door for privacy like he had always done and has to . Carrie went over to Elliot sitting in the chair beside him while Malcolm stood watching be brave Elliot he willed him to like you said to me .

Eliot what's going on what's happened " Elliot looked at Malcolm shaking his head. Be brave . Please Malcolm thought Carrie looked over at Malcolm. And back at Elliot Carrie went to take Elliot's hand they look at each other " whatever's happened I'm here for you ok " Elliot nodded Carrie held out her arms they hugged Elliot sobbed Carrie patting his back reassuring him .Carrie looks up at Malcolm he gives a faint smile while Carrie rubs Elliot's back .

MALCOM WAITED IN RECEPTION at the police station while Carrie and Elliot went into one the rooms for him to make a statement about what happened Elliot had put the clothes he wore that night in a bag and brought them to the police station with him .

Cameron came inside and went over to Malcolm after he had called him letting him know where he was. He didn't say what happened to Elliot, he would tell him later .

" Elliot's making a statement I might need to also since he confided in me " " ok are you ok " .Malcolm looks round at Cameron he nods this is the hard part for people he thought this isn't a great part of the job he does but it had to be done Malcolm thought .This is what I want to do help people whenever they could .

Malcolm took Cameron's hand for comfort and nodded. Cameron smiled " I'm ok " Malcolm smiled. Cameron squeezed Malcolm's hand for reassurance while they waited for Elliot to finish his statement.Poor guy Cameron thought whatever it is that has happened he is a nice kid. He hasn't done anything bad to us .

Carrie came out of the room after Elliot made his statement she saw Cameron with Malcolm they looked over at her Carrie looked a bit upset she sat beside them sighing leaning against the wall boy this had been some day she thought " The doctor needs to you know " .Malcolm knew exactly What Carrie meant Malcolm thought he went to take her hand Carrie looks round at Malcolm .

AFTERWARDS ELLIOT LOOKED up at the sky and took a deep breath closing his eyes he felt a little relieved Malcolm praised him for being brave he looked round at Carrie talking to Cameron and Malcolm , Malcolm came over to Elliot at the car " The hard part is over Elliot you were very brave " Elliot nodded Malcolm patted his arm " Thanks Malcolm at this moment I don't feel brave just scared "." I know at least you made a statement " . Malcolm patted Elliot's back and gave a faint smile nodding at Carrie who looked worried. Elliot thought " c'mon let's get home " Carrie said, leading Elliot to the car while Cameron and Malcolm waited .

MALCOLM AND CAMERON watched Carrie drive off. They looked at each other " I feel for him right now Cam " " I know c'mon let's get you home " .All of s sudden Malcolm felt drained after all it's part of his job and it's what he wanted to do he liked his job most of the time .But the abused or homeless were the hardest off the job .At least he was helping those who needed help that's the good part .

AUNT MAE HAD SAT TOM'S ashes on the living room table while he and Malcolm the next day had been sorting out some clothes for the charity shop; they were due to give up the flat soon, which Sam had reservations about; he had said he wasn't quite ready to give up his dads house just yet it would feel weird but he had to give it up sometime though .

He and Malcolm were in the bedroom. Sorting out the piles of clothes to take to the centre and charity shop " How is Elliot " Sam asked Malcolm looked over at him " Carrie said he seemed ok it's just the waiting game now " Sam stood up remembering back to when Malcolm reported his uncle for abuse and how he was stronger for that now thankfully . " What " Malcolm asked Sam he was away somewhere thinking about something " Nothing just the flat you know I wish it could go to a family that needs a home " .

Malcolm thought he had a couple people from the centre looking for a place to stay. This one would be perfect for them " Sam, leave it with me. Ok, I might have the solution, gotta talk to Rhona "" Sure no problem " .Malcolm thought of a couple people could benefit from taking the flat .Who had been waiting a while for a place they could stay some places were not suitable before .

ELLIOT SAT ON HIS BED he was exhausted he had a long bath but still felt unclean did that happen with everyone he thought the door chapped Carrie came inside Elliot looked up at her " Dinners ready " " Not hungry " Carrie sighed she sat on the bed " I'll leave it in the micro for later ok " Elliot nodded Carrie got up she looked round at him . " Elliot don't wallow and make yourself crazy. The kids are asking questions I can't answer " . Eliot looked away, tears stinging his eyes. I can't explain it either. He thought Carrie touched his arm. He looked round at her. They hugged Carrie, patting his back. " It's going to be ok, it might take a while, ok " Elliot nodded. He understood what she meant .

MICHEAL DISHED UP THE kids tea when Carrie came into the kitchen she shook her head she did try and get Elliot to come downstairs for his tea " Mummy isn't uncle Elliot having tea " Molly asked looking between her mum and dad " Uncle Elliot isn't feeling well " Micheal announced looking at Carrie " There. a bug going around school " Jack said making a sick sound Molly giggled thinking it was funny Carrie shook her head kids she thought .

  " Room for one more " everyone looked round at Elliot standing at the door god he looked so pale Micheal thought Carrie went to get up " I'll get it " Elliot said going over to the microwave " Are you feeling better uncle Elliot " Elliot coming over to the table Molly asked he ruffled her hair . " A bit moles " looking at Carrie and Micheal . " There's a bug going round school " Jack announced again as they carried on eating .That's the thing they wouldn't understand his situation but Carrie had mentioned to the kids about strangers if they felt uncomfortable about it and they would know what to do .

CARRIE TOUCHED ELLIOT'S hand and nodded and looked round the table at his brother in law and the kids. If anything they will help me through this crisis as well as his friends .I need to be strong like Malcolm said he would get over it eventually but right now he just felt like retreating to his room and not coming out but I can't do that to make myself miserable.

Chapter 13

“ The place is perfect Malcolm " Stephanie one off the centres residents looked around the flat of Sam's Malcolm looked at Sam for his reaction " Gaynors approved it then " Stephanie asked sitting down on the couch " All yours if you want it right Sam " Stephanie looked at Sam this is incredible she thought she had been waiting quite a while for a new flat to come up now that it has she and her kids can have a home now instead off the centre .Which they had to get out of now and get to start their lives again .

" ALL THE FURNITURE is with the flat to we had to fling the bedding out though all my dads old clothes are getting picked up " " Really that's great I'm sure I can check out bedding stuff right Malcolm " Stephanie asked looking at Malcolm a big smile on her face " We can sort that out " .There were plenty charity shops around and deals on furniture if they looked in the right places he thought .

   " Great so when can I move in? " Malcolm sniggered. There was paperwork to sort first and the landlord to get in touch with first before she could move in after Stephanie left to pick up her two children from school. Malcolm helped Sam with a few bags to leave in the living room. " Hows Elliot doing? " Malcolm sat down. Elliot was to have a blood test to check for any diseases the guy could have been carrying . Elliot had always used protection but wasn't sure if the guy did that night or not " He has a blood test today Seems to be holding up ok "

SAM HOPED ELLIOT WOULD be ok although he had been a pain in the ass at the beginning he had turned out ok now just was a bit big headed at the beginning and the way he was acting around Darian to that Cameron and Malcolm didn't like .It was just a crush word of mouth about the club and possibly curious to see what the fuss was about .

AFTER THE NURSE HAD taken the bloods he would find out his results in a couple days his phone rang when he got outside the clinic he connected the call " Elliot Mathews Di Bentley " " Hi what's up " Elliot leaned against the railing his heart pounding " Elliot Grant Samson has been arrested pending the investigation " wow Elliot thought that was quick he thought and good to they were certainly very thorough that's for sure " Elliot " " Yes I'm here that's great news and the other guy " .

" That is also getting dealt with to Elliot we are also checking with forensics on the clothes you have given us to I will get back to you on that " " Ok thanks inspector Bentley " A car drove up just as Elliot got off the phone he looked up at his friend Patrick get out the car coming over to him ." Well how did it go mate " .Standing staring at him hoping Elliot was ok and wasn't too stressed .He and Bailey were worried about him after his attack .

" GET THE RESULTS IN a couple days Di Bentley just called they have Grant Samson has been arrested " That's great news Patrick thought tears stung Elliot's eyes Patrick came over to him took his arm leading him to the car and the both of them went inside Elliot looked over at Patrick . " Patrick " " Yea " Patrick looked over at Elliot as he was starting the car . " Thanks for being a good friend " Shit Patrick thought what's got into him looking over at Elliot Patrick lightly punched Elliot's arm playfully .

" What's this getting all soppy in me now " Elliot sniggered Patrick and him have been friends since nursery and when Elliot told him he was gay at 14 when he first come out he didn't care as long as Elliot was happy that's all he cared about he was there for him when Leyton died him and Bailey to .The three of them were close like brothers and looked out for each other which they have always done since they were younger .

"Elliot, do you think Darian will give me the job? " Elliot looked over at Patrick. He applied for the bar job at the club and since the new one will be open in a few months Darian was needing new staff . " Probably Malcolm mentioned about new staff for Glasgow Club " . Maybe Darian will want more staff for the club in Glasgow, Patrick thought . Maybe got a chance and can only apply to see what happens when they get into the car Patrick looks over at Elliot he is looking tired Elliot looks at Patrick . " What" " Nothing Mate where'd you wanna go " ." Let's go get some chips "

Good idea Patrick thought nodding then starting the car driving off to get chips at the nearest chippy Elliot's phone rang Bailey calling he connected the call " Hey can you guys pick me up " Patrick nodded Elliot snorted this guy is unbelievable Elliot thought " Yes we can pick you up on our way " .

A day later Carrie laid down her bag in her mothers room. She had brought some drinks and a couple cakes. Her mum lay in her bed looking sleepy Carrie thought The nurses had not long been in to see her repositioning her she looked comfy Carrie thought Carrie looked over and her mother had been sleeping and was just waking up ." Hi mum " Carrie went over to Martha and kissed her head her mum smiled looking over at the door .Carrie thought she was thinking Elliot would arrive since they came together most days .

" Elliots coming later mum after college " Carrie didn't want to mention Elliot's attack; it would stress her mum out and Elliot didn't want Carrie to bring it up either she brought out a French fancy for her mum, cutting up some bits for her to take whenever she wanted them Carrie chatting away to her mum while she listened to Carrie talk about her day and the kids .

AFTER HIS CHAT WITH the lecturer about his course and wanting to change it over to another for next year to do social studies And that he had to take a couple weeks off for personal reasons Elliot missed out the attack part his lecturer did mention if he had wanted to speak to a counsellor which Elliot had already organise. For next week his phone rang as he was coming down the steps of the clinic, his heart pounding. If it's bad news he thought his hands felt clammy and kept calm he thought " Hello " .

" Elliot Mathews " " Yes that's me " the nurse explained his results were all negative oh my god Elliot thought he sat on the steps hand to his mouth he was never more glad to hear off good news a car arrived his name called two people running up to him . " Elliot Elliot talk to me what's happened " Patrick asked looking at Bailey he looked up at him . " My results were all negative " " Bloody hell mate I nearly had a heart attack " Bailey said sitting down next to Elliot thank god Patrick thought .

ELLIOT LOOKED ROUND at Bailey wasn't he supposed to be at work he shook his head " Why aren't you at work" " Bloody protesters again " Elliot looked up at Patrick he shrugged his shoulders `` Have you eaten " Elliot sniggered that's all they think about is food he thought " I could eat " . The three of them all piled into the car and went to McDonald's drive through for their usual burger fries coke and a McFlurry .Elliot thinking about his negative result and it's going to be a while till I have sex again until then he will be celibate for now .

" MALCOLM ELLIOT'S HERE " Carly one the receptionists announced as he was coming out the conference room he thanked her and went into his office where Elliot and Bailey were " Well how did it go with your lecturer " Malcolm asked going into the filing cabinet looking over at Elliot while Bailey was sipping on his zero coke . " Fine, I shouldn't miss too much and he said it would be fine to defer over just the bursary to sort out. Also, my results are negative too ."

Malcolm sat down and looked over at Elliot he could tell he was relieved that they were " Good to hear " Elliot went into his bag and brought out a muffin for Malcolm he sniggered and shook his head " What's this for " Elliot looked at Bailey who was laughing into himself . " Just my thanks and I've still to hear from the police for updates " . That's so kind of him to bring him a muffin which he didn't need to .

" Thank you and why aren't you at work Bailey " " Protestors again " Malcolm shook his head. These protesters are getting worse, he thought .Bailey seemed ok Malcolm thought each time he was with Elliot they were good friends he noticed and looked out for each other which was a good thing just like he and Sam .

THE WEEKEND CAME SATURDAY the club was busy DJ night Patrick was on his second night with Elliot which he thought was crazy he should be taking time off but he insisted keeping busy takes his mind off stuff and hanging around the house would just drive him crazy at least Patrick was with him tonight . Elliot was collecting glasses Patrick took some orders as more members arrived The Dj had not long set up. It was nearing 9pm and some people were on the dance floor or standing listening to the music . " Elliot, come have a drink with me, " Mr Edwards asked him. Elliot looked at him and he said he was not allowed to Club rules " Mr Edwards I'm working Club rules " Besides Darian had said the waiters couldn't fraternise with the members .

He went to grab Elliot's arm he froze " Ahh shame what about after then " " " Mr Edwards " Ed had come over to see what was going on when he saw him grab Elliot's arm he looked at Ed " Mr Edwards your tab " Darian handed him his invoice off his drinks he hadn't paid for . " Ahh Darian you know I'm good for it " .Mr Edwards sniggered Taking the invoice tutting he needs to relax it will get paid .

" CAN YOU COME INTO my office to settle your bill " Darian insisting staring at Mr Edwards " Ok ok I'll pay my bill " Cameron came over and guided Elliot to the office Elliot sat on the couch Cameron handed him some water " Elliot are you ok " he looked up and nodded Cameron leaned against the table watching him . " He just " " Take your time " . Cameron stood watching Elliot take the water, taking deep breaths .I think it's too soon Cameron thought watching Elliot drink his water .

The door opened Darian came in they both looked over at him " You should go home Elliot " " Darian no I'm fine " " I insist " Darian sat beside him Elliot leaned forward he felt faint " Elliot your going home " Cameron said bending down in front off Elliot looking at Darian he nodded .I think he's having a panic attack Cameron thought .That's something that Malcolm did before while Elliot took deep breaths .

" Please let me stay i feel.safe here " Darian wondered what he meant, looked at Cameron " Elliot what's going on " Cameron asked " He got bail they both did " .What the hell Darian thought that's not right looking at Cameron Darian was furious Cameron could tell .But at the same time it's not right the men getting bail .

" What? " Darian shouted as he stood enraged. Tears ran down Elliot's face. Cameron stood up and went over to Darian to calm him. " Elliot , Why didn't you say "" I was trying not to think about it i'm sorry " .Tears running down Elliot's cheek Cameron lay his arm round Elliot comforting him reassuring him poor kid he's not having it great at the moment .

THE DOOR OPENED MALCOLM came inside went over to Elliot he sat beside him rubbing his back then Bill came into the office Patrick behind him who went over to Elliot sitting beside him fuck he thought he should have stayed at home after all going over to Elliot .

" I'm here mate, he won't hurt you again, ok " Elliot nodded and both of them hugged as Elliot's tears ran down " Bill will take you home Patrick go with him please Darian asked Patrick looks up at Darian Yea Maybe I should go with Elliot " " Are you sure?". " Yes I'm sure we have plenty of staff on " .

AS THEY WALKED OUT of the office Elliot looked up at a bright light. Someone standing at the top of the stairs was dreaming of Leyton standing there. I feel a bit weird, Elliot thought . " Leyton "I felt faint. Elliot thought his head was buzzing . Then it went all dark. Elliot fainted .Holy shit Patrick thought going to Elliot all the commotion did someone say get water he wasn't sure bending down making sure Elliot was ok .What the fuck happened Patrick thought while others rallied round Elliot making sure he was ok .

CARRIE CAME DOWNSTAIRS with a basin to clean it up for Jack to he hadn't been feeling well couple days and had caught the bug that was going around and now Elliot Bill sat at the table with Micheal they looked over at Carrie " I think it's going to be another sleepless night again "Micheal groaned now that Elliot was sick to .Great he thought no rest again tonight scrubbing his face .

" DO YOU NEED ME " BILL asked Micheal looked at him he can look after his family he thought maybe taking it the wrong way Darians being to over protective he thought " Bill we will be fine " Carrie said looking round at them Patrick came into the kitchen " He wants water " He went into the fridge to get a bottle water and went upstairs. To Elliot's room " My no if you need me ". Bill scribbled down his no and left it on the table and left .Do we really need his no both Carrie and Micheal thought but they guessed it wouldn't be too bad just in case .

" Seriously Carrie Darians " " Michael I know " the door chapped Bailey appeared he waved and went upstairs to Elliot's room " MUM " oh no Carrie thought not again Micheal got up " I'll go " .Thank god Micheal is home it's bad enough when he isn't here when one the kids is ill I do hope I don't get this viral thing that's going around to Carrie thinks .

ELLIOT TOOK A SIP HIS water his throat hurt and lay back down just as Bailey arrived god he thought he's so pale Patrick sitting on the bean bag he looked up at Bailey coming in " Mate are you ok " Bailey asked going over to Elliot sitting beside him "Does he look ok " Patrick scolded him " Guys please " Elliot croaked.Shaking his head he didn't want his friends fighting he hasn't the energy to get them to calm down .

" Sorry " Patrick said as he held out his hand to Bailey he shook his hand " You want me to stay over to " Bailey asked Elliot nodded .The three of them hugged Elliot and were so thankful for his friends being with him they are just the best bunch . Later that night Patrick beside Elliot Bailey at the bottom Elliot had a nightmare he woke up in a sweat looking at the both of them laid back down looking up at the ceiling. I don't want to wake them up, he thought , and hopefully fall back asleep again. He reached over to take some water. The thing with Leyton was weird earlier. He thought he was dreaming it or imagined it. Who knows .

A COUPLE DAYS LATER Elliot entered the community hall for group therapy there were a few people already there ok he thought I can do this he thought " Hi " Elliot looked round at who spoke to him a young girl in dungarees a beanie hat a nose piercing " Hi " " New right " she asked Elliot nodded " I'm Freya I've been coming for a couple weeks now "" Ok right " Freya looked round at the group with the two therapists as Elliot and Freya went over to the group .

Elliot sat beside Freya looking around the room at the other people and the counsellors; they were all mixes of ages, not too bad I guess .

" Hello everyone a reminder I am Amanda this is Colin I see we have a couple new people to the group. Don't worry if you don't want to talk, that's fine, no pressure . They seemed ok. Elliot thought looking round the room again at the other people " I'm Thomas " Elliot looked over at the person who spoke to him. He seemed shy. Elliot thought, hugging himself . " Elliot " Thomas smiled and nodded, chewing his lip .He wore a big baggy jumper, also a beanie hat and combat trousers .

" Now what we normally do, let's all stand up and do some relaxing exercises " Colin announced to them all standing up and doing some breathing control Well this could work Elliot thought copying what the counsellors were doing Malcolm did mention something about that before that he normally did whenever he felt anxious .

AFTERWARDS EVERYONE said their goodbyes before Elliot left. Daniel explains that some of them go for drinks and food at the local pub and if he wanted to come along sometime he was most welcome he would go the next time not ready for that yet he thought .But he did have a good feeling about the group and thought Yea I could get on with them in the future .

Patrick was waiting for Elliot when he came out with the others he got into the car Patrick looked at him " Well how did it go " " Good they seem a good bunch and it's helped to " . That's good Patrick thought hopefully it will help him going to group therapy even if he wanted to talk about things to him and Bailey he could .But then again if he didn't that was fine or struggling that's what friends were for to help each other through the bad stuff .

Chapter 14

Julia chapped on the office door she looked round at Jake and they went inside Darian at his desk Cameron on the couch on the computer " You wanted to see us boss " " Yes have a seat " Cameron looked up smiling when Darian looked round at him Julia looked at Jake "Your not in trouble " Darian huffed Thank god for that Julia thought .Looking At Jake he shrugged his shoulders also wondering what's going on to .

Julia let out a breath thank god she thought Cameron put down his computer and came over to the desk leaning against it looking round at Darian `` How would you like a.step up " " What do you mean " .Julia asked looks at Jake again and back at Darian what does he mean .

" with Claudia going on maternity leave soon i need a co manager for here and the new place and i'd like the both of you to co manage together " " Us boss i mean that's great right jules " Julia nodded she and jake had worked for Darian ten years now she loved the job and Darian is a great boss .And they both loved the club even though sometimes it had its problems but they were quickly sorted out .

" I have applications for Glasgow and I wanted your opinions on them. Malcolm has already said to his right Cameron " Cameron huffed that he did, he thought " he did " .Some the applications were ok some not while some had worked in the hospitality field for some time and some wanted a new challenge .

" Between here and Glasgow with co managing I've sorted out an apartment for staff thanks to Frank and Lucy " " Boss that's great "Jake said looking at Julia she smiles that's good to know .And very kind Frank and Lucy to help out with the living arrangements too .At least it was something for the staff .

Darian got up and handed julia and Jake the applications they took them " Once we decide to interview i was thinking of asking Patrick to work between here and Glasgow as.well as training him up he's expressed interest in doing hospitality management "

" That's good isn't it Jake " " He is a worker that's for sure " Julia and Jake left Cameron went to open his computer Darian stopped him Cameron looked up at Darian he.cocked his head Cameron shook his head Darian leaned down to kiss Cameron. Gong to slide his hand down Cameron stopping him shaking his head smirking .Oh no he doesn't Cameron thought moving near to Darian a puzzled look on him .

" Steady on stud " Darian huffed Cameron stood up moving Darian to the table " The door " Cameron rushed over to the door and locked it he looked over at Darian watching him coming over to him " Could you not wait " Cameron asked he cocked his head they kissed Darian went to touch Cameron's groyne again he took his hand away again Darian looked at him .What is he playing at Darian thought shaking his head .

" Let me " Cameron bent down unzipping Darians jeans he looked up at him as he sprang free his cock he was erect mm nice Cameron thought "Mmm. So ready " Cameron licked the inside off Darians leg while pumping him he groaned " You know it's not good interrupting someone while they are in flow off working " Cameron said looking up at Darian his face was flushed .Looking down at Cameron smirking .

Cameron took him in his mouth Darian held onto his head while he sucked him off Darian held his head back letting Cameron do his thing Cameron stood up again Darian stared at him why did he stop he thought they kissed again Cameron licking his ear unbuttoning Darians shirt kissing all down his chest . " this .. isn't .. fair " Darian whispered Cameron looked up at him , taking him in his mouth again and sliding a finger inside him teasing in and out .Damn he has overpowered me again next time that won't happen Darian thinks .

BAILEY CAME DOWN THE steps and was about to chap Darians office door when he could hear noises oh my he thought are they having sex whoever was in there he blushed and was about to go through to the bar area when Claudia appeared " Can I help you " Bailey looked over at the door blushing again Claudia pretended not to hear what was going on behind the door . " Bailey Elliot's friend " " Come on through Bailey " . Bailey looks round at the door and someone is having a fun time in the office he thought .Good on them sniggering into himself and an afternoon as well oh wow .

   " My application " Handing it to Claudia she took it he noticed a slight bump Claudia noticed Bailey looking " I'm 5 months "Claudia felt her bump looking down and rubbing her belly " Wow great " They went over to the Vip area Bailey looked round the place wow Elliot was right the place is amazing he thought of pretty cool decor to I like it he thought .And it's the talk off the town the place to come to for a drink or pleasure .

CAMERON TUCKED HIS shirt back in his jeans he looked over at Darian fixing himself he looked over at Cameron and cocked his head " You didn't play fair " Darian said Cameron came over to him touching his chest " Ahh did my poor baby feel violated " Darian huffed Cameron kissed him i will get him back for that since he initiated it . First Darian wrapped his arms round Cameron he turned his head " What " Cameron asked holding onto Darians arm " Rain check for later " Darian grins Cameron shakes his head .He certainly has some sexual appetite that's for sure and he wouldn't change that at all my man is just sex on legs .

   " Maybe besides we promised Philip we would take him to the park remember " That's right Darian thought he had forgotten Cameron turned to Darian they kissed " Um don't start again " Darian looks down and back up at Cameron grinning again Cameron shaking his head .Seriously he just needs to tone it down now giggling and giving Darian a quick peck on the lips .

CLAUDIA AND BAILEY were finished talking when Darian and Cameron came through to the bar area Bailey looked over at them Elliot was right he looked intensely taller than he thought looked like he kinda worked out his dusty blonde hair greying a bit at the sides to a good looking man also that's for sure Blair thought .And he could see why everyone thought Darian was a sexy Italian fuck what am I thinking about that for Bailey quickly thinking about something else .

   Cameron fixed his glasses. He also looked smart, his brown hair glistening from the lights Claudia sniggered. Bailey looked at her " Everyone is mesmerised at first " she said what did that mean he thought .well I have eyes he thought and definitely could see the appeal not that I'm into guys but yea the both them definitely had it .

   " How are we doing? " Darian asked. That's a lovely accent so didn't Elliot say he is from Italy. " Darian, this is Bailey. " Bailey blushed and looked round at Darian and Cameron " Ahh Elliot's friend right `` .Darian asked smiling at Bailey Jesus am I blushing again Bailey could feel his cheeks hot .

" That's me " " where do you work Bailey " Cameron asked looking at Darian " The slaughterhouse it's pretty shit at the moment and extra money would be handy ."

Claudia handed Darian the application he nodded " we will let you know on the application Bailey " " sure " .Thats ok Bailey thought while Darian handed Cameron his application they both look at him " What do you think of my club " Bailey cleared his throat " Nice I've heard good things about it . Nice Darian thought huffing Cameron dunted his side Darian looked over at him . " Thank you and we will be in touch" " Cool thanks " .

Darian and Cameron left to go back into the office intensely or what he thought Claudia sniggered again Yep new people just don't get him she thought which now she was used to that's just the way he is with everyone except with the staff off course . Bailey looked at her " He is so intense " " something you get used to Bailey ":

" What about you? " Claudia shakes her head. He is a little frazzled looking. She thought Claudia patted Bailey's shoulder " Bailey you have nothing to worry about Darian is a big teddy bear really " he hoped so Bailey thought Claudia seemed nice and easy to chat to Like Cameron too .

SOME OF THE STAFF STARTED to arrive for their shift. Bailey noticed when he was leaving his phone rang Patrick calling him " Well how did it go " " Fine mate he's so intense " Bailey looked up at the sign Bailey giggled. Yea he was right Darian could be intense .But a nice guy was nice you get to know him everyone had said .

" you got that to him isn't too bad " " I guess and yea it seems a good place to work if everyone seems ok " .

Chapter 15

S am , Geraint , Malcolm and Daisy Mae took a trip to the Isle of Arran in the west of Scotland a few days later Sam decided he would like to scatter some off his dads ashes at Brodick pier when he was a child his parents had taken him there a couple times for the holidays one time Malcolm came with them after his parents died they were good memories Sam thought Especially staying at the caravan park had in Brodick which was still there it was a popular tourist spot for many a traveller .or locals to that area that fancied going over to Arran for a day or a couple days even school trips to .

They stood at the water's edge Sam had brought some flowers to set out to the sea he had sprinkled some off the ashes into another tin tying it onto the bouquet of flowers he bent down pushing out the flowers into the sea as Malcolm and Geraint watched him they looked at each other and nodded so touching they both thought Daisy Mae looked up at her dad holding his hand .My Daddy is sad Daisy Mae thought Sam looks down at Daisy Mae watching him he smiles down at her squeezing her hand he bent down to her pinching her cheek . " Ok " Sam asked her Daisy Mae nodded Sam brought Daisy Mae to him hugging her then kissed her head .

Sam stood up looking round at the three of them, a tear in his eye Geraint came over and wrapped his arms round Sam whispering words of comfort to him while Malcolm and Daisy Mae watched Malcolm sniffed, whipping his nose .Emotional moment he thought but it's what Sam wanted to do and he came with them for support .For his best friend anything he asked for and wanted to he would

support him like he had always done and Sam the same for Malcolm
.

They all wrapped there arms round each other Sam lifted up
Daisy Mae he kissed her cheek she wrapped her arms round her
dads neck " Anyone wanna say something " Sam asked " I miss you
grandpa " Although it was only a short time she knew him Sam
could tel, his dad enjoyed seeing her even though he didn't say it
but he knew . " I know baby me too " .Daisy Mae wrapped her arms
round Sam's shoulders and Sam gave her a tight squeeze. Yep he
thought it was an emotional day .

SAM LOOKED OVER AT Geraint he smiled " Daddy swings "
Malcolm huffed that girl he thought " honey lets get food first ok "
Geraint said Daisy Mae pouted Sam pouted to and pinched her nose
she giggled "Daddy stop " .Daisy Mae giggled Geraint laying his arm
round Sam he nodded at Geraint letting him know he was ok .

" I've thought of an idea," Sam said, looking round at Geraint and
Malcolm. " Climbing goat fell in memory of dad " . They all look ok
at each other, not a bad idea Malcolm thought Yes we can do that
why not he thought .

" Yeah we could organise that " Geraint said looking between
Sam and Malcolm he would be up for doing it why not he thought
and if he wanted to scatter more ashes there that would be ok .

" i'm in " Malcolm said the shock on Geraint's face Malcolm
thought " Besides Tom didn't manage that time i remember " Sam
nodded he did remember he still had some of his dads ashes and he
could leave a little up there to Malcolm couldn't make it the last time
they tried to his legs giving up halfway up ." Thanks Guys I really
appreciate it " Sam said he really did. They all hugged again, patting
each other's backs for reassurance .

THE LADY THAT OWNED the bed breakfast was accommodating to look after Daisy Mae for them since she had her grandkids with her today and Daisy Mae could play with them while the boys went off on their adventure until the goat fell the next morning because it would have been too late in the day to climb. It's better. Day time . " Thank you so much Mrs Watkins " " No problem and I have your nos " Daisy Mae was drawing with Mrs Watkins Grandkids. They were chatting away. Geraint went over to her, gave her a kiss on the head and spoke to her. She nodded her understanding as Sam watched them .Daisy Mae looking over at Sam waving at him he waved back then they left making their way to the trail god he couldn't believe their daughter could adjust to anything Sam thought he knew she would be ok with the landlady of the hotel .

THERE WERE A HANDFUL of people walking up goat fell when Sam and the others got there all three got bottles water for their backpacks Sam made sure the box with the recast off his dads ashes were ok and secure they did a selfie at the bottom off goat fell they would do one after Darian called facetime with Cameron giving them words of encouragement before there climb up .Then all three of them hugged psyching themselves up before there big walk up goat fell encouraging each other while they walked .

STOPPING HALFWAY UP taking another selfie as well as other walkers passing taking photos the views were amazing since it was a clear day their legs ache a bit they drank some water then carried on the rest off the way .Chatting laughing about silly things and about

Sam's dad his little ways and Malcolm chatted about his parents to which he didn't talk much about before it was good to hear them both chat about their parents Geraint thought .

After an hour they made it to the top, all three exhausted with the hike up more water and a snack they sat on the rock arms round each other enjoying the view Sam looked at Geraint he took his hand he looked at Sam . " I love you thank you " " Love you to and your welcome " They kissed Malcolm shook his head and sniggered Sam playfully punched Malcolm's arm they both laughed .Pretend kissed which Geraint thought was hilarious and took a funny photo of them which they thought was funny at that moment those two had a special bond .

Malcolm and Geraint watched Sam bring out the box he stood silent for a moment then looked up at Geraint and Malcolm Sam held out his hand Geraint took it they went over to a bit of rock made room to put the box inside and covered it back up . " You made it dad " He sniffed bowing his head, tears running down his cheeks Geraint hugged him Malcolm lay his arms round Sam to let him cry .They all lay their arms around each other looking out to the view then Sam felt a bit of peace come over him and thought that his dad was saying to him thank you for taking me here .That felt strange but Good Sam thought was it his dad telling him he was ok and he would be ok to .

THEY TOOK ANOTHER PHOTO again Sam hugged into Malcolm he lay his arm round Sam " Thank you " " Your welcome worth it " Sam felt lighter now it was like his dad was at peace now and Sam to an image off him and Malcolm came into his mind when they were younger with others making it up to goat fell .Malcolm stared at Sam is he ok he thought he looks a bit spacey maybe just thinking about stuff it's been a rough couples weeks for Sam .

" Sam, " Malcolm asked as he looked at him and nodded, " Just thinking back, I'm ok. " The three of them stood up. Sam went into his backpack , brought out a single flower and laid it on the place where he laid his dads ashes then stood up took a deep breath be at peace dad Sam thought he smiled and nodded he looked round at Geraint and Malcolm watching him .

" TIME TO GO BACK NOW " Sam said to Geraint and Malcolm they nodded they will definitely hurt in the morning they all thought because he was starting to hurt now a bath when they get back would help For Definite they would just take their time to get back down .

THAT NIGHT LAYING IN bed on FaceTime with Darian and Cameron Malcolm s legs definitely hurt now he had a bath to help which did a bit a little bark Cameron looked down and picked up there new husky puppy bluebell " This one has been naughty " Cameron said Malcolm guessed she had been chewing things which sometimes puppy's do especially when there teeth were growing she would soon learn and Frank certainly told her off a couple times .

" i could do with a back rub right now, " Malcolm groaned, laying on the bed. A little whimper came from bluebell and a bark from Frank because he heard his dads voice Cameron reached down, picking him up. He sniffed at the screen Malcolm giggled. He is confused and didn't expect to see him on the screen .

" when are you getting the boat " Cameron asked clapping Frank " We should get the 10 am one be back afternoon hopefully "

" OK LET ME KNOW IF you want picked up can come get you " Malcolm shifted on the bed leaning the phone on the headboard " Haven't you got book club " Malcolm asked leaning on his arm " Delayed till next week " .After there chat Malcolm called Darian at Work Face timing him to he was in the office checking memberships again Malcolm thought .

DAISY MAE SUCKED ON her thumb when Geraint tucked her in she was sleeping in the spare bed in the room while Sam got ready for bed his legs ached a bit but worth it he sat on the bed he had texted his aunt Mae that there walk up goat fell went well he sent her some pictures. And complained how sore his legs were now but it was definitely worth it .

Geraint winced when he got on the bed Sam noticed maybe it was too much for him especially after his Cancer which he was in remission now . " Geraint " he looked up Sam looked concerned he moved nearer to him " its ok its just the climb up I'm fine " Geraint kissed him.touching his face. Sam looks concerned he better not have done any damage he thought Geraint kissed his nose .

"ok but if " Geraint put his hand to Sams mouth " Sorry i " " i know let's get into bed " They both got in the covers Sam lay on Geraint's shoulder his arm around him " it's been a good day " " It has " Sam looked up at Geraint no sex tonight he thought not in front of Daisy Mae when they get back they kiss again and snuggled into each other until they feel asleep and thinking of good memories from today .

Chapter 16

C arrie stood at the patio doorstep it had been a couple days since Malcolm got back from Arran Darian looked round at Cameron and Malcolm and back at Carrie she had to process on what she had just heard about her brother Julius " He did mention about someone before but not a name " Carrie looked round at them her mum had a visitor a few times the nurses had mentioned before now it was confirmed Darian had visited her mum a few times in the past .But what was the reason for his visit to her maybe to do with Julius who knows maybe Darian not sure to why either .

" And now I know who it was that visited mum " " Carrie I wanted to make sure she was ok after Julius told me that time off her diagnosis' ' Carrie nodded. Malcolm felt nervous he didn't want anything to kick during their visit off Carrie went over to the kettle and went to fill it . " Whose for tea? "They nodded their agreement and all sat at the table, Carrie looking at the three of them .Still processing what Darian had said .She herself could not help Julius because he had his demons and it was good of Darian to get him clean and sober .

" I JUST WANT YOU TO know this doesn't change anything Julius had his demons. I did try so did Micheal and when he came to visit mum after a few months he was looking great " Carrie looked up at Darian he nodded then looked at Cameron and Malcolm . " Things got complicated after a time Julius wanted more but at that time not the business of my club well " .Understandable Carrie thought it was just a casual thing between them .

CARRIE PUT HER HAND on Darians she shook her head " Darian you don't have to explain you have two wonderful men that love you I can see that please don't beat yourself up about it " Darian nodded Cameron and Malcolm lay their arms round him he nodded " Carries right you have to stop carrying that burden " Cameron said looking at Malcolm " Cams right " Malcolm smiled but knew how Darian was feeling towards Julius .

" I KNOW YOU TWO ARE my rock " Carrie smiled at their affection towards each other and their love for each other "Have you heard from Julio " Darian asked "Not for a while but he seemed to be doing ok last time i heard from him " .

Elliot listened from the top of the stairs their conversation so Darian was the guy that Julius was involved with that Carrie and mum didn't know about that revelation. He felt angry that his therapy session was due this week that would be something to chat to the group about .Elliot stood up to go back into his room just as Darian , Malcolm and Cameron were leaving they looked up at Elliot he looked down "Going out " Carrie asked Elliot he nodded " Patrick's on his way going into town " .

" How are you " Darian asked Elliot looked down at them the three off them looked at each other "How do you think I am " " Elliot " At that Elliot went into his room Darian looked at Darian " Sorry about that he's just you know " Malcolm touched Carries arm she looked at him " He isn't angry at anyone Carrie you know " . He just needs time to heal Malcolm though and I know that feeling too well Malcolm thought .

" I know anyway thanks for coming over " Darian and the others left Elliot watched from a distance in his room as his heart ached but the therapy session exercises helped a text come through from Patrick he was on his way as he came downstairs. Carrie came out of the kitchen before Elliot went out to the car " Elliot that was a bit rude earlier " " Sorry " He looked round at Carrie then went over to hug her " love you sis " " love you to " .They look at each other I just wish he would be open more with her but maybe didn't want to just yet .He just needs time Carrie was thankful that he had his friends and therapy to go to and if he wanted to talk to her well he can she thought .

ELLIOT GOT INTO THE car Patrick looked at him he looked a little stressed he thought " Whats up " " Did you get them " Patrick nodded he looked round at the back seat Elliot looked round to at the flowers card and some beers to take to the cemetery " Thanks " " Mate you know I'm always here for you " Elliot nodded this day is hard especially since it's Leytons 20th birthday .God he thought those two half years have passed so quick Elliot thought and he would be turning 20 in a couple months to .

ON THE DRIVE HOME CAMERON driving Malcolm in the back Darian thought what was up with Elliot with his outburst. Maybe he is just feeling down. Cameron's phone rang, Steven calling and he pressed his hands free to talk to him . " Hey, what do you think about Dublin?" Cameron looked at Darian Dublin Malcolm thought " What about it I'm driving Steven Darian and Malcolm's here "

" BACHELOR WEEKEND GOLFING sightseeing " " Sounds ok to me hotel ",

" Sure that would be great " They both said they wondered what about Jordan what was he going to do " Steven what has Jordan organised " Cameron asked Steven huffed and sighed " He has not decided yet " Cameron sniggered looking at Darian who shook his head . "Why aren't you combining it Steven " " We decided to separate gotta go talk later ok " .

MALCOLM SAT FORWARD thinking why Elliot was being weird he thought " Steven sounded off is the honeymoon period over " Cameron sniggered no he didn't think that maybe just wedding stuff he thought .Steven had always been like that

" No babe he's being a groomzilla " Darian huffed and shook his head as they went to the pet shop to get food and puppy pads for the dog's groomzilla Darian thought what a weird term for it just like a bridezilla is .

ELLA AND IZZY FARAH got out of the car at the cemetery Ella got out the flowers for her son's grave she couldn't believe he would have been 20 years old today it was just like yesterday he was just born she missed him every day just like her daughter Izzy .

" Mum " " in a minute " Ella looked up izzy was looking over at Leytons grave Elliot and Patrick were there Ella sighed Izzy looked worried " Mum " " Izzy its fine hes every right to be here to " There was no bad feeling towards Ella and Elliot since Leyton died she didn't blame him that Leyton took the ecstasy tablet that night . She had approved of her son's relationship with Elliot and they both were each other's firsts too .

" Elliot " " Huh " He looked up at Patrick looking over at Ella and Izzy coming over to the grave Elliot stood up wiping his eyes he sat down the beer when Ella came closer . " Mrs Farah i " Ella hugged Elliot which surprised him he melted into her hug .Smiling she had always approved of him and Leyton she had no problem with that .

" Let me look at you " He looked thin dark circles under his eyes Patrick looked over at Izzy she smiled looking down at her brother's grave "Well isn't this a party then " Ella joked sitting down the flowers on her son's grave she noticed a can beer beside Elliots flowers she stood up looking over at the boys .

" You look to thin Elliot "He looked at Patrick and back at Ella " Lot going on " Patrick nodded Elliot looked round at Laytons grave Izzy came over to the gravestone bending down " Happy birthday " Sitting down a card Elliot looked up dont cry he thought Izzy looked round at everyone a tear rolling down her face Ella went over to her laying her arm round Ella .

Walking back to the cars, Izzy and Patrick chatted while Elliot and Ella chatted " How things " Patrick asked Izzy she looked over at him " I'm getting married " " " wow great Andy right " Izzy nodded and blushed "When " " Couple months " .

" Please come visit Elliot " Ella asked. It had been a while since they last saw each other. It hurt too much going into Leytons home " You are ok right " Elliot shook his head " Complicated i can't just yet " .

" I understand " They said their goodbyes. Elliot took one last look at Leytons grave then went into the car and they drove off. Elliot promised he would visit Ella soon he thought maybe they should have kept in better contact but it hurt too much to see Leytons parents at that time when Leyton died .

" SHIT FUCK " ELLIOT banged his leg on the kitchen table when he came home hours later drunk wobbling his way around the kitchen then the bag off chips he got burst and some fell on the floor " Shit " He bent down to pick them up then the kitchen light came on he up at Carrie standing at the door Micheal came into the kitchen to see what's going on . " I dropped my chippy, " Carrie signed. Micheal looked at her and back at Elliot who started to eat his chips .At the table seriously Carrie thought what a mess he had made Micheal picking up bits of chips from the floor .

" ELLIOT WHERE HAVE you been it's been it's been hours " Carrie said as Micheal helped to pick up the rest of the chips " Don't nag ":Elliot huffed Carrie shook her head sighing Elliot looked at her will she just leave me alone he thought " wouldn't get this if I had my own place " Micheal looked at Carrie then Elliot please don't argue tonight he thought he's just having a rough day because off Leytons birthday .

    " C'mon guys don't fight Eliot c'mon we know you're upset because of Leyton " upset he thought yea he's upset and yea it was because of Leyton birthday and what he heard about his brother and Darian .Which Carrie kept quiet about not being happy about .

    " Did you know about Darian and my brother " Micheal looked at Carrie and back at Elliot " Elliot I was going to speak to you about that I only heard today " Elliot huffed just what is it Darian wants from this family he thought " Lets not get into this right now ok Hun c'mon let's get to bed " .

    " Does he want to keep it in the family then now us " Carrie saw red she went over to Elliot and slapped him then immediately regretted it Elliot held his face shocked at what she did Micheal held her back tears running down her face " Elliot I can't take back what happened to you but your self destructing I can't take it anymore

" Carrie about turned and ran back upstairs into her bedroom flopping onto the bed .screaming into the pillow Damn him she thought I'm only trying to help .

" Micheal i didn't mean to say that " Micheal lay his hand on Eliot's shoulder " I know look ill clear up go to bed " Elliot nodded and went up to his room Micheal came into their bedroom Carrie was sitting still crying Micheal went over to her they hugged . "C'mon now dry those tears he's ok " " I didn't mean to slap him " Micheal lay his arm around Carrie comforting her .Yep she is feeling bad Micheal thought hugging his wife hopefully they will talk about it in the morning

This is such a mess the two of them need to hash it out Micheal though .

A jerk of the legs arms splaying Elliot was having a bad dream his throat hurt he couldn't breath then an image off Leyton Elliot trying to reach him as Leyton was trying to say something g to him Leyton getting further away " NO LEYTON " Elliot screamed he sat up in bed clutching his chest feeling sick he got up ran to the bathroom to throw up .Fuck he thought retching spilling his guts into the .

Jesus he thought as he spilled into the toilet " Elliot are you ok " Carrie asked, coming over to him bending down rubbing his back as he threw up some more " Sis I'm sorry " Carrie looked up at Micheal Carrie got up and rinsed a cloth giving it to Elliot to wash his face . " Daddy " Molly wondered what was going on. He went over to her to take her back to her room while Carrie tended to Elliot .

" Don't worry about that Elliot how do you feel now " Elliot got up rinsing his mouth he sat on the edge off the bath while Carrie cleaned up " I had a nightmare again " Carrie looked at him she sat on the toilet seat " Maybe you should get an appointment with the doctor could be anxiety or something like that " .No way Elliot through not taking medication to make me feel better or like a zombie .

" I DON'T WANT TO TAKE pills to make me feel better " Maybe he was right Carrie thought that's not always the solution talking about it would help with therapy sessions "C'mon . Let's get you back to bed " .Maybe it is a stupid idea but it's something he could talk to his therapist about .

Carrie looked round at Elliot before she left his room. Maybe he's right. She thought maybe he didn't need medication but something wasn't right since his attack .Or doing one on one therapy might help her and Micheal will also help him through it as well as Patrick and Bailey too one thing that Carrie wished was for Elliot to open up to her but maybe he didn't want to which was ok by her .

MICHEAL SIGHED LEANING against the car watching the kids get in line to get into school Malcolm looked round at him he looked tired he thought Micheal checked his phone for updates with Carrie " Whatsapp " Malcolm asked Micheal looked round at him " Rough night reason I'm doing the school run today " " Elliot " Micheal nodded Alice shouted her goodbyes to everyone Micheal and Malcolm waved . " Carrie thinks it might be anxiety they had words yesterday also it was Leytons birthday too " .

Ahh Malcolm thought it could be the reason he was acting out to Malcolm nodded. Micheal moved to get to the car Malcolm stopped him. He looked at Malcolm " Be patient with him Micheal he's been through a trauma talking to his therapist will get him through it I can guarantee it " .Micheal hoped so and yes it had been traumatic for him which was a kind thing to say Micheal thought .

" I hope Malcolm can help you. I know it's silly of me to ask Micheal up to Elliot now I can only give advice " He was probably right. Micheal thought and yes it was up to Elliot to sort himself out which he hoped he would do .

Chapter 17

Thursday night at the club Darian chatted to some members walking around seeing if anyone was ok, asking how the new club was going letting them know it was going good. Still a few inspections to get checked out Elliot was busy serving and taking champagne up to the vip and private rooms . Darian was yet to talk to him about stuff Since Malcolm came home from the school run letting him know what had happened with Carrie and Elliot the night before . The way he had been acting Darian thought therapy was helping .

Darian went into the office Cameron at his desk on the computer writing his novel he stood for a moment watching him shaking his head Cameron looked up at him watching him Cameron smiled " All ok " "Uh huh " Darian came over to him hovering over Cameron " Cam " " Mm " looking up at Darian lolking down at him " What " .

Darian closed the computer Jesus Cameron thought I was getting to a good bit he looked up at Darian " Darian Longstrom that better had saved " Darian moved the chair so he could get access Cameron cocked his head " what if it didn't " Cameron slid the chair over to him stood up and wrapped his arm round Darians waist bringing him closer to hm . " Then you get punished " . Darian hummed and grinned " I see " Darian went to slide his hand to Cameron's crotch he took his hand and held them down moving closer to Darian .

" I've locked the door " Darian said they kissed grinding into each other then the door knocks Damn Darian thought not now " ignore who it is they will come back " Darian says Cameron fixes himself goes over to the door opens it to Elliot standing there . " He wants to see me " " Elliot come in " Cameron looks at Darian he nods. Elliot comes inside Cameron goes over the couch and sits as Elliot stands . Looking pissed Darian thought but every reason to be but he will have to curb the attitude while in the club Darian thought .

Darian comes round to the front of the table and leans against it " Am I in trouble " Elliot asks he looks tired Darian thought " No you're not in trouble Elliot , there is something I do want to talk to you about " .Elliot buffs noticed by Darian which he will speak to him about that another time .

" My brother right " Cameron looks up Darian looks at him he nods and looks at Elliot again " What's your side then cause Carries only told her side " Cameron sighs shaking his head why does this boy have such a beef about his brother he hardly knew . " It was complicated between Julius and I. Elliot , your brother had a lot of problems " Right Elliot thought he had heard bits regarding their on-off relationship.

" That you didn't want to know about " " Not true " Cameron said Elliot looked at him. What does he know ? He thought " I didn't want this poxy. Job " Darian sighed looking at Cameron he shrugged his shoulders ." Enough Elliot " Elliot huffed shaking his head who he thought was trying to rule him .Because that ain't happening showed his dominance to him all he wanted to know about his brother.

" There is someone you can talk to " " Nope not doing more therapy " The door chaps Cameron gets up to answer it Ed standing " He is here " Cameron looks at Darian who comes to the door what's going on Elliot thought .Ed looks round as a tall man long black hair and amazing piercing blue eyes appears he is wearing a blue suit white shoes Darian smiles and holds out his hand Cameron can't stop staring at him .

" Lucien thanks for coming " " Pleasure " Lucien walks into the room wow Elliot thought he is very tall he thought Cameron still can't stop staring at him Elliot feels faint and sits down he also can't stop staring Darian sniggers Cameron looks at him which isn't funny he thought . " Lucien this is Elliot " Darian introduced him Elliot stands up why am I bowing he thought Lucien looks at Darian and Cameron .Has he .

" My husband Cameron " Lucien nods and looks at Elliot who looks nervous. Juliet said it was urgent " What was urgent Elliot thought and that voice it was angelic like when Lucien spoke " Yes you know the brief " .What brief Elliot thought what is going on I should stop staring he thought .

" I do Elliot please don't be scared no harm will come to you " " What " What is he talking about Elliot thought and why can't I stop staring at this guy again before Cameron notices that Elliot is staring at Lucien .Well I can't either he just seems so angelic looking .

Darian went over to Elliot laying his arm around his shoulder " Lucien is an empath and he can let you talk to people that have passed " Tears formed in Elliot's eyes as Elliot thought, looking at Lucien and back at Darian . " I can talk to Leyton , " Darian nodded. Why is he doing this for him? He felt so bad being nasty to Darian . " Darian you didn't need to " .Fuck me Elliot thought do I want to talk to Leyton I do miss him so much so many things I want to tell him do I need this he guessed so .

LUCIEN AND ELLIOT SAT on the couch while Darian and Cameron watched " Hold my hands Elliot when your in a trance you will see a white room with a door don't go through it wait there you

have ten minutes when you hear a ringing that's when you come back
" Elliot thought that's not long for what he wanted to say he nodded
his Heart was beating fast Lucien held out his hands Elliot placed
his on Lucien . Warm hands Elliot thought he felt a calmness off
him like electricity running through him .He was also light headed
a sense of euphoria came over him But went with it this is weird but
peaceful .

ELLIOT DRIFTED OFF his mind swirling until a while room
appeared he looked round where is the door he thought Lucien
spoke to him in his mind calming him " Elliot " he knew that voice
he turned round Leyton standing in front of him he smiled holding
out his arms for Elliot to go to him .Elliot ran to him they embraced
" Leyton " Elliot whispered they looked at each other " We only have
ten minutes " .He looks different Elliot thought is that a glow around
him to fuck this is hard .

" HE SAID " LEYTON touched Elliot's face he leaned into his
touch " Elliot you need to stop blaming yourself I was the one that
decided to take the tablet " They held hands Elliot nodded tears
running down his face Layton wiped them away " I miss you so much
it hurts " . God this was hard Elliot thought seeing Leyton again the
love of his life .Elliot moved nearer to Leyton slipping his arm round
Leytons waist they hugged Leyton smoothing his hair just like he
used to .

" ELLIOT LISTEN TO ME you will find love again you have to
move on " Elliot looks up at Leyton what if it don't want to or am I

ready to find love again but how " But I don't know how to Leyton "
Leyton kissed Elliot's head he closed his eyes " Are you happy Leyton
" He nodded laying his arm round Elliot's shoulder " I'm at peace
Elliot like you should be have you found it yet " .Found what what
does he mean staring at Leyton .

" FOUND WHAT " " THE box in the cupboard in my room the
shoe box " Leytons mum hasn't touched any of Leyton things since
he died she couldn't bring herself to do it she had wanted to keep it
the same way until she decided it was time to move on and decorate
the room . "No she hadn't touched any of what's in it " .Elliot was
curious to know about the box in the cupboard.

Leyton took his hand and looked up at Elliot again smiling " An
engagement ring Elliot" What the hell Elliot thought he was gonna
propose and didn't get the chance to " He is here " " Who " they
looked around at who Leyton was looking at Julius stood Elliot ran
to him not enough time he thought they hugged .So many thoughts
going round his head that he also wanted to speak to Julius about to
.

WAS HE OK CAMERON THOUGHT as Tears ran down
Elliot's face was that normal Darian held his hand reassuring him
that he would be .What was Elliot seeing Cameron thought
watching on Lucien and Elliot still holding hands .Elliot was smiling
to everyone noticed must be good .

" Julius you're here to " " We only have five more minutes "
Leyton announced god so quick to quick he thought " Elliot what
happened between me and Darian was my doing I wanted more "
" I don't care about that anymore I just want closure and the other
thing " Leyton hugged him as well as Julius " Sorry " .Julius was

right he had wanted more from Darian which they had fought about constantly but Darian did not want that .

" It's ok oh Zeke says hi to " " Zeke " Julius and Leyton looked at each other " Just say to Darian Zeke said hi " A faint ringing sound Elliot heard no he wasn't ready to go Julius and Leyton looked at each other and nodded time for them to go no I'm not ready yet Elliot thought I want more time .

" I'll never forget you Leyton " Leyton nodded touching Elliot's face the ringing got louder " LEYTON " Darian got worried Elliot didn't wake up Cameron held his arm then suddenly his eyes opened . " Elliot wake up " Lucien said snapping his fingers then Elliot woke up disoriented looking round " Elliot are you with me " Lucien asked he nodded . Looking at them he felt weird as if he wasn't in his body feeling faint. Someone handed him a glass of something to drink ." Zeke Elliot said Darian looked at Cameron" What did he mean " Elliot what about him " Then he went on with the mumbling again as if he was drunk and not able to speak properly .I hope he is ok Darian thought staring at Elliot while Lucien saw him .

" Is he ok? Cameron asked, looking at Lucien as Elliot lay down. " Not enough time. " Elliot said " He will be fine. " The door opened. Claudia came inside wow she thought and she stared at him so he is handsome Claudia blushed oh my Where did that come from . " Claudia please take Lucien to the vip Lucien you have time for a drink right " .

" I do thank you " Bill appears staring at Lucien while he and Claudia go through to the bar " is he "Bill asks looking at Elliot laying on the couch mumbling Cameron beside him " Bill can you take Elliot home I'll call Carrie " .What's happened to Elliot Bill thought he seems a bit out of it helping him up.

CAMERON HELPS BILL with Elliot into the car Dean appears from the club Darian looks round at him Bill looks over and nods Dean smiles looks at Darian " Alright " Darian asks him " We will be " Dean looking at Bill driving off .Taking Elliot home ." Dean are you guys ok " Darian asks Dean sighs nodding " Yea we will be Thanks Darian " .

Darian goes back into the office Cameron sitting on the couch he looks up at him as Darian goes over to the drinks cabinet pouring himself a whiskey and drinks all the contents `` Darian " Cameron asks Darian looks down at his glass the. Look round at Cameron . "Do you think Zeke said something to him? " Cameron got up and went over to Darian, wrapping his arms around him . " I'm here, don't think too much into it Love " . Darian leans into Cameron just weird that Elliot said Zeke's name .

They look at each other. Cameron gave Darian a kiss on the cheek. " You're tired, we should go home. " He was probably right. Darian thought lots were going on. Maybe they should go home. " I love you, " Darian says. Cameron takes his hand " Ditto ".Cameron hugged Darian he shouldn't think too much into it Cameron thought .they hugged Cameron kissed Darians head Yea it's been a day we should go home and get some rest now .

" HE WILL BE OK WON'T he? " Carrie asks Bill, standing at the door. She looks at him and back at Elliot asleep. " He will be fine. " A text comes through from Dean. When Bill checks it he smiles and sticks his phone back in his pocket . " That smile is not nothing, who is she? " Carrie asks while they go downstairs . Carrie looks at him damn maybe she should've said he or she thought .It's not her business regarding Dean's personal life .

" We Have been together a few months " " Lovely " Micheal comes into the kitchen getting a drink before they go to bed " Elliot ok " " He's fine " Carrrie goes to the door to see Bill out he looks round before he goes to his car . " It's a he just so you know " Oh Carrie thought he didn't need to tell me that Carrie thought . Bill nodded then left to get into his car and drove off .

" FOUND IT " ELLIOT said while rummaging around the cupboard in Leytons bedroom a day later Ella stood waiting Elliot came out the cupboard holding a box he looked at Ella and sat on the bed he looked down at the box thinking at what Leyton said his hands shaking . Ella sat beside him.she sniffed wiping her eyes Elliot looked round at her he lay an arm around her shoulders . They wanted to know what was in the box that Leyton was going to give Elliot .Good I'm shaking Elliot thought holding the box I'm too scared to look .

" Ella it's time to move on " She nodded brought out a hankie to blow her nose again his hands shook he was nervous to open the box " i know its just " Elliot carefully opened the box wrapping paper around the small box he looked at Ella and back at the box taking it out the shoe box .Ok be brave Elliot don't be stupid he sighed taking a deep breath to open the box .

Elliot opened it up 2 white gold rings. Oh wow he thought that must've cost a lot " There beautiful " Ella said Elliot nodded they were he thought he had a spare chain at home he could use for them .He would treasure them forever Elliot thought rubbing his thumb across the two rings a tear in his eye .Jesus Leyton what have you done to me Elliot getting all emotional .

" Have you thought what to do with his room " " Was thinking about an office " Ella had been thinking of decorating Leytons room for some time but it was saying goodbye to him first but she expected that Leyton would approve .Elliot looks round at Ella it's time to move on now he thought Ella needs to redecorate Leytons room and his clothes etc .

" Good idea Ella i can help with the decoration it will be good for my therapy " good idea Ella thought she patted Elliots back " Also there are a couple things i would like to take if it's ok" " Off course you can there are things we need to sort out take to the charity shop to " .

" I can help you with that Ella " Good to know because she wouldn't have the strength to do it all. I miss my son so much but it's time we moved on now it's what he would have wanted .

MALCOLM OPENED THE office door Darian was sitting staring into space for a moment bluebell cane running in over to a Darian he picked her up Malcolm had just come back from taking her and Frank for a walk Bluebell liked his face Darian screwed up his face bluebell liking it " Yes yes I know " Darian had been quiet since Elliot had his talk with Leyton at the club he didn't say anymore about Zeke and Darian had wondered if Zeke had visited him to ." Darian " he looked up at Malcolm " What " .

" Are you still worrying? " Darian clapped bluebells head He shook his head at Malcolm bullshit. Malcolm thought then the front door opened when Philip Came inside Cameron had picked him up from school and he came running into the office . " Daddy look what I made " Darian sat Bluebell down Philip sat on Darians knee Philip sat his makeshift volcano on the table Malcolm huffed " Wow that's amazing "" We have to make the lava " Oh great Darian thought another mess to be made .But he didn't mind that it was the fun in making stuff and Philip was artistic Darian wondered if he took it off from Cameron his artistic side .

Cameron stood behind Malcolm. he looked round " He still sulking " Malcolm nodded Cameron shook his head he's got to get out off this mood he thought Cameron went into the office " Philip go get changed buddy and put your volcano in a safe place ok " Philip went off upstairs to get changed taking his volcano with him Darian looked between Cameron and Malcolm . Are they ganging up on me now, Darian thought because it won't be happening, nothing to worry about .

" DON'T GANG UP ON ME " " Darian were not " Cameron said he went over to him leaning over him " This won't do right Malcolm " " Yes I agree " Darian was about to say something when Cameron put his hand on his mouth. " Maybe you need closure too " Darian shook his head then Cameron took his hand away . " I don't " "Bullshit " Malcolm said Darian looked over at him .Maybe he does, maybe not Darian thought Julius had his demons that's for sure that Darian couldn't help with .And they had an open relationship nothing more sometimes another person joined them he wasn't in love with Julius . Not like Zeke who he was in love with and now Cameron and Malcolm .

   " Could they you know " Cameron asked Darian shook his head " Will you two stop analysing me " Darian moved to get up Cameron stopping him looking over at Malcolm and back at Darian . " You want to talk about it, " Darian sighed, shaking his head. He made his peace a long time ago . " Honestly i am fine, can i go see my son now " .Darian glared at Cameron and Malcolm then looking at each other .

   Darian got up touching Cameron's face " i don't want to fight " Cameron nodded Darian looking over at Malcolm laying out his arm he went to him the three of them hugging .giving each other kisses and hugging Darian closed his eyes taking a deep breath It's ok I'm ok he thought .Maybe I do maybe I don't need closure I am certainly not doing what Elliot did .

That might after his shower Malcolm sat on the edge off the bed clasping his hands either it will work or not " Hello i know what your gonna say " Malcolm looked up thinking this is silly now " i would be really grateful if you could help out my love he's feeling a little lost right now also i will try and well shit sorry i mean take our son to church if he wants thanks oh p.s it would be great if Philip could win his prize for his volcano thank you " .

Malcolm sniggered into himself and shook his head. Cameron poked his head through the bathroom door. " Did you say something? Malcolm looked round at him." No babe ".Cameron stood watching Malcolm he looked up at Cameron " Do you think we should do something " Cameron asks Malcolm gets up leaning on the sink . " Maybe we shouldn't pester him so much" " Yes Maybe You're right".

But they both had to think of something to try to get Darian out of this funk he is in right now because of the message that Zeke gave Elliot .

A COUPLE DAYS LATER while at the Glasgow site Darian was going through CCTV sorting it out for different areas in the office working between the computer and the monitor in his office . There had been a lot of static things going on which was weird. He thought the Foreman didn't mention anything about that so he would phone him about it . Dariam went outside to the bar area. The lights were going haywire.flickering on and off . What the hell is going on? He thought he got out his phone to call Gary, the Foreman to ask him about the electrics so a weird thing happened: the feeling he had up his back .

" Darian " Darian froze he felt a tingling all over if i turn round i wont be able to hold it together he did i hear right Darian turned round and standing at the far side is Zeke dressed in a pale blue suit there was a faint glow around him "Holy shit " He was just as he remembered his shaggy brown hair smiling " Surprised " .Zeke asked smiling i sure am Darian thought.fuck I don't know what to say its just weird .

Darian went closer to him. How is this possible he thought and he needed a lot of answers to "How is " " I only have ten minutes " Tears stung Darians eyes he went closer to Zeke he could feel the aura around him .Mama. Mia thought " I didn't ask, I don't understand " .What is going on around here Darian thought who asked .

" Someone else did Darian, are you happy? " What he thought. Who would ask "Am i happy?" he asks " Yes now i am " Zeke screwed his face he cocked his head "Aren't you happy " " Yes i mean now i am Cameron and Malcolm are amazing Zeke I " .

" You need to stop blaming yourself. I did it to myself , shush I know " Zeke said "rolling his eyes " who was Zeke talking to Darian. Though Zeke took Darians hand he looked down at Zekes and it did feel warm. He looked back up at Zeke .That's weird should his hands feel warm Darian thought .I did wish sometimes I could have helped Zeke more with his addiction. Had gotten worse over the years even though he did get clean for a few months but he had triggers .

" i had the addiction Darian i didn't want to leave you oh Julius says hi " Darian wiped his eyes why didn't Julius come to he thought "We both can't be here same time yea yea I know " Zeke said shaking his head " He never shuts up he said he's happy for Steven " .Oh that was a nice thing to say about Steven he had moved on to and very happy with Jordan .

" Darian you guys are doing great, believe me I'm happy to see you have made a family " Zeke zoned out for a second he looked round at Darian " i have t to go now before I go you should sort out the storage " . Darian remembered he had put Zeke's stuff into storage at times he couldn't bring himself to get rid of Zeke's belongings and his paintings and art work " I will i promise " . " Oh

Christian please try to get on I know what you're gonna say " He is probably right Darian thought he should call Zeke brother Christian regarding Zeke work .They did talk about selling his work years ago .

" Close your eyes Darian " " Why " Zeke took his hands then touched his face Darian leaning into his touch " I want you to remember a happy moment between us ok count to 3 minutes then open your eyes ok ." Darian nodded he understood and it was good to see Zeke after all these years .

Darian shut his eyes and after 3 minutes he opened them to Zeke he laughed into himself wiping his eyes he felt a sense of peace since Zeke came . " Darian " Darian looked up at Gary the foreman he looked worried " Darian are you ok" . Gary was worried something was going on with Darian was he sick or having a seizure he thought .He looks a little pale Gary thought I hope he is OK.

Darian stood up coming over to Gary " I'm good I'm the electrics ok " " Yea fine why " .

Darian giggled into himself Gary stared at him is he really ok gr thought then Darians phone rang Cameron calling him he connected the call " Daddy i won " Darian giggled again smiling he looked up at the ceiling " Buddy that's great i told you they would love it i love you " .

" Love you daddy " Philip handed the phone back to Cameron " it's great isn't it babe " Cameron exclaimed to Darian ok he wondered he sounds a bit strange on the phone mind you it's been full on with the new place maybe tired .

Darian took a deep breath to stop himself from crying he nodded to himself " Darian " Cameron asked " I'm here yes it's great I'm ok Love you know it just been hectic " Cameron was well aware that his book schedules can be full on To whenever a new release comes out .He doesn't want Dariam stressed about the new place .

He disconnected the call Malcolm came into the club a worried Gary calling him Darian sitting at the bar Malcolm went over to him

" Darian " Malcolm sits beside him he looks kinda pale he thought he looks at Malcolm Malcolm. " Darian do you want to go home " " no love I didn't " Darian takes Malcolm's hand and they look at each other .Malcolm takes Darians hand staring at him he looks ok Malcolm thought are we worrying over nothing he thought .

" I saw Zeke " Ahh the big guy came through then he thought Malcolm nodded Darian touched his face " When " " Here just now " Darian pointed to the floor Malcolm looked over Gary had went back to work " Did you ask " Darian asked looking round at Malcolm he smiled "Well I did put in a word to the big guy " Darian sniggered shaking his head " Was he ok "Malcolm asked Darian nodded he stood up looking over at the floor area where Zeke stood . "Good he was good " Darian sniffed he reached over to Malcolm bringing him closer to him . Looking at each other Malcolm wraps his arms round Darians shoulders .

" Thank you " Darian gave Malcolm a kiss t" Are you ok now " Darian took Malcolm's hand again he felt ok more than ok he felt good " I'm ok now love " Thank god for that Malcolm thought he stood up Darian looked up at him . " Good cause you scared me c'mon let's get some lunch I'm starving " .

" Mmm I know what I'm starving for " Malcolm sighed, shaking his head, batting off Darian. They both giggled. " Hey, not that stud. " Darian pouted Malcom. Shook his head again and lay his arm round Darians . " you let's feed you " .Darian lays his arm round Malcolm he looks up at Darian he kisses Malcolm's head .

" What are you in the mood for to eat " Malcolm asks on there way out to the car " You decide " Darian suggests Malcolm looks at him he cocks his head grinning " c'mon you let's go get a Greggs " Darian groaned not his favourite shop but they did good sandwich selections I guess it will have to do then he thought .

Chapter 18

A week later for Steven and Jordan's bachelor weekend It was their second day in Dublin Darian hadn't been to Ireland before which he had wanted to visit for a while The others couldn't believe it all the years he had been living in Scotland he hadn't visited Ireland. The hotel was a good location at the temple bar area, good pubs, eating places Darian could just about make out what the Irish people were saying . The others thought it was hilarious and in the end Steven and Jordan decided just to combine their bachelor weekends together with a couple friends coming along as well as Jordan's dad and brother who all got on which was good .

IT WAS THEIR GOLFING day and they went into teams which would be more fun for them to do. They thought they were on the fourth course Darian was showing off with his golfing skills to everyone amusement he was so competitive Cameron and. Malcolm thought and they got a good view off his ass every time they tee off . Jordan's brother josh and father Albert were nice good job Steven got on well with them .while they walked to the next tee off Malcolm slipped his arm through Darians he whispered " Your ass looks great " Darian sniggered shaking his head he looks over at Cameron chatting to Steven and Sam he looks over at him and Malcolm wondering what they were whispering about .

" Thanks " Malcom bumped Darians shoulder and winked at him " Can you two stop flirting " Steven said shaking his head Jordan slipped his arm through Stevens waist he looked at him " Can I flirt with you " Steven giggled he kissed Jordan " Are we playing golf or not " Josh said laughing as they walked on to get the next round and where there balls landed .Seriously those lot need to calm themselves Josh thought hearing giggling from the back he looks round Malcolm and Cameron huddled in together watching Darian .

AFTERWARDS FINISHING off there golf which was a tie which was ok they were only having fun they went back to the hotel to freshen up before their dinner plans for tonight at one of the local restaurants and after dinner they went to one the gay bars called street 66 Jordan's dad and brother decided to go back to the hotel and let his son and others enjoy their night .Not that they were into going to gay bars they were told it was a good night but they would see everyone in the morning .

It was a cute bar Malcolm thought the cocktails were good for Sam , Malcolm and Geraint danced as well as Steven and Jordan Darian and Cameron sat and watched while they drank laughing at the guys' antics .Darian held Cameron's knee when they sat talking rubbing his thumb on Cameron's knee.Darian thought he will have to cut off Malcolm soon he gets drunk quick he looks at Cameron and Cameron thinks Darian is being to protective again .

There was a mixture at the bar old young people one particular guy Malcolm noticed was eyeballing Darian older with a moustache muscley he noticed . Malcolm lay his arms over Darian and Cameron they looked at him " Are you old farts gonna dance " Darian and Cameron looked at each other sniggering Malcolm looking between them Darian pointed to himself " " Love im not old " Darian said Malcolm cocked his head " Oh by the way your getting eyeballed "

.Malcolm announced I would To he is a total catch for sure that's my man .

They look over at the guy Malcolm mentioned at the bar collecting his drinks nope not my type he thought shaking his head Malcolm snorted Darian glared at him not funny he thought . " Cam c'mon dance with us " Steven asked, dragging him up to the dance floor Malcolm sat beside Darian wrapping his arms around his shoulders . " You're not an old fart really " Malcolm kissed him " I know I'm not ": They bumped heads, definitely not an old fart Darian thought touching Malcolm's knee .

" THE GUY IS STILL eyeballing you and you know what that means all the men think you're still hot especially me " Darian shook his head Malcolm was a little tipsy he thought maybe he should cut him off he thought or maybe not he didn't want to cause a fuss . " Mal c'mon a like this song " Sam grabbing Malcom to Dance to Jimmy Somerville .Cameron giggled laying his arm round Darian they look at each other " Do you think we should just give him water " Darian asked " Malcolm is Fine Darian try not fuss ok " Darian nodded looks over at Malcolm and Sam dancing with Geraint Yea Maybe I shouldn't fuss to much he thought .

Zeke and Julius watched them keeping themselves invisible, they looked at each other shaking their heads " You do know we can't interfere " Zeke said Julius looked at him and up to the ceiling " I know the big guy said " Julius grinned and they carried on watching the scene before them . Julius was happy for Darian that he found his happiness with Malcolm and Cameron and now Philip . Darian had always wanted a family and now Julius didn't at that time they just clashed at most things .He was his sire after all and he was grateful that Darian saved him when he came to the club to rob him that night .If only things could have been different he thought Zeke looks at Julius deep in thought while watching everyone he has to stop blaming himself " Julius stop it " He looks at Zeke and nods " Sorry I know " .

DARIAN ORDERED MORE drinks up at the bar while he chatted to the guy who had been looking at him. His name was Brendan Darian and found a nice chap he thought was from around the area . He seemed ok Darian thought he was Irish and was a local from Dublin `` I've got a bet on " Brendan said looking over at his partner padraig " You have what for " " The guy with the beanie over there " Brendan pointed to and with other friends ": " That's my Padraig `` Brendan smiled noticed by Darian Brendan looked at Darian . " We've been married for 10 years together 20 years `` " That's wonderful congratulations " Wow Darian thought that is a long time and well done to them for being together all that time .

Brendan pfft shaking his head looking round at the bar at the younger ones " I'm bloody 62 you know your man " Darian thought he was looking good for 62 he thought " My two " Brendan nearly choked on his drink when Darian said two " what really two men bloody hell " "We are in a throuple relationship " "Oh Jesus".Brendan patted Darians back congratulating him on his achievement to .

Darian laughed and Brendan explained to Darian about his bet with his husband that they would bet if they still could chat up anyone Julius shook his head listening to the conversation looking at Zeke . " I've got to " Julius said Zeke glared at him he better not think or they wouldn't get the privilege again .

Brendan took a sip of his beer and a shiver ran through him looking at Darian sorting out his drinks with the bar man " After all this time you're still not a beer man " Darian looked round at Brendan smiling at him he looked over at Zeke at the far side shaking his head . " Julius " Darian whispered Brendan leaned against the bar he nodded looking over at Malcolm and Cameron chatting . " Your happy Darian " Darian looks at Cameron and Malcolm and back at Brendan .

" I AM JULIUS " " DARIAN it's best this way I couldn't otherwise I'm ok you don't have to feel guilty anymore "What does that mean I don't have to feel guilty Julius made the decision himself Brendan shivered again Darian started " Bloody hell its all new now " Darian sniggered damn you Julius he thought nodding his head. Jesus Julius Darian thought stop doing this to me .

" FINALLY " MALCOLM said when Darian finally came back with the drinks giggling into himself what's up with him Malcolm thought " What is funny " Cameron asks as Darian shares out the drinks around the table " His name is Brendan he has a partner called Padraig the one with the beanie on they have been married ten years " Malcolm can't believe he got all that info he looked at Cameron open mouthed "And they have a bet on to " " I feel bad now " Malcolm Says pouting while taking a sip of his drink .

The bar lady comes over with a tray of drinks for them from Brendan and his partner which everyone thought was a lovely gesture Darian returned the favour and got a round off drinks for Brendan's table to which he also thought was kind.The Guys seemed ok Both Padriag and Brendon thought .A bit intense thought but he was a nice man after chatting to Darian .

Darian went to the Toilet he looked up at the ceiling " Seriously big guy what are you doing to me oh Hello and thanks for our sons winning his competition much appreciated. One more thing let my new club be a success please thanks oh and Amen " Darian crossed himself shaking his head what a weird night he thought .And he did hope the new club would be a success renovations were going well too .

Jordan wrapped his arms around Steven's waist looking up at him " I love you, take me to bed and love me forever " Steven snorted that's a line from Top Gun they kissed . " You just quoted Top Gun, " Jordan said giggling. Steven pinched his bum . " You mister are gonna get lucky tonight " Jordan announced Steven giggled shaking his head I certainly hope so and Jordan is a little tipsy .

Darian came back from the toilet he noticed Brendan and his husband with a couple there friends had moved to their table and into a conversation with everyone at the table . " Ok, " Cameron asked, sitting next to him. " Fine love, " Darian looked over at Brendan , Padraig and Malcolm, chatting , looking out onto the dance floor, some young ones dancing .Darian smiled. It was good everyone was having a good time .

" My man whats the name of your club " Padraig asked " Club Nero " Darian Announces looking between Malcolm and Cameron Malcolm reached over to Padraig whispering to him Padraig widens his eyes looks at Darian and back at Malcolm's " Jesus No way " Malcolm grinned and nodded Darian sat beside Cameron . " How Much is the membership my man? " Brendan asked " 1k for the year. " Padraig nearly spat out his drink in no way he thought that's pricey. " All members get the full experience " .Darian announced full experience in what Brendan thought we should check out the website when they get home .

ZEKE AND JULIUS STOOD watching them, they looked at each other smiling thinking that Darian could be ok he looks ok Zeke thought " Time to go " Julius said Zeke looked up at the ceiling shaking his head " Ok ok i know " Zeke sighed he wanted to stay longer and watch them all but couldn't at least Darian looks happy that's what Julius and Zeke want for him .

Darian looked over at the bar Julius stood watching him smiling he had shown himself Zeke looked over at Julius his glow had gone brighter oh no he's gonna get hell for that he thought .looks over at Darian smiling watching them only for a few seconds .Zeke cocked his head we really had good times together he thought and I loved him so much I was so stupid back then with his addiction Zeke thought .

" Darian " Cameron touched his arm he had zoned out for a second staring into space he looked at Cameron ` ` You ok you zoned out for a second" "I'm ok" Malcolm looked over at Cameron nodding his head Darian looked over at the bar again he had gone now maybe that's what he needed just to see there faces again . Cameron looked over at the bar to.and back at Darian he touched his face " Did you see something? Cameron asked, taking Darians hand "No love it's ok " Good Cameron thought it's been a bit of a weird night he thought .Cameron thinks he may have had a glimpse of Julius or Zeke will tell them in his own time if it was it what he would have needed and to know that they .

AFTERWARDS GOING BACK to the hotel Steven pushed Jordan against the door off the bedroom grinding into him kissing lifting each other's shirts up discarding them to the floor Steven kissing Jordan's neck sliding his hand down to his crotch " Steven " Jordan said breathless Steven looked at him " What " " I love you " Steven touched Jordan's face kissing him again sliding his hand down again unzipping his jeans sliding his hand inside Jordan hissed Steven working his way down pulling down Jordan's jeans .Springing free his cock Steven looks down grinning Steven looks at Jordan they kiss grinding into each other again .

Jordan held onto Stevens' head taking him in his mouth. That's so good Jordan thought then Steven stuck a finger inside him while sucking him off then Steven got back up moving to the bed more clothes were discarded . Steven licking Jordan's ear he spat on his hand and rubbed it between Jordan's ass cheeks. Jordan bent over Steven entering him he held onto the bed post Steven pounding into him and wrapped his arms around Jordan getting into a rhythm . Jordan bowed his head stroking himself while Steven licked and kissed his back.

Steven stilled when he came holding onto Jordan then he came he turned his head they kissed then they collapsed onto the bed holding each other "Ok Steven asked touching Jordan's face " More than ok husband " Steven sat up looking down at Jordan looking at him . "Shower, " Steven asked Jordan, smiling. Steven got up holding out his hand for Jordan to take and they ran to the shower for another make out session .

CAMERON KISSED MALCOLM'S back, his arms wrapped around him on the bed he turned his head to kiss him Darian watched them make out on the chair masterbating Malcolm watched him Cameron worked his way down Malcolm's back nipping his bottom he arched up giving Cameron access . Cameron kissed and licked his ass Malcolm bit his lip whimpering at the sensation Cameron was giving him what a beautiful sight before him Darian thought Cameron giving Malcolm pleasure .

Cameron moved back up licking Malcolm's ear Darian got up went over to the bed reaching over to Cameron to kiss him and Malcolm he got on the bed Malcolm reached down and took him in his mouth Cameron entered him getting into a rhythm Malcolm whimpered again kissing Darian .Jesus Malcolm thought Cameron guiding himself into Malcolm he whimpered again Darian holding onto Malcolm's head while he licked up and down his shaft .

The three of them went onto their side Darians arms wrapped round Malcolm Cameron entering him again all three kissing Darian lifted a leg up for Malcolm to get better access easing his cock inside him .Malcolm whimpered all three engaging in each other's pleasure entwined in one Malcolm squished his face into the pillow .

All three of them getting into a rhythm in sink Cameron held onto Malcolm's side he was gonna come soon Malcolm to as a Darian pulled at his cock Malcolm kissed his shoulder he still came spilling into Durian the same with Cameron.All three thinking the same about there lovemaking in sink with each other .Malcolm turned his head he and Darian kissed .

AS THEY LAY ALL STICKY and stated cuddling into each other saying their love you's to each other Darian sat up and got up Cameron and Malcolm looking at him "Shower " They grinned, Malcolm smirked shower make out is the best got up and they bundled into the shower together and another quick make out session .Darian loves showering together it's his favourite thing with his two favourite people .

" YEP STILL GOT IT PADDY " Brendan said sitting down all 5 phone numbers emails they had got tonight he looked round at Padraig laying down his to looking up at Brendan smirking " Cough up love " Padraig holding out his hand he counted at least 7 Brendan sniggered shaking his head " You lied that's not fair " Padraig moved closer to Brendan kissed him " No I didn't besides isn't this stupid now " .

Padraig thought Brendan was going through a midlife crisis; he loved his husband; he wouldn't exchange him for anyone; the party they met tonight was ever so nice, he thought and Darian saying anytime they visit Scotland, come visit his club . " I know I suppose it was' ' Brendan got up to go into the Toilet padraig sniggers into himself. I'll show him what he thought .Singing to himself my man is the best, that's for sure Padraig thought .

Brendan came back out the toilet and got a shock at padraig laying on top of the bed starkers. Well now he thought it was my husband flirting with me he shook his head " Padraig Cormack what are ya doing " " What ya think I'm doing " .Smirking and pouting

Brendan sniggered bold he thought .But they always had a good sex live since they meet those years ago even though they schedule the date nights since they meet .

BRENDAN WENT OVER TO him this isn't there sexy time night he thought dirty bugger he thought " I'm being spontaneous Brendan " Ok he thought going into the drawer for the lube looking over at his husband watching him smirking Brendan reached over to his husband they kissed then giggled Brendan got onto the bed Padraig scooted over to him .Brendan laid his arm round Padraig thinking about tonight it was a good night he thought the young man Darian seemed an ok bloke he thought .And two boyfriends lucky him and the club Darian runsthey heard about .

Padraig looks up at Brendan " What are you thinking about " " Nothing in particular just the couple we meet " Yea they seemed nice people Padraig thought they both kissed Brendan laying his arm round Padraig " Love you Paddy " Love you to " .

THE REST OF THE DUBLIN stay was good. They visited the sights, ate, drank, played more Golf before they left and all decided they would definitely go back to Ireland for longer next time so there were so many sites and places to visit in Ireland .

Chapter 19

2 weeks later The day off Steven and Jordans blessing ceremony arrived Cameron fixed Stevens tie he was never good at sorting ties Cameron thought he looked up at Steven rehearsing his vows he shook his head " Cam " " Hmm what " Cameron looked up at him again then stood back he looked handsome in his kilt Cameron smiled " Thanks " " For what " .They looked at each other Steven smiled then he hugged Cameron .

" Being a good friend and not Being to mad at us for the first time " ""Your welcome and it ok understood why "

Steven sat on the bed and put on his shoes " Are you happy Cam " Steven asked Cameron what a strange thing to say he thought of course he couldn't imagine his life without Darian and Malcolm now . " Yes I'm happy Steven why" " Good no reason I can see you are " .Steven looks up at Cameron I'm happy he is happy I don't want him to be sad again what he went through his break up with Darian that time .

A chap at the door Stevens mum coming into the room she looked amazing in her cream dress tears forming " Mum stop that " " I'm sorry dear I'm just happy that's all " They both hugged Darian chapped and also came inside with Philip who was wearing his kilt he looked so handsome Cameron thought .Our little guy looking cute and brave for his uncle Stevens blessing .

" Oh my, who is this handsome boy? " Margo said Philip hiding behind Darian still at the shy age Darian thought he looked up as Darian Cameron bent down in front of Philip he held out his hand

and gave him some pennies . Philip's face lit up looking up at Darian " it's for uncle Steven and uncle Jordan. It's lucky to throw money at them . Philip screwed his face up what a silly thing to do he giggled and thought it was great he had a lot off pennies " Cmon Philip let's find dad " Darian left holding Philips hand " He is so well mannered Cameron " " Thanks " looking at Steven another chap at the door Jordan coming inside .

" Can I have a few moments with my husband? " Everyone left, leaving the two of them alone. Jordan touched Stevens' chest looking up at him. " I'm glad we reconnected. " Jordan said, " Steven bent down to kiss him, ready to do this again "" You bet " .Jordan touched Stevens face they look at each other for a few seconds it was the best thing for them to do elope and no fuss even though they decided to do a blessing but it was no hardship to organise .

STEVEN AND JORDAN HELD hands while reciting their vows again Jordan's brother one side Cameron on the other Darian looked round at Malcolm he took his hand Malcolm looked at him he smiled squeezing his hand mouthing I love you to Darian Philip sitting on Malcolm s side . Cameron looked over at Darian and Malcolm smiled at them , noticing him looking over at them he looked so handsome Darian thought while holding Malcolm's hand.

After photos were taken everyone mingled around before dinner taking photos Steven and Jordan getting their professional photos done around The gardens of the hotel with family and friends each taking turns to get their photos done the kids playing which was good . Philip with them which Malcolm was pleased about because sometimes he can be a bit shy meeting new people .

ELLIOT BENT DOWN IN front of Leytons grave he touched the rings on the chain smiling " i found them Leyton " Elliot looking down at the rings on his chain a tear in his eye I will keep these forever he thought.

Leyton looked over at Lucien then looked over at Elliot back at Lucien " We can't interfere " " I know I feel I want to hug him though ", Lucien looks round at Leyton he knows he can't do that .

" Leyton if you were here i would have said yes " Elliot wiped a tear away " Leyton i've got to move on not right away i will meet someone I know someday maybe you will like him " Leyton agreed nodding he should meet someone else in the future .I really want that for him and hopefully Leyton would approve of the person Elliot meets in the future .

Elliot stood up and looked round thinking someone was around no one there he shook his head am I overthinking things Elliot thought Leyton stood beside him smiling at him . " I know you're here, " Elliot said, looking around the grave site .Elliot had a feeling that Leyton was with him, maybe he can't show himself yet which is ok .

Leyton wraps his arms around Elliot Lucien watching him look up at the sky Leyton made sure Elliot didn't feel him hugging him .Which was hard because Leyton wanted to hug Elliot properly really badly right now .

Leyton looked round at Elliot one more time and looked at Lucien " He is going to be ok " " yes he will be Leyton " " i hope so " Leyton didn't want Elliot sad he wants him to be happy like he always was I hate the guy who hurt him Leyton thought .

Elliot looked everywhere in his room for a jumper he used to sleep with hands on hips shaking his head. Where could it be he went downstairs and noticed washing out on the line with the jumper on the line . No way he thought running outside taking the jumper off the line smelling it Carrie watched from the door what's he doing she thought .Why is he taking the jumper off the line weird thing to do .

Elliot hugged the jumper his smell had gone from it this was his comfort blanket " Elliot " He looked round at Carrie he felt angry why did she bloody wash it he thought " His smell is away " Oh no Carrie thought going over to him " You washed it "Oh god he is " sorry but it did smell a bit " i can't smell him anymore ".Tears running down Elliot's cheeks dammit why can't people leave my stuff alone .

Carrie went closer to Elliot laying her arm round his shoulder it's not the end of the world at least he still has Leytons jumper " I'm sorry I should have asked first Elliot " Yea she should have Elliot thought " it was the one thing that comforted me Sis " shit Carrie thought I feel really bad now .

Patrick answered the call from Elliot while driving home he sounded upset " she's washed his sweater Patrick " Patrick sighed hs git to stop this he thought ok he's going through stuff just now but he has to get over it " Elliot c'mon Carrie probably didn't realise " Elliot hugged Layton's sweater against him he wiped his nose am I being stupid he thought .

" Patrick I need you " " I'll be there soon " Elliot touched the rings Patrick sometimes calms him down whenever he felt anxious

Cont

STEVEN AND CAMERON clinked Their glasses while they sat out in the patio off the hotel watching Philip , Daisy Mae and Stevens sister and brothers kids play in the Garden Darian watching Sam and Geraint watch from the patio Door with Malcolm. " it's been a good day " Steven said looking over at Cameron he nodded and thought they would need to get Philip to bed soon " it has "

" Those kids are gonna be hyper tomorrow " Steven said and thought that be us and Jordan hopefully this year Cameron sniggered thinking his right arms wrapped around Cameron Malcolm s face appeared Cameron looked round at him . " That kid is gonna be shattered tomorrow " They looked over at the kids Darian was giving Philip a drink looking over at them . " Better rescue him " Malcolm said, getting up and going over to Darian and Philip .Malcolm bending down to face Philip Cameron watching him " There good dads right " Steven asked Cameron looks at him and nods ":Jordan and I are thinking of having kids" " You and Jordan will be good dads " Steven hoped so now that he and Jordan were now stable .

" IT'S INCREDIBLE ISN'T it how it's all turned out " Steven said looking at Cameron he looked puzzled at what he said Steven sat forward taking a sip his whiskey " Steven what is it " He smiled looking down at his ring and looked at Cameron " That Jordan and I found each other again after all this time you Darian and Malcolm " it is Cameron thought if He and Steven didn't go to Australia who knows what would have happened.

Cameron touched Stevens knee he kinda knew what he was meaning he wondered if he also needled closure with Julius " Cam I don't need closure regarding Julius I closed that chapter a long time ago we weren't even a thing just a benefits thing " Cameron nodded right he guessed they were just friends with benefits thing .Jordan came outside he sat on Stevens knee hugging into him he whispered in Steven earl Steven looked up at him grinning .

" STEVEN GOT UP LAYING his arm round Jordan's waist he looked down at Cameron " See you in the morning " " Have a good night " They went off to there bedroom Philip came running up to Cameron sitting on his knee Darian sat beside him " Are you tired buddy " " No daddy can I play some more " .

Cameron looked at Darian and shook his head. " Philip it's time to get to bed now all the other children are going to " Philip pouted and hugged Cameron, sucking his thumb. Yep he was right he's tired now Cameron smiled at Darian . " C'mon then let's go up to the room " .

" Can I sleep in your bed tonight ":"Philip asked while hugging into Cameron Maybe " Darian said Malcolm coming over to them overhearing the conversation

" Daddy " the three then look at Philip " What's a surrogate " The three then look at each other he has overheard a conversation again . They get to the stairs sitting on them Philip looking between his dads " Well it's something we will explain to you when you are older Philip " Cameron says first looked between Darian and Malcolm " Ok " Philip gets up oh wow he isn't going to ask more Darian thought Philip Taking Malcolm's hand while they went upstairs to there bedroom .

STEVEN LOOKED OUT THE window of the hotel room Jordan came over to him wrapping his arms around him Steven looked round at Jordan " Come to bed " " in a minute loo " Steven kissed jordan then went into the bathroom doing his business smiling to himself it's been a good day .

Steven washed his hands after using the toilet he looked up "He had a feeling that someone was watching him I know you're there " Julius appeared arms folded smiling Steven shakes his head " i was wondering when it would be my turn " . Julius sniggered looking at the door and back at Steven smiling again at him leaning against the door .

" So what is your amends then "Steven asked looking at Julius " Are you happy steven " Am I happy he asks shaking his head I have married the love of my life so yes .

Steven huffed stupid questions and he looked at Julius again " Yes im happy do you need your ashes released "Steven leaned against the sink arms folded Julius shook his head .No I don't Julius thought .

Jordan tried to listen to Steven talking to himself about what was up with him. He chapped the door " Steven, are you talking to yourself? "" Don't worry, I'll be out in a minute." I should check if he is ok shouldn't I Jordan thought then thought that's stupid he will be .

Steven glared at Julius he smirked " Can i get on with my honeymoon then " " I am sorry Steven " Steven sighed leaning against the sink again he nodded jesus not on my wedding night . " Thank anything else " " Just everything will be ok " .What does that mean Steven thought but cryptic " I am finally happy Julius he is the reason I get up in the morning I have been over you a long time ago " .

" Good I'm glad you are happy Steven " Julius heard a tingle he looked up and sighs what is up with him Steven thought " Your dream for a family will happen Steven " .

Jordan lay in bed. Steven came out of the bathroom and stood watching Jordan " Hi " " Hi " Steven went over to Jordan and sat next to him leaning over to kiss him " what's up " Jordan asked Steven to look at him . " Not a thing babe " Steven sliding his hand inside the covers Jordan smirked leaning up to kiss Steven . " Our honeymoon starts now, " Steven sniggered, shaking his head .

" Technically kinda had a honeymoon " " Proper honeymoon now " Jordan said they kissed again then hugged steven closed his eyes Julius stood at the window gave a thumbs up then disappeared damn him he thought.Just leave us alone Steven thought they kissed again .

The door chapped. Who is it? They thought Jordan went to the door and opened a bottle of champagne sitting at the door. Nice he thought he looked both ways in the corridor, no one there .Jordan held up the champagne and wow Steven thought who gave them that . Really kind of the person who left it, Jordan sat it on the table and looked over at Steven. " Husband " Steven asks while Jordan comes closer to him " We can drink it tomorrow " .

PHILIP SLEPT IN THE middle of the bed with Cameron , Darian and Malcolm leg over Darians as all four of them hugged each other Darian woke up thinking someone was there no one was weird . He thought he sat up, scrubbed his face and he looked round at his son , Cameron and Malcolm. He smiled at his little family. He looked at the window again and saw Zeke and Julius gone . Then a thought of the storage unit came into his mind, a hand on his shoulder he looked round at Cameron looking worried . " What's wrong? Cameron asked, coming over to him leaning into Darian. " nothing love i'm ok just thought about something that i've been ignoring for a while " .

" What rong " Malcolm said all croaky they both looked over at him Malcolm sitting up.looking at the both of them " All good " Darian said Cameron kissed his cheek " love you " He said then they all lay back down . Yes Darian thought when they get back he will sort out the storage unit .He can't keep putting it off Cameron and Malcolm would help out and he would have to contact Zeke's brother regarding his artwork .

Chapter 20

Malcolm lay the flowers down at his parents grave he couldn't believe it had been 20 years they had passed it would have been his mums birthday today Philip held onto his dads hand Malcolm looked up at him and round at Darian and back at the grave he pulled Philip close to him he held onto his dad .My Daddy is sad Philip thought .

" Daddy are you sad " Malcolm looked at Phillip,he smiled " Just a little " " Daddy you don't have to be sad " Philip hugged him which was comforting Darian came over to them Malcolm stood up Darian took his hand looking down at the grave Philip looked up at his dads . " I miss them everyday " " I know I'm here " .Darian said laying his arm round Malcolm Darian kissed Malcolm's head Malcolm leaned against Darian he is just too good to me Malcolm thought .

WHEN THEY GOT IN THE car Malcolm had one last look at his parents grave Darian took his hand he looked round at him and smiled " let's go get those 80s outfits for your party " Malcolm announced Darian groaned trying not to think about it they decided on a 80s theme birthday party at the club which would be closed to the members family friends had been invited . Nero's in Glasgow was on schedule, renovations were nearly completed and new staff would be starting soon and doing some training in the Edinburgh club. First Darian hoped the club would be open in a couple months once all the inspections had been cleared they would be good to go

.It had been a long few months with renovations inspections etc but he was excited to see how the new club would do

THE NIGHT OFF DARIANS birthday party celebration family came from Italy Cameron's dad came to celebrate and have a couple weeks stay in the Uk much to Philips delight he even gave his staff except for the security a night off to celebrate with him he got caterers in for the night and mostly everyone came dressed up in 80s outfits they all looked amazing .

Luca and Sydney came to Darians party. Other people were arriving at the same time Darian greeted them. Luca handed him his birthday present ." Thank you " " Luca Sydney how are you " Cameron asked " Good the place is looking good Darian " .

Looking aroDarian was pleased that Luca and Sydney approved and it was good to see them to .und the club at the decorations they noticed the buffet was up the vip area to and dj for the night " Uncle Darian " Darian looked round at his great niece as more people were arriving Darian excused himself to greet them with his niece Carla .

" More champagne " Luca and Sydney looked round at the server a new person dusty blonde hair nice smile they both thought Elliot smiled waiting for the, two take the champagne from the tray " I'm told it's the good stuff " Sydney took two glasses from the tray handing the other to Luca then Elliot left . " He's new " Sydney said looking at Luca he nodded Sydney sniggered leaning into Luca " Brings back some memories " Sydney looked up at Luca he looked at Sydney smiling . That's true Sydney thought there was a quickie in the bathroom which was fun .

" it does " " Care to reminisce "Sydney asked leaning into Luca , Luca shook his head laying his arm on Sydney's back he grinned " I'd love to " They kissed and bumped heads " Get a room you two "

They looked over at Malcolm coming over to them a big grin on his face " Malcolm how are you " .

" Good and shows Betsy Jean " " she's good Philip " .

" Doing great loving school ".

CLAUDIA STRETCHES MADE new friends to " ed her back as the baby kicked. Nick looked at her while they added food on their plates. He placed his hand on her back. She looked at him " Don't fuss, I'm ok " Nick smiled, touching her stomach. Claudia looked down and looked back up at Nick . " Your beautiful" Claudia playfully punched his arm she giggled .I love this man and he will be a good father. She hoped they had waited so long to conceive and was grateful it finally happened.

Julia watched their interaction. She smiled. It was cute. She thought she looked over at Jake talking to Cameron. He noticed her staring at him. She quickly looked away and placed a couple bits of food on her plate then went over to Claudia and Nick to chat, aware that Jake was watching her .

DARIAN MADE A SPEED while he chatted to Darian .He thanked everyone for coming to the party and for the presents and thanking Cameron and Malcolm for their patience on the new Club .Cameron looked at Malcolm sliding his arm round Malcolms waist leaning into him .

Claudia , Jake and Yep they both thought thankfully the new Club Darian is happy with it .ulia brought out Darians Cake which he liked: a square one, a bed in the middle with three stick people, two dogs and a little one. Everyone took photos and loved the gesture . There was a card Darian opened it saying thanks for being a great boss Darian nodded .

Cont from his staff

JAKE AND JULAND LOVED the cake which looks good .ped on the office door they looked at each other before they went inside Darian was at the files he looked at his desk two of them came inside " you wanted to see us both " Jake asked Darian went over to the tableCame round the front of f them sat down Julia and Jake looked at each other and at Darian " are you two fighting "Are e looked at Julia and back at Darian " boss we " " if there'sBoss obleJake said and was about to say something else wIf you two working with each other we have to Iron it out"

Jake looked at Julia.I won't have any animosity with my staff Darian thought .. He smiled . Darian was confused. He thought they both looked round at Darian `` Boss I love this woman " " Jake " wow Darian thought they kept that quiet he thought but he did have a feeling the two of them had a thing for each other . " I do Jules, ' ' Julia smiled. He reached his hand out and she took it and they looked at Darian . "Will this change for us for the new club? Jake asked Darian, got up and went round the front of the table leaning against it .

" No it won't, how lHe smiled he kinda knew something between them now they have finally decided to be together .ife has been going on " " on and off for a whileOn Jake said Julia blushed " Polly thinks Jake is amazing " " and I do to " those two And a room D'Those thought " I love this woman " .

MALCOLM CAME DOWN TJAKE announced Julia looked at Jake and they both looked up at Darian grinning . " You two have definitely got something " Darian says and I am happy for them both .The steps just as Julia and Jake came out of the office holding hands.

What Malcolm thought were those two together Darian came to the door Malcolm looked surprised at those two "" yep together " wow M Yep thought thWow amazing coming into the office .

" You are missing, " Going over to Darian wrapping his arms around his shoulders.it's your party mr ":Darian wrapped his arms round Malcolm's waist bringing him closer to him. They kissed Malcolm and could taste whiskey off him " I just want to hold you." Cameron came inside and saw them hugging . "Everyone is asking where you are, " Cameron said, coming over and getting in the middle of them kissing Malcolm and Darian . " Julia and Jake " " all good "

" They are together," Cameron asked Darian, grinning. Cameron thought, looking between Darian and Malcolm . "That's great said Cameron looked between the two. Wow, he thought that's news " Can we go party now " Malcolm asks Darian, slides his arms round Cameron and Malcolm the three kiss each other " Yes Love we can "

.

Darians birthday party Carried on till 2 am then everyone left individually until it was time for Darian , Cameron and Malcolm to go home. It was after two am when they got back home .

MARION AND GRANT LOOKED down at their grandson asleep in his bed. They looked at each other. Grant laid his arm around Marion then they heard the car door looking out the window. Marion smiled. Malcolm looked happy. She thought I really hoped so and wished that they were still alive now that they have a grandson . " Grant, do you think he is happy? "" I think they do look happy " .

Malcolm looks up at the window thinking he had seen something there, probably his mind playing tricks on him. He thought it was Philips room. " Malcolm, are you ok? Cameron asksthought Malcolm looked a bit spacey. Darian looks round before he goes into the house and notices Malcolm looking up at Philip's room .

" Huh " Cameron lays his arm round Malcolm he looks up at the window " I uh it's nothing " they go into the house Malcolm looks up the stairs that weird feeling again it might be nothing and maybe overthinking stuff . Did he see a reflection from upstairs or was it just the lights outside ?

MARION HELD HER HUSBAND Grant's hand looking down at their Grandson Philip they looked at each other Grant squeezed Marion's hand " Dad " Philip sat up rubbing his eyes and yawning . Marion had tears Grant held her while watching Philip sitting up in bed. The bedroom door opened Malcolm came into the room going over to Philip sitting beside him..

" What's wrong buddy " Philip lay back down Malcolm lifted up his cover " I heard noises Dad " Cameron and Darian stood at the door while Malcolm tended to Philip " It's ok only dads and I coming home " .Philip did have an imagination sometimes Malcolm thought tucking Philip back into bed reassuring Philip that it's ok and try go back to sleep .

Malcolm kissed Philip's head and went over to the door. He looked round. Philip tucked into the covers. He then looked round the room. I'm just overthinking what Malcolm thought before he left the door halfway open. Malcolm looked round into the room again .

" Mum Dad he's cute right " Malcolm huffed, shaking his head. Well it could be them who knows what he thought and then goes into the bedroom Cameron and Darian are already in bed they both look over at him standing at the door .Is Malcolm ok Cameron thought .

" Philip ok " Darian asks while Malcolm gets undressed " Fine " They get into bed kissing each other Malcolm sits up Cameron and Darian looks up at him " Am I overthinking that my parents are watching over Philip " . Weird question Cameron thought " Yes I think you are overthinking love lets get some sleep " .Malcolm sighs yea I'm probably overthinking yawning then snuggled into a Cameron him laying his arm round Malcolm .

LATER THAT NIGHT MALCOLM got up to get a drink he shut the fridge turned round and there standing were his parents holy shit Malcolm thought his parents smiling at him tears stung his eyes. " Mum , Dad " Malcolm ran to them, his Dad patting Malcolms back . " I miss you guys so much " .

" Malcolm look at me " Marion asked Malcolm look up at her wiping his eyes " Mum , Dad were you here earlier " " " Yes son " .

" I don't understand why are you here " " " We wanted to see our grandson Malcolm you are doing good right " This is really confusing he didn't ask maybe Cameron or Darian did Yea he was doing good he was happy in their relationship there son Philip . " I'm good Mum Cam and Darian are the best thing that's happened and having Philip too " .

" That's good son your mum and I wanted to see Philip "

Who is Malcolm talking to? Cameron thought when he came halfway downstairs and he could hear him talking Malcolm had disappeared downstairs half an hour ago Darian was asleep when Cameron checked the time which was four am .

MARION TOUCHED MALCOLM'S face her hands were warm that's weird he thought then they hugged Malcolm felt a sense of peace come over him which was weird was it because he has seen his parents maybe " We have to go now son " Grant said taking Marion's hand Marion placed her hand over Malcolm's heart tears running down his face . " We are right here Malcolm we always have " Malcolm placed his hand on his mum's and nodded . " Mum , Dad, can't you stay longer? " His parents shook their heads. Malcolm had so many questions, not enough time .

" YOU ARE DOING GOOD with Philip. I know it's hard but he is a good boy. We love you ok " Marion hugged Malcolm, tears running down his cheeks. This is amazing to see his parents get the best present he could ask for . " Malcolm " Cameron appeared in the kitchen. Malcolm wiped his eyes, looked round at Cameron standing at the kitchen door and saw that Malcolm had been crying. Cameron came to him embracing what happened . Cameron thought .

" I'm here what's happened " Malcolm looks up at Cameron he wipes Malcolm's tears away " " I just saw my parents " Wow Cameron thought nodding Malcolm grabs the wipes from the kitchen table wiping his eyes he looks round at Cameron . " Did you ask" " No wasn't me c'mon let's go back to bed" .

" What's going on " Darian appears in the kitchen looking between Cameron and Malcolm. Malcolm had been crying. He thought " c'mon let's all get back to bed. " But Malcolm goes over to Darian, gives him a kiss, looks round at Cameron and takes Darians hand . " Can someone tell me what's going on " .

" Tell you in the morning " Malcolm says while going upstairs Darian looks at Cameron while they go up to their room " He saw his parents " Wow Darian thought that's great no wonder he was upset looking . " Did you? " Cameron asked Darian, looking at him . " No, it wasn't me, did you? " .

" Not me either" Cameron wonders who it could have been asking for Malcolm to see his parents; it was definitely not him or Darian .

Chapter 21

❝ Oh my god " Malcolm said opening up the canvas he Cameron and Darian visited the lot a week later that Darian had to have Zeke work in storage Cameron looks up from looking at other stuff Darian comes over to Malcolm who turns the painting round Ahh that painting Darian thought which was one that Zeke did when Darian was sleeping the covers half off him .

Malcolm smirks looking at Darian " Oh that one " Cameron comes over to them oh wow indeed he thought Malcolm sitting it down all three them looking at it " This one would definitely make a lot of money " Malcolm says looking at Darian " Oh no no not for anyone else's eyes " .

" Really where will we put it " Darian lays his arm round Malcolm's shoulder looks at Cameron " Our bedroom " Cameron smiles and nods " Best place to have it " Cameron says then going over to the other boxes Darian places the canvas over to the other boxes they will be taking home with them today.

" ANY OTHER SURPRISES Darian " Cameron asks looking up at him " No Love " Darians phone rings off he connects the call from Christian Zeke brother " Christian how are you " " Good Darian I will be around tomorrow some ideas I was thinking about " .

"Ok see you then " .

AT HOME THEY STAND and look at the bedroom wall above the bed of the painting of Darian I'm not sure this is a good idea to have it there since Philip comes into the bedroom " I think it looks good up there " Darian looks round at Malcolm " Me to " Are they teasing Darian thinks shaking his head I guess it does look good hanging up there .

" Ok it can stay there " Malcolm snorted Darian glares at him and Cameron " What " Cameron lays his arm round Darians shoulder " You really want to leave it up there " I'm confused now Darian thought either it stays up there or the Office " You are both ganging up on me again " Cameron giggled shaking his head " No were not Honestly I would leave it up there right Malcolm " .

" YOUR PLACE IS NICE Darian " Christian stood in the kitchen Darian looked over at him while in the fridge bringing out the wine " Thank you Wine " Christian sat down at the breakfast bar " Thanks but I can't drive " Darian put the wine back in the fridge while Cameron came into the kitchen . " Christian Cameron " " Hello " They shake hands Cameron goes over to Darian he looks over at Cameron .

" Malcolm not here " " Picking up Philip from a friends "

Christian looks over at the boxes stacked in the conservatory Darian notices him looking over " There are more in the lot " Christian nods and sighs " Darian I have an idea that Annie and I want to let you know I'd like to do a piece on Zeke work at the gallery " . That would be a good idea Darian thought when Zeke was living he did do a gallery opening although it didn't do that well that time only some of his artwork sold .

" your warry Darian I can tell from the last time " Darian looks over at Cameron and back at Christian " I trust you Christian and I think it would be good it will be weird handing it over to you to be honest with you Christian it's just going to waste " . That's true Christian thought " Some personal ones I have kept "

" No problem, it's an anniversary gallery we would like to do. How does that sound and I'd like your input on it "" I'm sure you and Annie will do a good job Christian " .

After going through the boxes and Darian giving Christian the key for the storage unit Darian and Cameron stood outside watching Christian drive off just as Malcolm arrived home with Philip they went inside Cameron getting a drink for Philip . " How did it go " Malcolm asked " Good Christian is planning a gallery opening for Zeke's anniversary " .

" Dad whose Zeke " Darian ruffles Philip's hair he goggles `` Someone I used to know did you have fun at Mollys " " U huh' ' Then Philip goes over to Frank and Luna clapping them . " You ok about that " Malcolm asks it be weird Darian thought but a good idea to remember his brother ." He seemed ok " Cameron said yea he was ok this time Darian thought even though they had the old spot whenever Zeke was alive and when he died but they kept in touch throughout the years after Zeke died .

" Christian is Fine we had our od spats in the past But I trust him with the gallery project " Cameron lay his arm round Darian kissing his cheek he seemed kinda sad talking about Zeke Darian smiled leaning into Cameron " Don't worry love I'm ok " " Good right I'm going to do a couple chapters takeaway tonight " .

" I'm in " Malcolm says from the door while watching the dogs run around the garden with Philip is that boy not tired Darian thought after being at Molly's he thought .

" OH WOW " THAT IS SOME painting Sam thought when Malcolm brought him upstairs to see what the fuss was about this painting that was done of Darian the likeness and well it was a bit

revealing to Malcolm snorted Sam looks over at him . " Anymore " "
Zeke just did this one the others are tame compared to this one " .

" Really and Christian is gonna be doing a gallery opening for
Zeke's anniversary " " Yep " Nice Sam thought while they stared at
the painting Sam liked it very Darian he thought .

" Are you both done gawking " Sam and Malcolm turned to
Darian at the bedroom door Malcolm and Sam looked at each other
and back at Darian Sam pointed to the picture " Great portrait
Darian " Chewing his lip Malcolm snorted and looked away I will
get him back for that Darian thought . " Thank you Sam " .

" Oh is that the time better go pick up Daisy Mae from Dance
classes " Sam left Darian came into the room going over to Malcolm
sliding his arm around his waist Malcolm looked up at him " It is
not nice to tease " Malcolm grinned gave Darian a peck on the lips .
" Darian relax, I wasn't teasing Sam. I wanted to see the painting " .
Darian hummed moving closer to Malcolm he felt Darians haRdness
against him . " Hey stud, a time and a place " Darian raised his
eyebrow .

" Take aways here " Cameron shouted as Darian sighed and
looked at Malcolm " Saved by the bell " Malcolm giggles and slaps
Darians ass and goes to leave to go downstairs leaving Darian in
the bedroom staring at the painting it does look good up there he
thought smiling to himself .

Cameron and Malcolm he,led dish out the take away putting
some out for Philip he liked his sweet n sour Chinese the dogs in
there beds after being fed Darian comes into the kitchen staring at
everyone Cameron looks up at him is he ok he thought coming over
to Cameron . " Smells Good " " That one is yours Wine " .

Cameron pours himself and Darian the wine while Malcolm
opted for a soft drink " I like Chinese dad " Malcolm bends to Philip
patting him on the back " Me to buddy " The dogs bark in there beds

everyone looks over at them " Don't worry some left For tomorrow " Cameron says Frank panting and whining Luna not even bothering .

" New season Headtsopper starts back today " Malcolm announces checking his phone for updates on what's new on Netflix " I've lost count which season is it " Darian asks tucking into his meal " Season 3 " Malcolm s phone beeps of a text message checking from Jenny announcing her engagement that's great news Malcolm thought . She has now been living in Australia on the Gold Coast for three years now with Josh who comes from there .

" JEN GOT ENGAGED " Malcolm turns his phone round to show Cameron and Darian the photo of Jenny showing of her engagement ring " That's great news isn't it Darian l " It is " " Daddy whose Jenny " They look over at Philip someday he will know who she is but right now he is to young to know ." A friend I know who now lives in Australia with her now fiancée " .

" like where Grampa lives " " Yes Philip Where Grampa lives "

ZEKE FOLDS HIS ARMS standing in the bedroom smiling, a good place to put the painting he thought he thought back to the day Darian found out about it for his birthday and afterwards was pretty great too . " Nice " Zeke sighed looking round at Julius grinning Zeke shook his head " I thought you had an. Assignment " Julius shrugged his shoulders going over to the painting looking round at Zeke " All done now this " Julius pointed to smirking and looking back at the painting .

" Julius " Zeke sighed Julius giggled coming over to Zeke patting his shoulder " I'm just messing Cameron's coming upstairs " They heard footsteps coming upstairs followed by other footsteps Julius laid his arm round Zeke he looked up at him smiling .

" Get Your jammies Philip I'll be in a minute " Cameron came into the bedroom he felt a shiver is the window open he thought looking over at the window which was shut weird he thought then he heard the shower running Philip was getting more independent especially getting into the shower himself but sometimes he needs more help . Cameron looks round the bedroom and up at the painting smiling to himself about it giggling at himself while Zeke and Julius watch on .

" Daaaaad I'm ready " Philip shouts from the bathroom Cameron huffs shaking his head turning to go out the door Cameron looks round the bedroom " Zeke , Julius I know you can hear me You don't need to worry about Darian he's ok " Zeke and Julius look at each other smiling at each other they look over at Cameron standing at the door .

" A LITTLE FAVOUR FOR Sam look out for his dad please " Dad " Cameron looks round at Philip his jammies on hair still damp staring at him " Daddy who are you talking to "Cameron goes over to Philip ushering him into his bedroom " No one son just thinking out loud " Philip screws up his face while Cameron towel drys his hair . The door chaps Darian comes in with Philips hot chocolate and latest book for his night time ritual Darian sits beside Philip on the bed while Cameron tidies up Philip leans into Darian going under the covers while Darian reads him his book .

LATER THAT NIGHT WHILE asleep Geraint's arm over Sam's stomach he was a bit fidgety dreaming he was in a white room Sam looks around where am I he thought this is some weird dream " Sam " Sam looks round at his mum standing there smiling at him tears stinging Sam's eyes holy shit he thought she still looks the same he thought . " Am I dreaming Mum " Rhôna comes over to Sam there. Embrace she pats his back they look at each other again .

" Mum I miss you " Rhona nods touching Sam's face " You are doing great Sam Daisy Mae is beautiful you have both done well bringing her up " Sam nods wiping his nose " Dad " " Your Dad is doing fine Son grumpy as ever " Sam giggles typical still his grumpy self " You Don't worry now his heart was bad I'm looking after him "
.

Sam nods looks around and wonders why his dad wasn't here to looking back at his mum " Mum didn't dad want to see me " " He does But not yet he needs more time to process what's going on " A tingle came through Rhona she looks up and smiles " Your dad says hello " Rhona lays her arm round Sam he smiles that's good he thought at least he had acknowledge him.

" Sam I have to go now " " So soon " .

"MUM " SAM WAKES UP looks round Geraint looking worried since Sam had been thrashing around the bed " Sam it's ok I'm here " " Geraint " Sam held onto Geraint tears streaming down his face Jesus what's up with him Geraint thought did he have a bad dream . " I saw Mum " " You did " Sam looks up at Geraint then lays his head on his shoulder.

" I was worried you weren't waking up " I'm ok babe Mum said dad is ok " .

GERAINT LAY HIS ARM round Sam they should get some sleep he thought " That's good right " Geraint asked kissing Sam's head " Mm at least I know Mum is with him " .

Sam lay his arm round Geraint's stomach and thought at least he knows Mum is with his dad and looking after him Mum seemed happy that he misses her a lot but at least he had his aunt Mae to confide in also Malcolm . " Go back to sleep don't overthink ok I love you " Geraint kisses Sam's head " I'm not Love you to ".

JULIUS STOOD OUTSIDE the house looking up at Darians bedroom window smiling he is happy I can see that he thought and he has every right to be to he had his family that he wanted for so long Julius just wished he had that to and fucked it up with Julio . Then he wondered how Julio was. Maybe he should see how he is doing. Julius huffed he would certainly meet someone else that's for sure and why not he wouldn't grieve Julius forever surely .

Zeke appears Julius looks round at him Zeke looks over at him " Julius " Julius sighs, looks at Zeke again and back up at the window Julius was aware of something glowing bright . " Julius " Julius feels a sense of peace come over him looking round at Zeke mouth open " Julius your wings " .

JULIUS STRETCHES OUT his arms he is all a glow oh my god Zeke thought he has upgraded and now got his wings this must mean he is free from guilt in his past " Zeke it's amazing look " " I can see Julius " Julius whooped Zeke giggled Julius bent down spreads himself out his wings all spread out I don't know wether to laugh or cry Zeke thought .

Then there was a whoosh and Julius flew up into the air wow amazing sight to see Zeke clapping then he sensed someone beside him looking round at Lucien looking up at Julius up a tree " Don't worry Zeke you will get your wings " Lucien looks round at Zeke why would I be worried Zeke thought " I'm not Lucien I'm happy for Julius he has earned his wings " .

LUCIEN FACED ZEKE PLACING his hand on his shoulder " You need to stop feeling guilt Zeke " Zeke looks down maybe I should but I did it to myself even though Darian tried many times for Zeke to get clean Zeke nodded looks up at Lucien just as Julius flys back down going over to them notices Zeke isn't to happy .

" Zeke " Zeke looks over at Julius in all his glorious glow " C'mon let's head back and celebrate getting your wings " Zeke walks away is pissed Julius thought looking at Lucien " His time will come Julius " " I hope so " .I really do Julius thought I don't like to see Zeke sad .

AS ZEKE WAS ABOUT TO walk away Lucien stopped him Zeke looked at Lucien his eyes gleaning " Lucien " " Don't keep it to yourself Zeke " What does he mean he thought Zeke huffed and shook his head walking off Lucien looks round at the house Julius has made his peace now Zeke and hopefully soon.

Julius overheard the conversation between Lucien and Zeke. They are just friends right and bonded over Lucien, meaning he thought he would have to talk to Zeke about it soon . Does he feel embarrassed maybe because there is certainly something between them he could see ?

Chapter 22

Zeke was in a happy slumber Julius watching him he smiled looking down at Zeke he was mumbling something he couldn't make out what he was saying Julius bent down going over to Zeke " Zeke wake up " Julius leaned on his arm laying beside Zeke on the bed Zeke slowly opened his eyes at Julius staring at him " There he is " .

Zeke sat up and stretched looking around his room and at Julius watching him he handed Zeke a brochure Zeke looked down at it opening up a picture of his brother Christian about Zekes art work " Whats this " " Your brother has the gallery opening in a few days in memory of you " . Zeke sighs and lays back down Julius face appears .

" What's up " " Nothing really just Christian doing that for me " Oh no he's is not doing this Julius thought doubting himself again Zeke looks up at Julius `` What else is it " What is he on about Julius thought sitting up he looks round at Zeke `` I have my first assignment " . Wow Zeke thought that was quick he only got his wings a couple weeks ago I'm really happy for him .

" THAT'S GREAT WHEN " " Soon Nathaniel is guiding me c'mon get up let's get breakfast " Zeke snorted shaking his head we don't eat he's just being silly Zeke thought getting out of bed while Julius sorted Zeke's clothes while he showers Julius grins looking at the bathroom door shaking his head thinking naughty things .

THE SHOWER DOOR OPENS Julius steps in and Zeke looks round at him " Julius " he goes nearer to Zeke touching his face " Julius this is inappropriate " Julius cocks his head looking down Zeke is very erect he quickly covers himself Julius takes his hand away . Julius bends to kiss Zeke he pushes Zeke against the tile kissing grinding into Zeke he whimpers do Angels have sex he thought .

Julius tingles Seriously now he thought closing his eyes Zeke looks up at him as if he is ok " Julius " they bump heads " I'm sorry rain check " Zeke nods Julius kisses him and leaves the shower Zeke stands against the sink closing his eyes. Dammit he thought .Zeke looks down he is hard Oh no not had that feeling in a while he thought chewing his lip sniggering into himself then starts stroking himself while the water flows over him he goes with the feeling stroking faster while he leans against the tile it doesn't take long for him to come that feels so good Zeke thought .

THE DAY OFF THE GALLERY opening arrives two weeks later Cameron , Darian and Malcolm take a walk around while Sam and Geraint walk around the gallery to check out Zeke's paintings and artwork Christian is chatting to a couple reporters about the gallery opening. Darian stops at one painting he smiles remembering when Zeke painted it at the winery he loved the scenery there and had always admired it . " I like this one " Cameron says Darian hums and looks at Cameron and back at the painting " Why didn't you keep this one? " Malcolm asks Darian though he thought it was a good one to be added to the display

Zeke stood watching them admire the painting. Yes he liked it himself smiling to himself and so wished to be back in Italy. Those were happy memories. " What are you smiling about? " Zeke jumped

when Julius spoke behind him. Zeke shakes his head Julius smiles "
A warning next time anyway why are you here ".

" Assignment over and I wanted to see you " Zeke rolls his eyes
tutting what's up with him Julius thought isn't he happy to see him
while they walk around the gallery and see Tobin staring at Luca and
Sydney Zeke looks at Julius he shrugs his shoulders .

" Tobin " He looks round at Zeke and Julius " Hey Guys great
event Zeke " they look around and still Christian chatting to
reporters " Thanks Yea What are you doing here " Zeke asked
looking round at Christian again Tobins points to Christian and his
wife Zeke looks over at Tobin again . " I'm sorry Zeke it's his wife "
What the hell he thought, not his family looking over at them again.

" WHAT IS IT " ZEKE asked Tobin clucked his finger a file appears
he hands Zeke the file looking over it shit he thought Cancer he
looks over at Tobin " I'm sorry " Julius goes to lay his arm round Zeke
he pushes him away going round the corner to the other paintings
and sculptures . Julius looks at Tobin " I was about to say she will get
better " Julius nods patting Tobins back he means well he thought .

" Christian a Mr Fitzwilliam has bought one of the paintings "
His Assistant Annabelle came over to him to tell him " The online
bidder " Yes " brilliant Christian thought who is this Fitzwilliam
Darian thought and which painting was it he thought .

Julius grinned while he stared at the painting Zeke glared at him
Julius looks round at him " What did you do " " What do you think "
Julius looks over at the painting the one of the winery Zeke did what
he bought it for real shaking his head he didn't need to do that . "
It was to cheer you up " Julius whispers to Zeke cheer me up I don't
need to be I am perfectly fine while he walks around the gallery Julius
watching him . " What's up with you two? " Tobin asks because they
both seem tense with each other .

" Zeke thinks it's a sin if we you know " Tobin snorts it certainly is not that way he should know since Luca set his ashes free he has had a few indiscretions since he will talk to him about it if need be .Poor Zeke he must be frustrated Tobin looks over at Luca and Sydney looking at some of the paintings they are certainly happy which is good a tingle went through him he sighs and looks up just a few more minutes Please he thought the tingle went through him again " Ok ok I'm coming " .

" GREAT EVENT DARIAN " Darian Thanks Sydney Yes it has been good he thought and people seemed interested in Zekes work thanks to Christian then Darian notices someone from Zeke's circle of friends who he hasn't seen in a long time " Polly " Polly looks round at Darian surprised to see him they hug she looks good Darian thought .

" How are you " " Good Darian and you " Darian pointed to Cameron and Malcolm and scrolled his phone for a photo of Philip " That's wonderful Darian he is cute " Polly looks up at Darian he looks happy and two men in his life now that's great she thought . " What about you is Ben still around " Polly smiles looking over Darians shoulder he looks round " Yep we're still together we have three kids now " .

That's great to hear Darian thought and to hear they have kids. Another added bonus: Polly explained they now live in Spain. Ben opened a new business, a bar which was going well in Tenerife. They love it there and the kids do too .

Christian was ecstatic that the memorial gallery opening did so well and some paintings were brought to which was even better the gallery would stay open for visitors to come and check out the art work displayed .

Everyone went home after a good success first day opening Which Zeke was pleased about to he left after everyone was leaving and went back to his place sat on his bed thinking about today he looks over at the blank canvas in the corner of the room smiling to himself he was also pleased for Christian and the gallery opening to .

JULIUS WALKS ALONG the corridor a day later carrying a canvas wrapped up grinning to himself on his way to see Zeke he bumps into Tobin and wonders what he is carrying " It's a present for Zeke " " What is it " Lucien walks along the corridor and notices Julius and Tobin chatting while he is reading his next assignment passing the guys saying hello while he passed . Both Tobin and Julius thought Lucien seemed distracted lately; it's not like him " What do you think is up with him? " Tobin shrugs his shoulders and wonders .

" Catch up with you later " Julius goes off to see Zeke Tobin goes in search of Lucien Julius chaps on Zeke's door and looks in his canvas painting Julius smiles he hasn't been painting for a while Julius thought .

" HEY " ZEKE LOOKS ROUND at Julius smiling at him they both look at the painting " What is it " Zeke sighs shaking his head while Julius sits down the canvas for Zeke who looks over at it " I bought you something " Julius looks over at Zeke who is staring at him " What is it " .

Zeke goes over to Julius he hands him the canvas and Zeke opens it up revealing his own painting the one off the winery he loved so much " Julius why I don't understand " " You love it so I bought it for you " This is to much Zeke thought he didn't have to buy him his own painting " Mr Fitzwilliam " Zeke asked Julius nodded " Now where could we put it " Julius looks round the room Zeke checks the time he will have to go to his art teaching class soon " .

" Can we do this later I have my art class " Julius goes to take Zeke's hand he looks up at Julius he brings Zeke closer to him " Zeke your ok right " Zeke sighs he wishes Julius would stop worrying so much " Julius I'm fine stop worrying ok " Julius bends down to kiss Zeke him responding to the kiss then stops " Talk later " Zeke nods smiles " Thank you for the painting " . Julius grins then a tingle goes through him " I've been called check in later " Sure " .

DARIAN LOOKS AROUND the new club while at the bar which was getting busy. It has now been open a month now and Jake and Julia were doing great both co managing the bar. The staff were also doing a good job at the Glasgow site; he had no worries with them thankfully .

Cameron's face appears sliding his arm round Darians waist Darian holding his hand " First draft done " Darian asked Cameron hummed smiling at Darian " Some Which I need your opinion on " Darian turned to face Cameron sliding his arms round Cameron's waist " You have notes Love " Cameron whispers in Darians ear " I need more notes " .

They look at each other Darian grins Cameron takes his hand leading him to the office and goes inside locking it . Where did Darian go Julia thought while sorting out a tray of drinks and nibbles for the Vip . Jake turned the handle of the office about to go in and it was locked huh he thought we don't normally lock it he thought then he heard the noises from the office Jake's face went red holy shit he thought not my office to be sniggering to himself and going back into the bar .

Julia came over while Jake was at the till he looks round at her " What's up " Julia asked Jake shook his head Julia sniggered and slaps his bottom " Hey " Julia goes to whisper in Jake's ear " We Can christen the office to " Jake looks down at Julia smirking at him then she walks off cheeky little minx he thought Julia looks round at Jake while she tends to the tables I so love that woman he thought .

CHRISTIAN WAS GOING through the sales at the gallery and some of Zeke's art work was selling which was great. At least his work was getting recognition Christians gallery opening for his brother was in a couple of papers and online reviews which were great positive reviews which Pleased Christian .

Christian was about to go back through to his office when the lights flickered. That's happened a couple times now he thought will have to check that out " Christian " Christian looked round at Zeke standing at the door smiling at Christian he looked like good tears running down Christians face .

" Zeke " Christian goes nearer to Zeke holding his arm Christian was aware of a glow around Zeke " I've missed you so much Zeke " " Me to " Zeke looks round the gallery Christian following his view " Zeke are you ok " Zeke nods taking Christians hand looking up at him .

":Christian thank you " " For What " Zeke lets go of Christians hand walking round him Christian looks over at Zeke going over to one of his artwork " For doing the gallery opening for me I really appreciate it " " You're Welcome Zeke are you happy " .

" Yes Christian I am " That's good Christian thought patting his back Zeke smiling at him I'm happy he's ok now has he been looking after him Christian thought he has had a couple weird feelings past while " Christian things will be ok ". Weird thing to say but ok not thinking about it too much Christian thought while his phone rang off .

" You better answer that " Christian looks down at his phone, his wife calling him. He looks up. Zeke has gone, could he not stay for longer? So many questions I wanted to know when he rang his wife .

ZEKE STOOD AT THE BRIDGE looking down at the water he was aware of someone standing behind him he looked round at Julius standing there smiling at him he came nearer to Zeke they looked at each other Julius touched Zeke's face leaning into his touch Julius leaned down to kiss Zeke .

Zeke places his hand on Julius chest they look at each other " Zeke " Zeke looks down " Zeke look " Zeke looks up he has a strange feeling he looks up a Julius smiling then Zeke's wings appear oh wow Julius is dumbstruck amazing in all his glow " Julius I got my wings " . Tears running down Zeke's face spread out his arms and his wings spread out. It's beautiful Julius thought he had now upgraded. Which is amazing which means all his guilt and past trauma must be over for him .

" Jules isn't it amazing " Zeke twirls, stops chewing his lip then he suddenly soars up to the sky Julius watching him Zeke flying around Julius laughing at him at his celebration. He's happy, which is good. He should be happy Julius thought .

Zeke swoops down and faces Julius " Are you done now " Maybe " Julius goes nearer to Zeke he takes his hand " Let's go home " Zeke screws his face home he thought cocking his head going nearer to each other again they kiss then bump heads . " Yea Let's go home " Zeke says smiling at Julius Then a tingle goes through them they both sigh Peter signalling them both to see him .

Guessed celebrations will have to wait for Julius though taking Zeke's hand and willing themselves away back up to heaven they go along the corridor Peter is waiting for them " Congratulations Zeke " Thank you Peter " Zeke looks between Peter and Julius .

" Julius your report " " still to finalise Peter " .

" Very well Zeke let's talk " Peter indicates the way Zeke looks round at Julius " Catch up with you later " Julius nods and watches Zeke and Peter walk into the office well I better go finish off my report then .Then Julius thought Peter was being weird or was I just imagining it Julius thought going into his room going over to his bed laying down arms round his head .

Way too much overthinking on things on my part Julius thought it's time he and Zeke talked properly it's obvious we like to act other times he like me back Julius wonders, smiling to himself .Julius looks over at the folder well I better get my assignment finished off since I have time to kill But first I will take a visit to Mum first .

Chapter 23

Elliot was going through boxes of Photos he and Leyton took with friends and then together Elliot touched the rings hanging round his neck laying the photos back in the box his phone pinged of a text from Patrick on his way to pick him up for work . Elliot got up laying the box of photos in his cupboard to stop this wallowing. He thought I would meet someone someday. It's only been two months since his attack therapy was helping and his one to one to they even said he had to heal first before venturing back into a relationship.

A car horn beeps Elliot looks out at Patrick waiting for him he picks up his rucksack and runs downstairs shouting to Carrie he was off to work and getting into the car Patrick looks at him is he ok he thought Elliot looks at him ",Mate " "I'm ok Patrick " I'm overthinking again Patrick thought I shouldn't worry about him to much Patrick thought I know he's getting stronger and therapy's helping .

Elliot looks over at Patrick he's chewing his lip thinking " Patrick let's go " Elliot sniggers Shaking his head where did he go while they drove to the club some the staff just arriving and the day staff leaving . Sam is at the bar setting up Geraint sitting at the bar while Elliot and Patrick sign in for their shift a few members arriving " Another beer Babe " Sam asked Geraint " " I'm good for now " Sam smiles Elliot notices their interaction it's cute while Julius sits at the end of the bar watching everyone it's so cute to see .

Darian appears with Rosters Julius admires him and his interaction with everyone maybe I should stop coming to visit Julius thought but it's like a comfort blanket that I just want to see everyone and how they are doing and Sam seems more happier now since his dad died I wonder how Tom is and how he is adjusting maybe I should reach out and see him Julius thought . Malcolm and Cameron arrive and all of them hug. I wasn't jealous of their relationship but with history with Darian it was hard at that time and I didn't handle it well .

Zeke came into his room went over to his canvas to do more work on the piece he was doing and wondered where Julius was he had thought he would be in his room he wasn't there which was weird Zeke Carries on with his painting an hour passes Julius comes into the room . Stands to watch Zeke painting " Are you just gonna gawk " Zeke looks round smiling at Julius he sniggers Zeke has a spot paint on his nose .

Julius comes nearer wiping Zeke's nose they look at each other " Where have you been " " Around " Zeke glares at Julius shaking his head Julius goes to kiss Zeke again he stops him what's wrong with him Julius thought .

" I'm busy " Zeke goes to get over to his canvas Julius takes his hand Zeke looks up at him " Julius we have to discuss things " " I know " Julius notices an envelope on the bed he looks over at Zeke.

" What's that? "" My assignment " Julius goes to Pick it up Zeke stops him " Leave it Julius " Zeke goes over to the bee picking up the folder laying it on the table he looks round at Julius ." Why do you want to be with me Julius " .

Strange question to ask he thought why is he being weird with him " I like you Zeke " Zeke sighs leaning against the table Julius goes nearer to him "Tell me it's not the connection with Darian Julius' ' .

" What no course not I like you for you silly " Julius touches Zeke's face he huffs " Are you serious " " Yes Zeke " Zeke moves going over to the bed sitting on it Julius goes over to him bending down in front of Zeke . " Are you missing Sex Julius? " Julius snorted, shaking his head looking up at Zeke .

" No Zeke I'm not " I'm not ready for that yet Julius " Julius gets up sitting beside Zeke taking his hand " That's ok I don't mind waiting " . Zeke lays his head on Julius' shoulder Julius lays his arm round Zeke's shoulder kissing his head .

" Sleep here tonight " They look at each other again " Are you sure " Zeke nodded Julius went to kiss Zeke he held him back " Just a sleepover " " Ok " Zeke smiled Julius laid his arm round Zeke's shoulder he leaned into Julius who looks over at the folder again .

" Julius stop it " Zeke looks up at Julius " Sorry and yes I will Lets get into bed " Zeke snorted sits up smirking keen isn't he he thought Zeke gets up grabs his towel looks round at Julius " Going for a shower myself " Julius pouts Zeke shakes his head boy he is making him sweat that's for sure . Julius gets up, takes off his shirt, keeps his bottoms on and gets into bed with his arms around his head .

It didn't take long in the shower Zeke quickly changed into his pj bottoms and went out Julius already in bed Zeke looks at him with no shirt on showing off his defined abs Zeke swallows Julius looks over at him smiling . Zeke goes over to the bed and Julius lays out his arm and Zeke shuffled over to him " We can cuddle cuddlings good " Zeke snorts Yea cuddling is good Julius kisses his head and they both put out the light . " Goodnight Zeke " " Goodnight " .

GERAINT GOT OUT THE car Sam came out the other side and went into his pocket for his keys while Geraint locked the car Sam had a feeling they were being watched he looked round at the trees maybe his imagination he thought Geraint looks over at Sam Looking at the trees is he ok . Geraint goes over to him " Sam " " Huh " Sam looks over at the trees again stupid imagination he thought .

" I'm ok," Babe just thought. Saw something " Geraint huffed laying his arm round Sam's shoulder leading him into the house Geraint's Mum was looking after Daisy Mae tonight she was having a sleepover at her grans tonight Sam looks round one last time before he goes back inside .

" Want a drink " No Thanks I'm gonna go up " He is Tired tonight Geraint thought it has been a busy night Geraint goes over to Sam sliding his arms around his waist they look at each other . " What" " I'm just checking if you are OK " Sam sighs Geraint moves closer to Sam " Babe I'm fine " Sam looks down and back up at Geraint who is smirking at him .

" Raincheck " Geraint hums cocking his head sliding his hand up Sam's shirt " Let me take care of you " Geraint goes to unbuckle Sam's jeans sliding them down and palms his cock with his boxers on . Sam looks down at Geraint sniffing at his boxers. He is hard Geraint looks up at Sam chewing his lip face flushed .

GERAINT PULLS DOWN Sam's boxers springs free his cock so ready for him Geraint thought looking up at Sam Geraint licks up his inside leg Sam opening his leg for better access then cupping his balls massaging them .That's nice Sam thought panting Geraint spits on his hand and starts stroking Sam he closes his eyes letting Geraint do his thing .

GERAINT TOOK HIS COCK in his mouth Sam bit his lip holding onto Geraint's head his head bobbing up and down so good Sam thought opening his legs wider again shit I'm gonna cum soon Sam thought leaning against the table " Geraint I'm " Geraint stopped looks up at Sam his face still flushed Geraint stood up they looked at each other Geraint touches Sam's mouth sticking his finger inside his mouth Sam sucking it that's hot Geraint thought . They kiss, then Geraint lifts Sam up onto the counter, the coldness hitting him. Sam wraps his arms round Geraint's shoulders, they kiss again then Geraint pulls down his jeans, discarding them and goes to lift up to Sam's leg . " Here " Sam asks, looking shocked Geraint grins Sam shaking his head then Geraint guides himself inside Sam while he wraps his arms round Geraint's shoulders again .

GERAINT KISSES SAM'S neck while he Pounds into him Sam whimpering Geraint is close to coming he stops bringing Sam closer to him and drives back in Sam moaning holding himself onto Geraint " Fuck Sam you feel so good " Sam kisses Geraints neck while he stills and cums holding onto Sam " Baby are you good " " Mmm " . Geraint looks up at Sam holding onto him until his orgasm subsides Geraint lays his head on Sam's shoulder " I needed that " Sam said they look at each other again . " Shower " Geraint asks a great idea Sam thought of helping Sam down by picking up their clothes Geraint goes to kiss Sam's neck he giggles .

" Just a shower " Sam suggests Geraint giggles, slapping Sam's butt he yelps and they race upstairs into the shower for another make out session in the shower .

ZEKE SLIPS OUT OF BED looks round at Julius still asleep Zeke smiles he is so cute when he sleeps Zeke gets up and goes into the bathroom to change comes back out he won't waken Julius and lets him sleep he won't be long anyway goes to the door looks round at Julius before he leaves he may not wake up till he gets back .

Julius turns round to snuggle into Zeke feeling his side no one there Julius sits up where did Zeke go he wonders rubbing his eyes he doesn't hear the shower running . Julius gets up going into the bathroom. No one there Julius goes back out and notices the envelope on the table .

Curiosity got to Julius and picked up the envelope opening it. What the hell Julius thought with his assignment was why he had got Sam's dads assignment. That isn't fair he thought I could have had. That is where Zeke is Julius thought he got his phone about to dial Zeke's no when the door opened Zeke came into the room with two coffee cups and a bag .

Zeke stops to look at Julius oh he is up already and holding the envelope " Where have you been " Julius asks Zeke goes over to the table sitting down the coffees and pastry he looks up at Julius. " I went to get us coffee and pastry " .

" Where " Zeke sighs, taking the envelope from him sitting it inside the drawer " Julius what's with the interrogation I went to Paris I was doing a nice thing for us " .

Shit Julius thought it was a nice thing for him to do Julius went nearer to Zeke touching his face " Thank you " Zeke went to move picking up his cup coffee and taking a sip " Peter asked me to deal with Tom Julius because it's too personal for you " Maybe so Julius thought he drank some his coffee and took a bite the pastry tasted quite nice biting into more off it thinking .

" I COULD TAKE YOU TO Paris " Zeke snorted shaking his head yea maybe he could one day leaning against the table also taking some the pastry " Sorry " Zeke looks over at Julius Looking glum looking at Zeke " It's fine Julius " Just then Julius got a tingle a guess i better go see Peter then . " I've been called " .

" Catch up later " Zeke asks Julius coming over to him they kiss " You bet we will " Then Julius leaves Zeke looks over at the folder then goes into his drawer bringing out another folder Peter had given him something that he and Julius will have to talk about soon putting the folder back into the drawer .

Chapter 24

A week later while at home Sam was clearing up the dishes Geraint had just left for work taking Daisy Mae with him to nursery he sat the dishes on the dryer the light flickered he looks up is the bulb faulty or needing renewed it's been flickering like that most the morning now Sam thought and went into the cupboard bringing out the spare bulb .

He sat the bulb on the table, went to dry the dishes and was aware of someone in the kitchen with him. He turns around and gets a shock from his dad standing there holy shit Sam thought he looks totally different now Tom smiling at him . " Dad " " Hello Son " tears stream down Sam's face seeing his dad again it has now been two months since he passed .

Zeke watches their interaction from the corner of the kitchen Sam goes to his dad, they embrace Tom patting Sam's back, Tom looking over at Zeke giving Tom a thumbs up, Sam wipes his eyes amazed at how good his father looks in front of him . " Dad are you happy " " Yes Son I am I'm with your Mum and Alannah " Oh Wow Sam thought that's good to know at least they are all together . " That's great Dad Couldn't Mum come to " Tom took Sam's hand they looked at each other " Sam it was important I come alone you have been struggling right " .

" Yea I just miss you guys Daisy Mae especially " " Sam it was my time to go that little girl is amazing just wish I had more time with her " Me to Sam thought and more time to get to know Geraint to Tom looks over at Zeke at the corner on the chair who is he seeing

235

Sam thought " Dad Who is with you " Tom looks over at Sam and between Zeke . " Zeke is over there" Tom points to the chair at the patio door Sam looks over no one their why can't he see him Sam wonders "

" Zeke is my guide Sam he recently got his wings right " Tom looks over at Zeke who nods at Tom guide what does that mean Sam thought " I know confusing right " Tom giggles wow it was good to see his dad laugh .He hadn't seen his dad that happy in a while over the years .

" Do you forgive me Sam " What a strange question Sam thought what is there to forgive does he mean them not getting on over the years . " I apologise for not being well " " Dad it's ok " Tom looks over at Zeke watching them look back at Sam .

" The big guy says I have to be more forgiving and accept you well you know " who is he talking about who is the big guy " You are thinking too much Sam " .Tom says maybe I am but it's the kindest thing his dad has ever said to him .

" 2 minutes Tom " Tom looks at Zeke and back at Sam " I have to go now Sam " . Soon Sam thought " Dad are angels real " Tom smiles and nods. Zeke taps Tom's shoulder, he looks at Zeke and nods " I Love you Son " .

Sam got dizzy then his dad wasn't there oh my god he thought that was like an out of body experience he looks around his dad gone fuck it was to short Sam fumbled for his phone dialling Geraints no . He picks up after a few rings `` Miss me baby " Geraint the weirdest thing had just happened " Sam explains to Geraint about his dad appearing weird to indeed Geraint thought what Sam had said .

" Sam do you need me " Sam snorts sitting on the stool " I'm ok Geraint besides I have work soon I love you " After his call to Geraint Sam got ready for work he sniggered into himself at what just happened seeing his dad but happy that he was doing good and that his mum and sister were with him . He picked up his keys for the car dialling Malcolm's no he answers straight away " Hey you ok " " Malcolm the most weird thing happened " .

Sam gets into the car and explains to Malcolm about his dad while driving along to get to work Malcolm has told Sam many times about the past experiences with Darian Sam had just laughed it off before until now. Malcolm asked if he was ok which he was and they arranged to meet in the middle of the week for lunch .

" THANK YOU ZEKE " " Your Welcome Tom Sam seems more happier now I'm happy to help " Zeke pats Tom on the shoulder and notices Lucien walking along checking his folder he had been very distant lately from what everyone was saying Tom looks round to Lucien disappearing into one the rooms . " Is Lucien ok " " Not sure Tom I have to go now we will catch up " " Off course and thank you " .

ZEKE GOES BACK TO HIS room and noticed red roses on the table Zeke grins going over and smelling them and picking up the card which was from Julius soppy Sod he thought but it was thoughtful of him the door chaps Julius with a big grin on his face .

" Thank you " Julius stands at the door he cocks his head " I went to Paris to get them " Zeke snorts shaking his head looks over at the flowers " How did it go with Tom " " Good " Julius stands behind Zeke wrapping his arms round Zeke's waist whispers in Zeke's ear . " Let's go on a date " .

Zeke turns to face Julius screwing up his nose a date he thought " Well I would much like to be wined and dined " Julius smiles bending to kiss Zeke him responding " I would very much like to wine and dine you Zeke " Julius moves Zeke back against the table opening Zeke's legs his hardness against Zeke .

They kiss Zeke is hard he whimpers Julius kisses Zeke's neck and5 goes to slide his hand down " Julius " " mmm " he looks up at Zeke " I do want to but can we wait " Again Julius thought he sighs and moves away he thought they were getting somewhere Zeke goes over to him .

" There is something else someone else you need to see to " " Who " Who else is there Julius thought Zeke slides his arm round Julius shoulder he looks down at Zeke .

" Julio " Julio is fine Julius thought he has met someone new and happy I don't need to make amends with him or do I Julius thought or is it Julio that needs to move on he thought . " Julius, for us to move on with each other we have to make it right with the people we loved before " Julius snorts he is quoting Bernard with his Therapy sessions again Zeke looking at him . " Ok ok I will do that will you be with me" " Yes Julius I will come with you " .

SAM LAY THE FLOWERS down on his mum's grave and stood up he looks round at Malcolm beside him Sam had asked Malcolm to come with him to visit his mum's grave he had a feeling he needed to because it had been a while since Malcolm looks at Sam he's just feeling nostalgic Malcolm thinks since his dad visited him a few days ago ." Thanks for coming with me " " No probs you are ok right " .

Sam looks at Malcolm and nods yes I am now since my dad visited me a few days ago and very strangely I'm not sad about it anymore Sam Though Helen watches on from the tree Sam and Malcolm talking she looks round at Zeke and back at her son . Malcolm laying his arm round Sam's shoulder " Ready to go " Malcolm asks Sam smiles at him leaning into Malcolm " Lets go and thanks for doing this with me " .

" Anytime C'mon you let's get back " Malcolm dunted Sam's shoulder while they headed back to the car " Malcolm " Malcolm looks round at Sam standing at the car what's up with him he thought " You don't regret it do you " Malcolm comes round to Sam's side he slides his hand onto Sam's neck I know what he is talking about the time they went to Blackpool . " No Sam I don't if anything it's made our friendship stronger " That's true Sam thought he nods Malcolm smiles " Why you wanna go again " They both giggle and bump heads then hug Helen smiles at their interaction so cute and can't understand why they are not together with different partners .

They get into the car and drive off. Sam looks at Malcolm and their bond will never be broken. He thinks Malcolm will always have a special place in his heart for him that's for definite " What you thinking about " " Nothing special but does Darian really wanna do a themed bar ."

Malcolm giggles thinking back when they went to the themed bar in Edinburgh Frankenstein's that man has so many crazy ideas going around his head at the moment " That's a no at the moment you know what he is like when we go to different places " Sam knows that but someday he could do other theme nights for the two clubs that were running great . The new one in Glasgow was running great even though the members from Edinburgh often visited and new members were wanting to join nearly every day which was great .

" SAM " " WHAT " SAM looks round at Malcolm while driving along the road he smirks then glances round at Sam again what's he smirking for Sam thought " Were you thinking about Blackpool " Sam snorted shaking his head unbelievable of all the days to ask that " No I wasn't thinking about Blackpool " Malcolm hummed smirked again " Get your mind out of the gutter Malcolm Mackenzie " .

They both laughed which Sam needed to kill the tension between them " Fancy a McDonald's " Malcolm asked " Sure that be great and get a burger for Geraint to " " Sam " He looks round at

Malcolm he glances at Sam " love you Mate " Sam smiles and nods Malcolm squeezes Sam's hand " Love you to " .And he always will their special bond between them .

Epilogue

Julius and Zeke watch Julio work the bar area he has set up a new bar in Malaga went on his own with his fiancée Caro nice looking Julius thought they look happy he thought and the bar looks good to which is at the marina area not that big of a bar by the size of it Julio had talked about running his own bar when Julius meet him .

Zeke took Julius and he looked round at Zeke giving him a reassuring squeeze Julius nodded and looked over at Julio " Going to get a box wine " Julio says to Caro and goes off to the cellar Julius looks at Zeke now is his chance to go talk to him .

While Julio is in the cellar he thought it strange the lights flickering maybe needs a new bulb he thought while getting a couple bottles wine " Julio " Julio looks round and standing at the far side is Julius " Surprised " .

" Yes you could say that I don't understand why " Julio went over to Julius. Is he a ghost coming to him to help tears stung Julio's eyes. " Julio it's all good I'm happy and " Julius looks round at Zeke standing beside him smiling who is he looking at Julio thought .

" ARE YOU GOOD JULIO " Julio lifts up his hand Julius smiles " I still miss you " Julio says Julius nods looking at Zeke Julio thought why doesn't the other person show himself " Julio I'm sorry the way things happened Zeke says " .

" Zeke " Julio asks Julius looks at Zeke again he nods laying out his hand for Zeke to take Zeke holds Julius hand and appears to Julio

" Julio we have both upgraded and got our wings recently and he says I have to see you well you know " Julio snorted suddenly there was a woosh of air Julio looks at the both them Zeke and Julius wings outstretched what an amazing sight .And Yes he knows what Julius means .

" Julio " Caro shouts down shit he thought how long has he been away " Julio " Tears run down Julios's cheeks at the sight of Julius and Zeke " Be happy Julio " .

Caro comes downstairs and notices Julio staring at the wall " Julio " Caro goes over to him he looks round at Caro tears streaming down his face . " Julio what is wrong " Caro laying his arms round him " I'm ok Caro " Julio wiped his eyes I was worried Caro thought . " I saw Julius" " What" .

" I know I'm ok Caro he's ok " Are you sure" Julio lays his arm round Caro kisses his cheek " Yes c'mon let's get back to the bar " .

JULIO HAD ONE LAST look round the cellar. It was good to see Julius. He had a feeling about Zeke that they might be together which is good they are all moving on and I'm happy with Caro now it had taken him a long time to get over Julius until Caro came along

.

JULIUS AND ZEKE SAT on the wall at the beach eating ice cream watching the sunset and other people walking along the beach to Julius seemed happier now that he had seen what Julio Zeke thought . Julius looks at Zeke staring at him.while they eat their ice cream " What " " Nothing just making sure you're ok " .

" I'm ok Zeke " That's good Zeke thought I don't want him to be sad after seeing Julio Julius looks at Zeke again Julius takes his hand " What are you thinking " " I'm ready " Julius nearly chokes on his ice cream did he hear Zeke right looking at Zeke who is chewing his nails . Julius takes Zeke hand getting closer to him " Say that again " Zeke digs into Julius rib looking away Julius turns Zeke's head back round they stare at each other .

" Are you sure " " You said you were gonna do what I asked it's so sexy " Julius giggles moving nearer they kissed Julius wrapped his arms round Zeke they bumped heads " Lets head back " " Can't we stay overnight here " why not Julius thought no harm in doing that he guessed " Sure we can do that " .

THEY WERE ALL HANDS kissing when Julius tried opening the door to their room eventually he managed to open it falling through the door nearly onto the floor Julius pushed Zeke against the wall grinding into him Zeke whimpered " Julius " Julius looks back up at Zeke "What " " Slow and steady " Julius grins shaking his head Zeke pushes Julius off him going over to the bed Julius watching him undress Zeke looks round at Julius dropping his jeans showing his ass Nice Julius thought grinning I like what I see .

Julius comes over to Zeke sliding his arms round Zeke's waist kissing his neck both their cocks hard Julius slides his hand down starting to stroke Zeke he whimpers while Julius kisses his neck and ear loving the sound of his moans while stroking him..

Zeke moves up the bed Julius coming over to him he hovers over Zeke all a glow Zeke amazed at the sight of Julius he leans over to pick up the lube looking at Zeke . " Do we need that " Zeke asks they are angels after all " well I kinda thought it would be easier " Zeke giggles Julius cocks his head .Julius hasn't had sex with anyone since and wondered if Zeke had n't be stupid thinking things like that Julius thought .

Zeke sits up bringing Julius closer to him they kiss Julius lifts up Zeke's shirt taking it off and his own Zeke looks at Julius chest a nipple ring Zeke bites his lip his abs defined Julius slides down licking and nipping at Zekes stomach he groans .

Julius licks up and down Zeke's cock lifting up one hind leg. He looks up at Zeke, his face flushed. Julius spits on his hand, rubbing his spit onto Zeke's cock and taking him in his mouth . " Oh God " So Good Zeke thought tingles all up his back with Julius giving him a blow job Julius looks up at Zeke his eyes shut Julius smirks and moves up nearer to Zeke he opens his eyes startled that Julius stopped . Julius hovers over Zeke and looks up at Julius " What's wrong? " Zeke asks, " Nothing, I just want to look at you " .

ZEKE SNORTS SHAKING his head Julius bends to kiss him again lifting up both of Zeke's hands kissing his neck licking his ear " Are you ready " Mmm " Julius positions himself in the middle of Zeke's legs " By the way I've warded the place " Julius says good job Zeke thought . lifting one up licking the inside of Zeke's leg Zeke chewing his lip his leg tingling " Julius " He looks down at Zeke and bends down " Can I go on top " Julius smiles and nods as they change positions . Better view Zeke thought Julius so ready Zeke licks his lips and bends to kiss Julius and he positions himself easing himself onto Julius cock and Julius sliding his hand round to keep him steady and getting into a rhythm.

Zeke holds onto the bed frame his orgasm looming this is so different from when he was alive the sensation different and heightened from before his whole body vibrating Julius feeling the same " Look at you ,you're glowing Zeke " What a sight to see Julius thought seeing Zeke all a glow while they make love Julius wrapping his arms round Zeke's waist . " I Love you " Zeke says first kissing Julius he smiles touching Zeke's face that's the first time he had said it to him .

ZEKE'S ORGASM RIPPED out of him laying on the bed Oh Wow unbelievable sensation when he orgasmed Julius coming after him they both laying beside each other Julius looks round at Zeke smiling he looks over at Julius who is staring at him . " That was amazing " Julius moving closer to Zeke they faced each other " I meant it when I said I l love you you don't have to say it back yet " Julius smiles and touches Zeke's mouth " I do love you " .I really do Julius thought staring at Zeke then touching Zeke's face .

Zeke smiles they move closer Zeke resting his head on Julius shoulder " You ok " " Mmm" Julius kisses Zeke's head " Wanna go again " Julius asks Zeke giggles during Julius side Zeke sits up looking down at Julius and oh man he thought he is hard again Zeke looks at Julius who has his arms over his head smirking Zeke gets up Julius watching him go into the bathroom coming out with a towel to clean themselves .

Zeke straddles Julius Looking down at him " I will even let you top me if you want " Julius says Zeke smiles bending to kiss him Julius did bottom sometimes when he was living which didn't bother him whatever the other person preferred sometimes he and Darian reversed roles sometimes .Thinking back to their time together " Julius " Julius looks up at Zeke he reaches up for him to come nearer to him " Where did you go " " nowhere "

After their second love making they sat up on bed and got Pizzas and fries they got hungry and watched trash tv and laughing at some off the silly adverts and watched half of a movie until Zeke fell asleep he is cute when he slept light snores Julius and Zeke snuggled into each other while they slept And legs wrapped around each other .

TWO DAYS LATER THEY eventually left their room at the motel in spain during that two days they mostly made love had food and declared their love for each other over and over and they decided to become a couple not just fuck buddy's. It was evident their feelings for each other was mutual who would have thought Angels falling in love even though they did see others pairing up before .In the past would Darian have approved of their relationship who knows what Zeke thought .

" I NEED ANOTHER VACATION " Zeke said sighing Julius snorted shaking his head Zeke looks over at him what's funny he thought " We will soon " Zeke smiles looks away " Promise " Zeke asks looks back at Julius " Promise "Definitely Julius thought " I love you " Zeke said first Julius takes his hand " Love you to " .

The End

CLUB NERO SERIES WILL Return

BY

Dale V Mcfarlane

Club Nero Series
Club Nero
(Vol 1)
Club Nero Series
(Vol 2)
New Beginnings
(Vol 3)
A New Start
(Vol 4)

His Cold Heart Series
His Cold Heart
(Vol 1)
Warm Heart
(Vol 2)
The Warmest Heart
(Vol 3)

LINKTREE
https://Linktr.ee/dalevmcfarlane[1]

PATREON
Patreon.com/dalevmcfarlane

DISCORD
dalevmcfarlane

COPYRIGHT
Dale V Mcfarlane

---

1.   https://linktr.ee/dalevmcfarlane

Don't miss out!

Visit the website below and you can sign up to receive emails whenever Dale v Mcfarlane publishes a new book. There's no charge and no obligation.

https://books2read.com/r/B-A-WMJU-SZKYC

BOOKS 2 READ

Connecting independent readers to independent writers.

Also by Dale v Mcfarlane

The Little Coffee Shop On The Corner - Vol 1
The Little Coffee Shop On The Corner- Vol 1

Vol 1
Club Nero
His Cold Heart
Club Nero Series Novel - Little Pretty Things - Vol 1

Vol 2
His Cold Heart - Warm Heart - Vol 2
Club Nero

Vol 4
Club Nero Series - The Next Chapter - Vol 4

Vol one
Club Nero - Vol 1

Standalone
Club Nero Series - New Beginnings vol 3
His Cold Heart - The Warmest Heart - vol 3
Club Nero Series - The Reunion

About the Author

Hi i am Dale i live in scotland writting is my passion i also write fan fic to please check out my socials